The **RN** *Diaries*

Dolyn Keys

You can discover more information about Dolyn Keys and future releases here:

https://www.facebook.com/DolynKeys

https://instagram.com/dolynkeys

https://twitter.com/dolynkeys

Email: dolynkeys@gmail.com

This book is dedicated to all who follow their dreams, and to those who are determined to do their best in all things.

Table of Contents

Chapter One

Diary Entry #1

I'm a registered nurse at Ellerton Memorial Hospital in Los Angeles, California, and I'm also an event planner. I can expose you to things that may give you a heart attack, but don't panic because I can perform CPR and save your life. I meet plenty of people in both my fields of work. I've never slept with a patient, but everyone else is fair game. To describe me as promiscuous would be an understatement, because I've had them all, from dentists to NFL stars. My life's a little complicated right now, so a real relationship is out of the question. At the most random of times, I find that I'm ready to do it anytime, anywhere, and almost with anyone, trying to get that ultimate orgasm that holds me over until the next encounter. I'll settle down one day, but right now is not the time. V.C.

Vanity Carter

"If everyone could just get the hell out of the way, I could get to work on time tonight," Vanity scoffed as she honked the horn. She provided her fellow road mates with nice hand gestures, letting them know what she thought of their driving. She wanted to be anywhere but at Ellerton Memorial Hospital tonight and hoped to get called off due to low census. Magna Carta blasted through the speakers of the new corvette she'd bought herself for graduation; her cell phone lit up on the passenger seat. She hoped it was the hospital calling to cancel her for the night, but the caller ID displayed a number she didn't recognize. She usually didn't answer numbers she didn't recognize, but she had time to kill sitting in this traffic. "Hello, this is Vanity."

"Glad to know you gave me the right number, Vanity. Do you know who this is?"

A smile spread across Vanity's face. Of course she knew who it was— Paul. She'd know that accent anywhere. He was six foot and Italian, with broad shoulders, a six-pack, dimples, and thick black hair that she'd fantasized about getting her hands in again. But, she'd never let him know that. Instead, she answered, "No. Care to refresh my memory?"

"I'll give you a hint. Last month we were at your place, and I made you scream my name while I was buried inside of you."

Last month? Was he serious? Last month was like last decade in her sex book. She'd had several more encounters with several different guys since him, but that accent made her name sound like velvet rolling off his tongue. How could she forget that? It was like an aphrodisiac. She'd given him her number because he used his mouth to make her orgasm over and over again. In her opinion, his tongue should've been the ninth wonder of the world.

"Scream your name?" she replied. "That's tooting your own horn. But. I'm starting to recall. How can I be of assistance?"

"I was calling to see if you'd like me to come over tonight." He was quick and straight to the point, characteristics Vanity always held in high regard . . . outside of the bedroom.

Without sounding anxious, she said, "That sounds nice. Around what time were you thinking?"

"What time would you like me to be there?"

"Around ten. Do you remember how to get there?" Vanity asked with a slight arrogance in her tone. How could any man forget his way to her? Each guy she ran across thought of her as a fantasy come to life. She was five-six, had long, blonde healthy hair, green eyes, perfect high cheekbones, a tight, toned body, and a natural double-D cup.

"How could I forget?" And with that, he ended the call.

The men Vanity dated weren't much for fulfilling her fantasies completely, but they were great at being temporary fixes to her cravings, and for stroking her ego.

His arrogance and sureness of himself was attractive. Though she had long since cleared "Sex with an Italian man" off her bucket list, Vanity was still turned on by his accent and more than ready to engage in another sexual encounter with him. Then again, she couldn't remember a time in her adult life where she wasn't ready to fuck. She'd been having sex since she was fifteen, and at twenty seven she was still searching for the sex of her lifetime. Vanity had graduated from vanilla sex a long time ago, and she wondered if Paul would be willing to kick up the kink a notch. It was worth the try.

Vanity called the floor at the hospital and asked to speak with the charge nurse. She was taking the night off with a mysterious case of stomach flu. She had plans to do far more interesting things for the evening.

Chapter Two

Diary Entry #2

I don't like to be told what to do, but it gives me great pleasure to give out the orders. My sexual appetite is always in overdrive. I've been called insatiable by a few, but I prefer the words "extraordinarily un-sat-isfiable." I like to tie my men up, and use my whips and chains on them until they yell out "Nadia" in sweet agony. I once met a sick, twisted freak who liked to be tied up with barbwire rope. He said the self-in-flicted pain from pulling against the restraints taught him discipline. He was my favorite of them all. I meet a guy and we keep at it until I lose interest. Then I'm back on the hunt for my next thrill and that can take months . . . and months . . . and months. Believe it or not, a lot of men like being told what to do. So, finding a partner is easy, but finding a good, attentive, obedient partner is something else in itself. N.H.

Nadia Hollinsworth

Her pupils dilated each time the leather met his flesh. Watching his body bow backward and listening to his screams brought Nadia closer and closer to orgasm. Nothing was more attractive to her then a man on his knees begging her to keep pleasuring him.

Nadia stood back and released her wrist again, thrashing the whip down onto his upper back. The sound echoed off the walls, mixing in with her moans of satisfaction. In her knee-high spiked-heel boots, a skimpy thong, and leather bodice, she circled around to get a good look at his face. Bending down, she gazed into his deep gray eyes and kissed him sweetly.

Stopping only to catch her breath, she freed his arms from the bondage cuffs. He let out a sigh as he ran his hands through her thick black kinky hair. She placed his hand between her legs to let him know just how turned on she was by his submission. With her tongue, Nadia tasted his salty skin, slick from sweat, from his collarbone to his square jaw. Rubbing his thumb across her sensitive flesh, Nadia's breath began to quicken. Refusing to ask him to satisfy the ache stirring within her core, she bit down on his shoulder, then sucked his flesh, massaging it with her tongue to send him a message of what she needed. With a cry for release, he leaned back onto the floor, taking Nadia with him. He gripped her sides and placed her dripping core on top of his face, waiting for her to regain control. Without hesitation, she rhythmically swayed back and forth, circling her hips to create the right amount of friction. The strokes and teases from his tongue felt like silk sliding over her clitoris as she rode his face. She dipped her head back when she reached her climax, causing her entire body to shake.

"My turn," he grumbled as she straddled him. She placed his thickness at her core, then slid down slowly. He reached for her hips, but she grabbed his wrists and placed them above his head. She trailed kisses from his chest to his neck while maintaining a steady rhythm. Slightly letting her teeth graze his skin, she increased her speed and he moaned her name. He bit his bottom lip, and she knew he was close. Lifting her legs and turning around in reverse cowgirl, she grabbed his ankles and rode him, bouncing up and down to milk his length.

"Shit, I'm gonna come, baby," and then she felt him jerk and his leg muscles tensed. His release washed through her, and then she let go of his ankles, as she rode out the waves of her pleasure.

"That was amazing," he breathed.

Nadia got up, walked into the bathroom, and closed the door. *Maybe for you, but not nearly enough for me,* she thought while stripping out of her clothing. She'd come twice in less than fifteen minutes, but she still needed more. She always craved more. Some women barely orgasm once, but she'd rode out two orgasms back to back. Wasn't she lucky? She never had a problem having an orgasm, but stamina these days was as ancient as being monogamous. The more she thought about it, the more frustrated she became. She turned on the water in the shower and waited for the water to warm. She had a bomb-ass handheld showerhead and she was going to use it. After all, it lasted as long as she needed it to.

Chapter Three

Diary Entry #3

I'm the boss! I always have been and always will be. I treat men like tissues, take one, use it, and then throw it away. I say who, what, when, where, and how . . . with the exception of the bedroom. I'm a diva with a type-A personality, and I'm a little narcissistic, but behind closed doors, I like to be brought to my knees and dominated. If you're scared to be in control, then I am not the one for you. Orgasm by asphyxiation is the type of shit I'm into, and I'm able to swallow at least nine inches of cock and hold my breath for fifteen seconds before my gag reflex kicks in. I love sex—kinky, dangerous, out-of-this-world sex. You can keep that hair pulling and ass slapping for the little girls. I'm a gold member in the mile high club, and I've done it in the front seat of a Bugatti going two hundred miles per hour. I probably zipped past some of you motherfuckers on the freeway while I was chasing that orgasm. My sex life is fucking fantastic. I don't think it can get any better than this . . . K.D.

Kensington Dumas

Kensington sang on the elevator as she patiently waited to arrive on her floor. She really didn't want to work, but duty called. She entered the break room and put her things away in her locker. Kensi said the occasional "hello" to the coworkers she liked and pasted on a smile for those she didn't care for. She was ready to get this twelve-hour shift over with.

The other nurses were already in the conference room drinking coffee and talking about the previous night's patients and events. They all sat around a rectangular table with tonight's assignment stacked neatly in the middle, along with a phone and a pager, all the things administration felt the nurses needed to provide sufficient patient care. *Bullshit*, Kensington thought as she reached across the table. *If administration had a clue about real nursing, they'd give each nurse a lifetime supply of Xanax, Red Bull, and a raise.* As she looked at the assignment, she saw that Vanity's name had been crossed out with the words "called in sick" written beside it. A smile spread across her face. *That bitch isn't sick.* She'd call Vanity tonight first chance she got and see what the hell was really going on.

After sitting through pre-shift bed huddle, Kensi headed down her assigned hall. She peeked into the dictation room to see who was on call tonight and damn near dropped her clipboard when she saw a handsome guy spitting out orders like he was some type of captain in the army. He stopped for a second, locked eyes with her, and flashed her a megawatt smile. Kensington didn't return the gesture. Instead, she straightened her shoulders and proceeded down the hall.

"He's probably the typical MD asshole. No need to smile at him when I'm sure you'll be talking bad to him by end of shift," Brandy said.

Brandy had been a nurse for a long time, but she never had her shit done before the next shift. She was XXX years old, but still had the body of a teenager. While she needed some assistance on how to properly apply mascara and eyebrow pencil, she was still pretty for her age.

"Why do you say that, Ms. Brandy? Did you have to resort to such tactics earlier?"

"No, but I can see the arrogance in him, and I'm familiar with your take-no-shit attitude. So, let's just say it'll be interesting when you two cross paths, which will be shortly. I need to get this consent for blood signed, and I'll be back to give you the report."

Kensington rolled her eyes. "Probably had that damn order all day and she's only just going to get the consent signed now?" she said quietly to herself.

"Actually, I just gave her that order," a voice said from behind.

Kensi turned around and grimaced. The doctor she'd just passed in the dictation room was standing there with the same megawatt smile on his face. He was obviously pretending to look through a chart, since all the orders were put directly into the computer now. *I can either ignore him or smile back, but don't say anything.* Going with option A, she took a seat at the computer and began to log in to the system.

"So, you're just going to ignore me?"

Kensi placed her elbows on the desk and folded her hands. She flashed him a menacing stare. "I'm sorry, did you need something?"

"Yes. I'm guessing you'll be the nurse taking over for the patient in room 2916 judging from your comment."

Ignoring the latter, Kensi replied, "I will be the nurse taking over for night shift and —"

"I know you haven't looked at the labs yet, but her hematocrit and hemoglobin levels are low," he interrupted. "I'm putting in an order to have them redrawn at midnight. By that time both units should be given."

"Well, I have to see all my other patients and make sure they're stable first. Then I have assessments and charting that must be done. Not to mention nine o'clock meds to pass, and I'm sure a few Accu-Cheks. So, how about you change your little order to a nurse communication note that states to have the labs drawn after the units are completed?"

By this time, the smile had completely dropped from his face. "Regardless of your job responsibilities, the blood should be completed by midnight, so I'll leave the order as is. Thanks."

"Well, just go ahead and enter it however you like, and when the lab technician comes to draw blood I'll instruct them to come back when I call down for them. Problem solved."

Smirking, Kensi dropped her head and continued to log into the computer while he just stood there. Before he could respond, they both turned their head in the direction of snickering. Brandy stood there assessing the situation, laughing at the inevitable. "Kensi, I see you've met Dr. Randahl."

"Kensi, is it? I suggest you get the labs at the time instructed. I'll be coming back to the floor for the results at that time."

"It's Kensington. Only the people I like have the privilege of shortening my name." She turned to Brandy. "Are you ready to give me report?"

Without a comeback, Dr. Randahl headed down the hall to the elevators, and Brandy proceeded to give report to Kensi. Kensi sighed. This was going to be a long night.

Chapter Four

"Vanity." She could hear Paul calling her name. She'd hit the breaker on the lights in her condo. He'd have to find his way to her using his other senses.

"I'm here," she said.

Vanity could hear Paul's footsteps as he climbed her Victorian staircase. Her heart began to beat faster as she lay naked in a swing with her wrists secured to it.

"What the . . . ?"

"It's a sex swing," Vanity said. "It binds me in place while still giving you access to every part of me. I want you to take me right here, right now, just like this."

Paul, grinning like the Cheshire cat, ran his hand through his hair and slowly walked over to her. He placed his hand on her feet and gently began rubbing circles up her calves and her thighs until he reached her sweet heat.

"Stop," Vanity ordered.

Taking his eyes from his soon-to-be dinner, Paul looked her in the eyes.

"Take your clothes off. I want to look at you . . . all of you."

Paul grabbed the bottom of his shirt and began to pull it off, but Vanity cried, "No! Do it slowly."

He slowly lifted his shirt, pulled it over his head, and threw it on the floor. Then he kicked off his shoes and pulled his pants down. He stood there for a minute or two, letting Vanity bask in his masculinity. He pulled down his briefs and all nine inches of his excited manhood sprang free.

This man was gorgeous. Six feet of pure man, with ripples in his stomach to define his abs, hair glistening like he just stepped out of the shower, big hands, big feet, and a nine-inch Italian sausage to go with it. Paul had said something, but Vanity hadn't heard him. "What? Huh?" she asked.

"I said, am I free to please you now?"

When his question registered in Vanity's brain, a smile spread across her face. Still speechless from his naked body, she simply nodded her head yes. Before she could say anything else, Paul kneeled in front of her and let his tongue do the talking.

"Ahhhhhhhh" echoed off the walls of her condo. This man had a tongue like a feather and the motion of a vibrator. Attempting to run her hands through his hair, Vanity's plans were halted when her wrist pulled at the restraint. So far gone from Paul pleasuring her, she'd forgotten she was restrained. "Un-cuff me."

"No." Then Paul went back to teasing her with his mouth and touching her all over with his hands.

"Paul, please."

Ignoring her cries, he continued to stroke her back and forth slowly with his tongue until she cried out his name and exploded.

"Paul, please unstrap me."

She looked completely drained, so Paul unstrapped her and scooped her up in his arms.

"Where are you taking me?"

"To the bedroom. So we can finish what we started."

Without saying anything else, she wrapped her arms and legs around him, rested her forehead on his shoulder, and closed her eyes. There was no doubt in her mind Paul was going to care for her and satisfy her in every way she could imagine.

Chapter Five

After showering and putting "what's his face" out, Nadia got dressed. She wore her new Tahiri black bandage dress, five-inch Louboutin heels, and Chanel bag. Nadia was going out to see if she could find her next late-night conquest. She climbed into her Mercedes CLS and headed toward Studio City. The Blue Flame was always packed, and there were always nice, wealthy, and willing men who frequented the spot. Nadia parked her car in valet and entered the restaurant and bar. The atmosphere was perfect for the mood she was in—dim lights, old-school Al Green playing softly in the background, and people dressed to impress.

"Welcome to the Blue Flame. How many?" The hostess was a petite young woman, with a perky voice, wearing light makeup, and her midnight-black hair was pulled back in a chignon. Nadia wondered if she knew how hot she was, or if she'd like to go home with her so Nadia could show her how hot she thought she was. Nadia had never been with another girl. She'd been bi-curious for quite some time now but had never met the right girl to take home and experiment with.

Nadia smiled. "It's just me tonight . . . so far." The hostess raised her eyebrows like she was taken aback by the comment. Nadia just stood there staring at her, not letting her expression give anything away.

The hostess smiled. "Well, it's been busy tonight, but we can have a table ready for you in fifteen minutes. Would you like to sit at the bar while you wait? Who knows, by the time your table is ready you might need a table for two."

"You read my mind," Nadia teased.

"What name would you like to use?"

"You can put it under Nadia."

"Okay, Nadia, I'm Amber. You can have a seat at the bar. It's self-seating, and I'll come and get you when your table is ready."

"Thanks," Nadia said, and she took a seat at the end of the bar. She potted the bartender. He was handsome, but they all looked the same now. Tall, handsome, million-dollar smile, but most of them came before you were fully undressed.

Her phone vibrated, snapping her from her thoughts.

Kensi texted, *Vanity called in sick.*

Nadia responded, *Not surprised. You should've called in too. Then you could have been sitting here keeping me company.*

Kensi's reply was immediate. *Where? And FYI, there's a new MD here tonight.*

Nadia replied, *Blue Flame. Is he cute?*

"Is somebody sitting here?"

Nadia looked up from her phone and stared into a pair of Carolina-blue eyes. His Caribbean dark brown hair had the wild, messy look. He was clean shaven, wearing blue jeans, a black blazer, and a crisp white shirt with two buttons undone that made her wish buttons didn't exist at all. To say that this man was fine as hell would've been disrespectful.

"Depends on who's asking," Nadia replied. Without hesitation, he sat down and summoned the bartender.

"I'll have a French connection," he then turned toward Nadia, "and whatever the lady is having."

"Midori sour, please."

"Do you come here a lot?" the man asked.

"First of all, is that the best pickup line you have?" Nadia said. "Second, you already know that I come here a lot, because I've seen you before."

"So, you've been watching me?"

"I believe I asked you a question first. Let's start there."

"Sort of a show-me-yours-I'll-show-you-mine type of thing?" he said with a smirk. Nadia returned an innocent smile. "Okay, well no that's not my best pickup line. I'm actually not trying to pick you up at all."

"No?"

"No." He leaned in closer and whispered in her ear, "Because if I were trying to pick you up, I'd tell you that those heels make your legs look even sexier than the tan ones you had on last week. That I love the way your ass looks in that dress, and that if I were your boyfriend there'd be a cold day in hell before I'd let you leave the house looking like that."

"Oh really? Well . . ." Nadia leaned closer. "Guess it's a good thing you're not my boyfriend."

They sat there starting at each other, trying to size the other up. "Excuse me," a voice said from behind Nadia. Nadia broke the stare and turned around to see Amber the hostess. "Ma'am, your table is ready."

"You don't have to call me 'ma'am.' I'm not nearly old enough to be worthy of that yet."

"And just how old are you?" the man asked.

"I'm old enough to be in the Blue Flame. I believe that tells you enough Mr . . . ?"

"I'm Mr. I'm Definitely Old Enough to be here. Enjoy your dinner. It was a pleasure meeting you."

He grabbed her hand, lifted it to his mouth, and placed a soft kiss on her knuckles. With that, he smoothly walked away.

"Right this way," Amber said.

Nadia headed toward her table, but with a stab of disappointment. She didn't know when she would run into him again, and she'd failed at getting his name. She left the house on a mission to find some relief from her sexual tension. Now she was more tense than she'd been when she arrived. Taking a seat at the quiet table Nadia pulled out her phone. She had three new text messages from Kensi.

Kensi: *He's actually very attractive. Probably an asshole though.*

How's the Flame? Any cuties there?

When's the next time you work? Are you off this Saturday?

Nadia replied: *Attractive and an asshole, huh? Sounds like your type. Blue Flame is dead tonight with the exception of one hottie, with no name might I add, and killer swag, who slick talked dirty to me and then left me hanging. I don't go back until next Tuesday. And what's going on this Saturday?*

As soon as her phone chimed again, the waiter approached. "Good evening. I'm Angelo, and I'll be your server this evening. I see you already have a beverage. Would you care for an appetizer, madam? Or are you ready to order?"

"Can I have a few more minutes, please?"

"Sure, madam. Take your time."

Kensi: *Vanity is hosting another private event, and it's about time you came to one. So, I was just wondering if you were going to be free this time. Let me know, and I wanna hear what happens with Mr. Hot No-Name.*

Nadia: *If you're referring to one of those sexclusive events that I've heard her talk about, you can count me in! We should all link up, have lunch, and find something to wear. Mr. No-Name is def my type, but I don't know where he went to.*

Kensi: *Yes, one of those. And okay, we'll do lunch and shopping that afternoon. Have you talked to Vanity? I was going to call her tonight, but it doesn't look like I'll get the chance.*

Nadia: *No. She must be a little 'tied' up :) I'll call her later and find out where she is and then let you know.*

Kensi: *Kay ttyl. I got a call I have to take about one of my patients.*

"Are you ready to order? Or do you still need a few minutes?" Angelo asked.

Nadia looked up from her phone and smiled. "Yes, I'll have the Scottish king salmon, another Midori sour, and a glass of Pellegrino with lemon please." *And that sexy-ass man with the look of promise I met at the bar for dessert*, she thought.

"Very well. I'll take your menu, and I'll be back with your Midori sour and water shortly."

Nadia had come out tonight with the intent of meeting someone new. She'd thought she found him but had no clue where he went. He made a hell of an impression, a lasting one, and then just vanished. However, she couldn't wipe the smile off her face. She sat there daydreaming of him while she waited on her food. Wondering if his soft lips would feel as good all over her body, as they did when he kissed her hand.

Chapter Six

Kensi was sitting at her computer checking the orders of for her newly admitted patient when the intercom clicked snapping her from her thoughts. It was the front desk secretary.

"Kensi?"

"Yes."

"Dr. Randahl is on line three."

Dr. Randahl? "Okay. Thanks."

Kensi picked up the receiver and took the call, "This is Kensi."

"Ah, is that permission for me to use your nickname, Kensington?"

"Who's this?" Kensi knew damn well who it was, but she wasn't about to admit to him or even to herself that she not only knew it was Dr. Randahl but was hoping it was him.

"Dr. Randahl, please forgive me. I didn't have the chance of properly introducing myself earlier. I was calling for the lab results of room 2916. Do you have them?"

"I don't. I've just now hung her second unit of blood. As I stated earlier, I asked lab to not come back until I called for them."

"I expected to have those labs by now, and I definitely expected her to have received both units of blood by now. What is taking so long?" He said.

Kensi looked at the receiver on the phone as if it had grown a human head. "I have more than one patient, okay?" she responded. "She's getting the units of blood, and as of right now, her vitals are stable and she's asymptomatic. Is it taking a long time? The answer is maybe for you. May you ask why? No, you may not."

"Well, that's ridiculous, because five hours to me is more than enough time to have hung both units of blood."

Without responding, she hung up the phone. He must be one of those doctors who thought that nurses just sat around and drank coffee all night waiting on them to write orders. She sat in her cubbyhole down the hall checking orders for the next fifteen minutes. She was still a little pissed off from Dr. Randahl questioning her, but she felt ballsy that she had been the one to disconnect the call. Maybe hanging up in his face was a little much. Maybe he was just looking out for the patient's wellbeing. Whatever the case might be, questioning her job performance just did not sit well with her.

The intercom clicked, and Kensi just dropped her head because if it was Dr. Randahl calling back she wasn't sure if she was going to be able to hold her tongue . . .

"Kensi, your patient in room 13 would like to see you" said the front desk secretary.

"Do you know why?"

"No. He just asked if I could send the nurse in."

"Okay." Kensi closed the chart she had open and headed down the hall. She'd been so wrapped up about Dr. Randahl and his comments that it didn't even register to her that she didn't have a patient in room 13. She was the only nurse on the back hall that night. She knocked and cracked open the door. Before she could back up, someone grabbed her arm, pulled her into the dark room, and slammed her against the wall. With one hand over her mouth and the other hand securing her wrists, pinning both arms over her head, she heard that distinct voice that she'd been replaying over and over in her head. Then she relaxed. . . but only a little.

"Do you have a problem taking orders from me, Kensington?"

With his hand over her mouth, she couldn't say a word.

"Nod your head yes or no."

Nodding her head no, he tightened his grip on her wrists and leaned closer to her ear. "Your actions tell me otherwise, Ms. Kensington. You refused to follow my orders and then you hung up in my face. If your body wasn't betraying you right now, I'd think you didn't like me, but your respirations have slowed and your pulse has quickened. I bet if I were to stick my hand between those thick thighs that wetness of yours would tell me different. Wouldn't it, Ms. Kensington?"

Kensi was caught off guard but so turned on. The way he kept saying her name made her want him right then and there, but she was at work and needed to get back to her patients. She tried to say something, but it was muffled.

"If I remove my hand from your mouth, are you going to behave, Ms. Kensington?" She nodded her head yes, and he removed his hand. "You were saying?"

"Let me go," she snapped, but the look in her eye betrayed the words that were coming out of her mouth. Kensi tried her best to wiggle her wrists away, but she was unable to break the death grip that she found to be both arousing and irritating. "You've got a lot of fucking nerve, Dr. Randahl. Is this a courtesy you provide to all the nurses? Is cornering them in vacant rooms your sick, twisted idea of foreplay?"

"Tsk-tsk, Ms. Kensington. You have no idea of my idea of foreplay." Still holding her wrists in place with one hand, he lifted the hem of her scrub top, reaching under her shirt until he reached the lace of her bra.

He caressed her lacy bra, then he reached in and pinched her nipple until a gasp escaped her mouth. She closed her eyes, arching her chest into his hand. "You're beautiful when you don't fight it, Ms. Kensington. It's perfectly okay to give in to temptation. I can promise you so much more than just a quick tease." He withdrew his hand and stepped back, releasing her wrists from his grip. "That is if you want more. Do you want more, Ms. Kensington?"

Kensi opened her eyes and straightened her scrub top. She took a deep breath and just stood there staring at him. He flashed his thousand-watt smile. Lifting one corner of her mouth and stepping toward him, she dropped to her knees, undid his zipper, and pulled out his cock. Nice, long, thick, and already rock hard. It pleased her to know that he was just as aroused as she was. When she wrapped her hand around the base, a drop of pre-cum escaped. She licked it and moaned to let him know she approved of the taste. Without any delay, she took him in her mouth to the hilt. Her tongue rubbed against the veins of his cock as she sucked and applied just the right amount of pressure to elicit a moan from him. She smiled at the sound and then stopped.

Jumping quickly to her feet, Kensi looked him straight in the eye and answered the question he'd asked her. "No. More won't be necessary. I believe I've had enough, Dr. Randahl. Besides, I have to get back to my patients. I have orders for blood transfusions that must be carried out in a timely fashion."

Without another word, Kensi left him alone in room 13. If he thought all he had to do was hold her in place and tickle her tits then he had another thing coming. But if he wanted to make it a competition she was all for that. Especially seeing that she had already won the first round.

Chapter Seven

Vanity awoke to the sound of her phone vibrating off her nightstand. She reached over and caught it before it hit the floor.

"Soooooo, I heard you called in sick to work last night. Care to share the reasoning behind it? Or, do you want to hear me beg for it?" Nadia asked.

Vanity groaned. "Nadia, it's way too early. What the hell are you doing awake anyway? What time is it?"

"It's seven. I figured you'd have put whatever guy you had over last night out by now. Was I wrong?"

"Oh shit." Vanity rolled onto her back and looked at the empty space on the bed next to her. *Where did he go?*

"Oh shit, what? Is he one of those who doesn't know how to leave? Don't tell me this will be like that time you had to—"

"Shhh, Nadia. I'll call you back, okay?"

"No, not okay! I want the tea, and it must be some serious damn tea if you're rushing me off the phone."

"Nadia! I have to—"

"Okay, yeah, I got it. Just make sure you meet me and Kensi on Saturday. We're doing lunch and some shopping before sexclusive event."

"What? I don't know if I'll have time. I have a lot to do."

"Look. Either meet us, or I'm on my way over there right now to see this secret that you obviously want to keep for yourself."

"No. I'll be there Saturday. Lunch and shopping, I'll see you then. I gotta go. Bye!"

Without waiting for Nadia's snappy comeback, Vanity hung up the phone and swung her legs over the side of the bed. Her snatch was aching, her arms heavy, her legs sore, and her butt felt like it had been lit on fire. She stood up and stumbled, but then she caught her footing. She couldn't remember the last time she felt this good. She grabbed her robe, tied it around herself, and then headed down the hall, letting her nose lead her toward the smell of bacon, syrup, and coffee.

Paul turned around and smiled. His jeans hung low onto his hips. "Good morning." He was standing over the stove bare-chested and barefoot.

My gosh this man is built like a God.

"Thought I'd wake you up, but then you were snoring so I figured if I woke you up I'd better have a good reason. So, I'm making you breakfast."

Vanity scoffed. "I don't snore."

Paul dipped his finger into the mixing bowl and started toward her. "Yes, you do, and it's kind of adorable. Now open and taste." Without an objection, Vanity opened her mouth and clamped down on Paul's finger.

"What is this?"

"It's my secret recipe for pancakes. It's basically . . ." Before he could get another word out, Vanity held up her hand.

"No, I mean this. All of this. Last night didn't go anywhere near how I planned it. Now you're invading my kitchen, cooking . . . What exactly do you think this is?"

Paul just stood there speechless, as Vanity waited for an explanation. He finally said, "Well, I thought last night went rather well. Was I wrong? I mean judging from the way you were screaming my name and begging for more, I'd like to think last night was pretty damn good." Vanity opened her mouth to interrupt, but this time Paul held up his hand. "I thought I'd get up early and make you breakfast, because that's what some men do in their attempts to woo a woman. However, I guess I was wrong. You don't want me 'invading' your kitchen then fine. I'm done here."

He stormed right past her, leaving her standing there alone in her kitchen speechless, and she was rarely ever speechless.

Diary Entry #4

Last night I came over and over again. I even fell asleep. Men *never* put me to sleep. I wanted to be fucked and fucked hard, and then I wanted him to put his clothes on and leave! Instead, this man laid me down, made love to me, fucked me hard, and then made love to me again, and then he decided to make me breakfast. So, what's my problem? The damn problem is that this is not what the hell I asked for. We are not dating, and this is not going anywhere. Now, if I wanted him to spend the night or cook me breakfast, he probably would've done the total opposite. Then he has the audacity to throw his hand up at me to shush me, and then slammed the door on his way out *without* cleaning up my kitchen! That was the last time he'll get some of this juice box! What's even more depressing is that I'm back to square one. Damn, where are all the no-strings-attached guys hiding? V.C.

Chapter Eight

Kensi had given report, grabbed her lunch bag, and headed straight to the restroom. She had been holding it far too long. She washed her hands and stopped to look at herself in the mirror. Even in scrubs, Kensi looked fabulous. Her chocolate hair was the same hue as her eyes. She was five-five and the actual measurements for her physique were of thirty-six, twenty-four, thirty-six. Her dad told her all the time that she'd reminded him of her mother every day. She licked her pouty lips; her MAC Candy Yum-Yum lipstick was still on even after deep-throating Dr. Randahl. She made a mental note to herself to buy more. Realizing she still had the taste of Dr. Randahl on her tongue, Kensi exited the restroom smiling to herself, and hit the time clock on her way out the front entrance of the hospital. The sun was shining today, and she had the night off. Her usual routine was to go home, take a nap, wake up and just chill at the house, and then fall asleep. Working the night shift for twelve hours was very tiring. It took a whole day before her body got back on regular schedule. As she headed to the car, she contemplated taking a nap and then going to the beach for a few hours.

Kensi unlocked the doors to her car, put her bags in the backseat, and then cranked it up. She plugged in her iPhone and then dialed her father's house.

"Dumas Residence."

"Hi, Madeline!"

"Kensi! How are you, my dear?"

"Great. Is Dad at home?"

"Your father is here. I was just about to take him the newspaper and his morning coffee. I'll go get him. It's so lovely to hear your voice. I hope you come to visit soon."

"Thanks, Maddie."

Madeline's voice was one that could put anyone in a good mood. She had worked for the family for years and had been around since Kensi was a child. When Kensi's mother died when Kensi was six, her father was in need of someone to look after her and keep the house in order. So, he'd hired Madeline as the nanny and housekeeper. He'd remarried when Kensi was nine years old, but it was to a woman who didn't have a maternal bone in her body. Sara was beautiful, but that was where it began and ended. Whether or not she had brains depended on the subject. She was a complete expert on Louis Vuitton and Prada, the "what to" and "what not" to wear." However, if you wanted her to tell you the end product of a simple math problem you were pushing your luck. If Maddie hadn't been around to teach Kensi womanly things, she just would've been shit out of luck.

"How's my favorite daughter doing?"

"Dad, I'm your only daughter. But I'm great, thanks for asking. How about you?"

"Same old, same old. Just taking it one day at a time."

"I called you a few days ago, but Sara said you'd gone to the doctor."

"Yeah, had to go in and make sure everything is okay."

"And is it?"

"It is now. I went to set up my next appointment and realized the doctor wrote, 'Consult cardiologist for S-O-B.' I stared at the paper for the longest, and then I just decided to ask the nurse what I did to get called a son of a bitch."

Kensi burst into a fit of laughter while shaking her head. Her dad could always make her laugh even when he wasn't trying.

"Then she told me it meant shortness of breath."

"I didn't even know you were having shortness of breath, Dad. Those are things you should tell me."

"Yeah, Blake's home. I decided to join him for an early run one morning and I couldn't keep up. We slowed the run down to a jog and then a walk, and I was still out of breath. Madeline made me an appointment, and now I'm waiting on the cardiologist to call me back."

"Okay, call me and let me know when the appointment is and I'll take off work and go with you. How long is Blake going to be here?"

"I believe he'll be here until Sunday. You should stop by and see him before he goes back."

"Dad, let's not even pretend like I'm the slightest bit interested in seeing Blake. And it's the middle of the semester. Doesn't he have classes?"

Blake was Sara's son from her previous marriage. He wasn't much of a stepbrother, but then again, he was raised by a woman who could probably throw a rock at the ground and miss. Blake had enrolled in college a year before Kensi went off to nursing school. She'd graduated and started a career, and he was still a super-duper senior on campus. He'd changed his major so many times nobody could even remember what he was studying anymore.

"He says he's on fall break. You kids and these breaks. When I was in school, the only break you got was lunch break, and—"

"Dad, I don't have time for the 'back in my day' speech. I was just calling to check on you. Give Maddie a hug for me, and don't forget to call me about the cardiologist appointment."

"Okay. You take it easy and don't work too hard, kid."

"You too, Dad. Love you, and talk to you later."

She disconnected the call and was getting ready to back out of her parking space when she spotted something on her windshield. "I hate it when people leave flyers on my car. It's so irritating." She rolled down the window and reached around to grab the flyer from under her wiper. But it wasn't a flyer. It was an envelope with her name on it. She carefully opened the envelope, and a small black card fell into her lap. It had elegant purple writing that read:

The presence of Kensington Dumas is hereby requested

Saturday October 28, 9:00 p.m.

52764 N. Henderson Lane

Beverly Hills, CA 90211

This is a by invitation-only event.

Your best masquerade attire is required.

~ When fantasies become a reality, then pleasure is certain ~

She opened the car door and looked around, but all she saw was the usual hospital traffic. People were walking in and out of Ellerton, patients being wheeled to their loved one's cars, valet attendants opening car doors, and white coats blending into the pedestrian traffic. She got back into the car and closed the door. She stared at the card a while longer, then put it above the overhead visor. Taking a deep breath, she backed out of her parking space and headed out of the lot. The beach was sounding better and better by the minute.

Chapter Nine

Nadia was tired but found the strength to finally roll out of bed and put on some clothes. She had an appointment to see her plastic surgeon, and there was no way in hell she was going to cancel it. The LA traffic was its usual pain in the ass, but she'd made it on time. She took a seat in the waiting room and was growing more and more annoyed by the minute. A teenage girl and her mother were bickering back and forth about why she couldn't get a nose ring. Nadia was contemplating telling them to shut up, but before temptation could get the better of her, the door near the reception area opened and a petite blonde girl called her name. Nadia quickly stood and followed the woman down the hall. They stopped at a small nook where the nurse got her vital signs, current weight, and asked if she was currently taking any new medications or if anything had changed since her last visit. Swiftly after the mini screening, the nurse escorted Nadia toward the end of the hall where they reached an exam room.

"Okay, I need you to get completely undressed and put on this gown, and Dr. Kaleb will be in shortly."

Smirking, Nadia stripped down, removing every item of clothing except for her four-inch heels. She took a few minutes to make sure her makeup was still intact and that not one hair on her head was out of place. She looked at herself in the mirror on the back of the door and admired herself. Nadia was Creole with milk-chocolate skin, hazel eyes, perfect eyebrows, long, thick, kinky hair, full lips, and thick hips. In her eyesight, she was only missing one thing— bigger breasts. She was already a 36C but she always thought bigger breasts were better breasts. As she was critiquing herself, the door opened.

"Ms. Hollinsworth, back again I see. Have you given much thought to what we discussed last time?" Dr. Kaleb said.

"Yes, I have. But can you go back over the process again, so I can make my decision wisely."

Nadia turned toward him, dropped the paper-thin gown, hopped onto the exam table, and lay down on her back. Dr. Kaleb walked over and looked at her body.

He took his finger and drew a line from her navel to the under-cup of her breast. "I'd make an incision under here." Then he moved over to her other breast, "and under here. Then, I'd insert the implants sub-muscularly. I'll close the incision with skin-bonding adhesive, and the lines will fade over time, but you'll still see a slight scar underneath."

"I've also been considering the vaginal tightening. You'll have to tell me what you think, Dr. Kaleb."

Before he could say anything, Nadia hopped off the table, pulled his white jacket down, and turned him around. Careful not to pull the jacket down too far, she secured his hands behind his back and tied the jacket in a knot. She rolled the small stool behind him and then sat him down. She circled around him, allowing him to get his fill of looking at her naked.

"I've been waiting all month for this appointment with you, Dr. Kaleb."

She unzipped his pants and pulled out his length. He was excited, and that excited her.

"And it feels like you have too."

Nadia took a condom out of her purse. She placed it on the head of his penis, got on her knees, and pushed the condom all the way down with her mouth. Then she straddled him and slid down slowly, eliciting a gasp from him.

"Shh, you don't want one of your staff members to come in, do you?"

She rode him, up and down, back and forth, fast and slow. The look on his face showed that he was close to coming, and the friction from his masculinity rubbing against her clitoris was sure to make her climax.

"Ahhhhh, Nadia."

She reached over, grabbed a handful of gauze, and stuffed them into his mouth. "From the look on your face and the sounds you're making, I'd say you disagree with me needing the tightening." A look of pure lust shone in his eyes. She tightened her vaginal muscles, and he moaned again, but it was muffled through the gauze.

"I'm trying to be as discreet as possible, but if you don't answer I may have to resort to other tactics. So, I'll ask you again—do you think I need that procedure done? Nod your head yes or no."

He slowly shook his head from left to right; he breathed heavily, trying to control himself.

"Good boy." She tightened up her vaginal muscles again and rode him faster. She knew he was close by the crease in his brow. She was close too. Grabbing his shoulders, she slowed down as her orgasm washed through her and he climaxed at the same time. She dropped her head onto his shoulder and reached behind him to undo the knot she'd tied in his jacket. Nadia removed the gauze from his mouth and then climbed off him. Dr. Kaleb stood up, pulled up his jacket, and discarded the condom.

Nadia walked over to the table, grabbed her dress, and stepped into it. While he was straightening his clothes, she walked over to him. "Zip me up behind, please."

He zipped her dress, rubbed his hand across her shoulders, and then spun her around. "We can't keep doing this, Nadia."

She glared at him. He broke eye contact and turned around to grab her chart.

"Okay, well, if you'll give me the date for my surgery and let me know what else I need to do, I'll be on my way."

"I didn't mean it like it sounded."

"You men never do. Always after you get the cookies, never before right?" He opened his mouth to say something, but Nadia stopped him before he could speak. "That's okay. I'm not sentimental anyway. If you were expecting me to get all dramatic, cry, or be heartbroken then I'm sorry but you've been fucking the wrong woman. However, it would be really nice if you could get me in here as soon as possible for my implants."

He cleared his throat. "Well, just stop by the front desk and my team will let you know the next steps and the exact date of your surgery."

Smiling, Nadia grabbed her purse and shades. She kissed him softly on his cheek. "That's just in case you change your mind about ending it." She opened the door and strutted down the hall. After almost an hour of reviewing and signing all the paperwork, Nadia just wanted to get home, shower, and relax. She sat outside the doctor's office in her car trying to think of the easiest route to take on the way home, and thinking of a few other things too . . .

Diary Entry #5

Screwing the doctor was a good start to my day. His office is a semi-public place. I personally prefer an alley, bathroom, or parking lot, but it's still a little risky being caught with him in his office. That thought alone gives me a bit of an adrenaline rush and intensifies my orgasm. But, I still can't get my mind off of Mr. No-Name. I vividly remember his hand grabbing mine, rubbing his fingers across my flesh,

and then softly pressing his lips to my knuckles. OMG. I keep trying to tell myself it was nothing, and that it was just a harmless kiss on the hand. But somehow he had managed to turn that simple act of kindness and flattery into something so sexual and left me wanting more. Sooooo much more. I'm trying to use my imagination and picture him in one of my fantasies, but I can't picture him on his knees, wearing a collar, and begging for more. I actually can't picture him submitting to me at all. Something about those scenarios with him is just not fitting. I don't even know who the hell he is, but I'm certain that I want to see him again. Who knows, maybe the next time he'll put some kisses in other places besides my hand. N.H.

Chapter Ten

"Girl, I just don't want to go. I'm not in the mood to answer any questions or call lights, deal with overbearing family members, admit patients back to back . . . I'm just tired of going to Ellerton overall. Hell, who am I kidding? I'm tired of all hospitals, not just Ellerton. I need something else. I'm just tired of the same thing, and I really want to do something else. Ya know?"

Kensington was in total agreement with everything Vanity was saying. They hadn't been nurses for long, but all of them were on the verge of "nurse burnout."

"I hear ya, girl. I was there last night," Kensington said. "Same old, same old. Discharged one patient and got an admit as soon as I got there. I had a patient with almost the entire pharmacy ordered PRN. Admitted two more patients, and then hanging blood all night on another patient. All while trying to chart and deal with the ego of some new doctor hospitalist who was there last night. Between giving meds, hanging blood, charting, and doing admissions, I don't know how I had the time to give him that blow job."

"Waaaaaaaait what? Give who a blow job?"

"Dr. Randahl, the new hospitalist at Ellerton. He's hung like a horse, but he's such an arrogant son of a bitch."

Vanity burst out laughing. "So, let me get this straight. You?"

"Uh-huh."

"And the new doctor?"

"Uh-huh."

"Engaged in sexual activities last night?"

"Uh-huh."

"Wooooooooow. Okay, well, I can't wait to see what he looks like."

"He's actually very handsome. Tall, muscular, dark skinned, and a million-dollar smile to top it off."

"Well, if he's here tonight I'll let you know what I think. I'm getting ready to walk in now, but I reaaaaaaally don't want to! Hey, before I forget, Nadia said were all getting together Saturday for lunch and shopping."

"Yeah, we all have some things we need to catch each other up on—one being the reason why you called in sick last night."

"Oh, don't worry, I'm going to tell you all about it, but it needs to be an early lunch, because we will definitely need some time to shop. The event this Saturday has a masquerade theme."

"Yeah, I got the invitation."

"What invitation?"

"The one you left on my windshield."

"Kensi, I don't know what the hell you're talking about. I didn't leave an invitation on your car."

Kensi took a moment to process what Vanity said before saying, "That's odd. Maybe it's for something else. I'll have to look at the invitation again. Where is this event going to be?"

"A mansion in Beverly Hills. It's really nice. They're doing the full decor tomorrow. I think you and Nadia will love it," Vanity said. Kensi had gotten completely quiet "Hello, Kensi?"

"Okay, early lunch, shopping, masquerade theme. Got it. I'll see you then, and have a good night at work." Kensi quickly hung up before Vanity could say anything else.

Kensi had been at the beach for a few hours and still wasn't quite ready to go. But after her talk with Vanity, she grabbed her bag, flip-flops, and snatched up her beach blanket. She hurried to the car and threw her things onto the passenger seat. Reaching above her head, she grabbed the invitation and stared at it. This had to be the same party. There was a slight chance in hell that there were two masquerade balls that night, and an even smaller chance that they were both in Beverly Hills. She had had an idea of what kind of party it was, but now that she knew it was one of Vanity's events, she knew for sure what kind of party it was going to be. The only thing she didn't know was who left her a personal invitation, and why he or she were requesting her presence at such an event.

Diary Entry #6

The hardest part about being promiscuous is remembering all of your partners. I'm trying to think back to all my partners. I can't imagine which one could have kept a close-enough eye on me to know where I worked, when I worked, and that I'd even consider showing up at a random address for who knows what. My instincts tell me that Dr. Randahl left the invitation on my windshield, but people at the hospital rarely want you knowing them outside of work. And I had just met him the night before the invitation was left on the windshield. Maybe he wanted some more of me, and the way he took control of the situation leads me to believe he could actually run in the same circle of people as Vanity. I'm definitely going to that party on Saturday, and my mission is to find out who sent me my own individual invitation. K.D.

Chapter Eleven

Vanity was sitting at the nursing station checking charts. It was three hours into her shift and she was trying to get as much done as possible before she got an admission. Taking a second to relax, she leaned back in her chair and her jaw dropped when she saw him breezing down the hall towards the nursing station. Ms. Gwen looked at Vanity salivating and said, "That, my dear, is Dr. Randahl."

"That's Dr. Randahl?" Vanity said a bit too loud.

Ms. Gwen looked over her glasses and eyeballed Vanity. Ms. Gwen had been the secretary on the telemetry unit for ten years. If you wanted to know who was who, or what was what, you asked Ms. Gwen. "Yeah, you know him or something?"

"No. I'd heard we had a new hospitalist on nights, but they failed to mention that he was ... um ..."

"Tall, dark, and handsome," Ms. Gwen said.

"Precisely, Ms. Gwen. Preeeeeeecisely."

"Good evening, ladies."

Vanity smiled casually, trying to keep her cool.

Dr. Randahl held out his hand to Vanity. "I don't believe we've met yet. I'm Dr. Kenneth Randahl."

Vanity, still smiling, held out her hand. "I'm Vanity. Pleasure to meet you."

Ms. Gwen cleared her throat. "I'm fine, Dr. Randahl. I didn't know you were on call tonight. I've been paging Dr. Ogbee. It's no wonder why he didn't call back."

"Yes, I'm on tonight. Gladly so," he said while staring at Vanity.

Slowly removing her hand from his, Vanity said, "Well, it was nice meeting you, Dr. Randahl." She turned and headed down the hall. Kensi had said he was handsome, but she'd failed to say that he looked like sex in human form. She grabbed her phone out of her work tote and started to text.

Saw the doctor. Next time be a little more specific when you say HANDSOME! OMGEEEEE! We'll discuss this further Saturday!

"So, how's your night going?" a voice said.

Vanity looked up and stared straight into the megawatt smile she had been warned about.

"It's fine, give me just one second." She quickly texted Kensi, *And he just flashed me with the smile.* Then she looked up at Dr. Randahl.

"Your night. How is it?"

"Fine and yours?"

"Just got better. You're beautiful, you know that?"

Before she could respond to his comment, her phone chimed. Kensi texted her, *Why do you think I gave him the BJ duh! Yes, we'll talk more Saturday.*

Vanity smiled and turned her attention back to Dr. Randahl. "Sorry about that. You were saying?"

"I was just saying how beautiful you were. How long have you been working here?"

"Thank you for the compliment, and not long. I moved here after I finished college and I've been here ever since."

"Yeah, I just moved here myself. So, what is there to do out here?"

"Well, of course there's the beach, my personal favorite being Manhattan Beach. Perfect place for surfing, the shopping is nice, and you can grab something to eat too. It's also a great place to meet people."

"So, where's a great place to take a beautiful woman on a date?"

"Well, Dr. Randahl, that depends on the woman."

"She's a nurse. She's beautiful, and she seems to be very fond of Manhattan Beach. Any ideas?"

Vanity paused and stared at him for a moment. She couldn't believe he was hitting on her after he'd just hooked up with Kensi.

"Dr. Randahl, that's very nice of you, and I'm flattered, but I don't date people I work with." She gave him her best smile. "You'll have to excuse me, but I have patients to check on." She walked off. It really didn't matter how hot he looked; if he thought he was going to run through the crew he was dead wrong.

Chapter Twelve

It's the Saturday of the masquerade and Vanity, Nadia, and Kensi had all agreed to meet up at a café in Santa Monica. It was Nadia's idea and closer to her place, but also the midway point for Kensi and Vanity, so they didn't object. However, they were trying to figure out how the person who lived the closest to the location was the one who was late.

"Where the hell is Nadia? She texted me at eight this morning to make sure I was still coming and she's not even here on time," Vanity said, taking another sip of her Bloody Mary.

Kensi stared out the window, still thinking about her invitation and whether or not she should tell Vanity and Nadia about it.

"Helllllllo, earth to Kensington!"

"Yeah, she texted me too. I don't know where she is. Maybe she's stuck in traffic or something," Kensi said.

"Well, you must be stuck in China. What's going on? You zoned out on me when we were on the phone the other day too. Then hung up on me before I could get the word good-bye all the way out. You want to talk about it?"

"I'm fine. Just thinking about work, my family, and this party tonight. I'm not even sure if I feel up to going."

Vanity put her drink down. "Is everything okay with your family? How's your dad doing?"

"He's fine. I'm supposed to be going to the doctor with him soon. Nothing serious, just a checkup, but I miss him. I need to drive out to Santa Barbara and visit, but I've been so busy."

"Let me know when you go back to visit, and I'll go with you. It's been a while since I saw him and Maddie. As far as work goes, I don't think any of us thought this was how nursing would be. The other night, I had a patient who could barely breathe but wanted to know if someone could wheel him downstairs so he could smoke! These patients never cease to amaze me. I love taking care of people, but they also need to take care of themselves."

"Sorry I'm late, you guys," Nadia said looking over at a laughing Kensi. Nadia was wearing a plain white t-shirt, ripped dark denim blue jeans, stilettos, and was making her simple attire look like it cost a fortune. „Well, looks like I've already been missing out. What's so funny, Kensi? Is Vanity telling you about another one of her sexcapades gone wrong?"

Vanity looked up. "No. Actually, I was waiting on you to get here, so I could grill Kensi about her latest conquest."

Nadia took a seat at the table and sat her purse in the vacant chair next to her. She looked over at Kensi again, who was now blushing. "Oh really? Then I'm just in time." Nadia had just picked up her menu when the waitress approached the table.

"Hi, I'm Ashley. I'll be your waitress this evening. What can I get you to drink?"

"I'll have a Midori sour please," Nadia said.

"Of course she will," Vanity said, reaching for her Bloody Mary.

Nadia looked over at Vanity. "Are you saying I don't try new things?"

Vanity raised her eyebrows and smiled. "No, honey, we know *you* try *new* things *allllllllll* the time. Just never a different drink."

Now blushing, Nadia turned to the waitress and said, "You know what? I think I'll try a French connection."

"Okay, a French connection for you, and would you ladies like to order anything else?"

"We're fine for now. Thanks."

"Okay. I'll have that right out, and again my name is Ashley if you need anything."

" French connection, huh?" Kensi said.

"Yes. It's the drink my potential conquest ordered the other night." Nadia smiled and looked at Kensi. "But, getting back to you, Ms. Thang. Give me the tea on what Vanity is talking about."

By the time Kensi finished going over what had happened with Dr. Randahl, both Nadia and Vanity were speechless.

"You have got to be kidding me? Dr. Handsome as Hell is a dominant?" Vanity asked.

"That's the impression he made on me. You should've seen the look he had in his eye when he pinned my wrists against the wall. It was some sexy shit, let me tell you." Kensi took a sip of her cosmo.

"Were you scared? I would've been a little shocked. That's a bold ass move to pull." Nadia said.

"No, it was more exciting than anything. If you could have heard the way he was saying my name you'd have given him a blow job too."

"Well, sounds better than my night. I met this guy named Paul with a body like a Greek God. I let him come over, had all the lights off, and was waiting for him in my sex swing. He released me from the sex swing, laid me down, made love to me, then fucked me hard, and when I woke up, he was in my kitchen cooking me breakfast," Vanity said.

Kensi and Nadia looked at each other, and then looked at Vanity. Nadia asked, "And this is a problem how?"

"It's not what I wanted. Sex, rough sex, wild, kinky, no-strings-attached sex is what I was shooting for. All the slow seducing, mixed in with the rough sex, and then breakfast in the morning is just not what I'm looking for right now. And it kind of pisses me off, because if I was looking for that I wouldn't be able to find it."

Kensi chimed in, "So a guy . . . correction, a hot guy, comes over, sexes you the right way, makes an attempt to feed you in the morning, and this is a problem for you? I'm with Nadia on this one. I don't see the problem here either."

"French connection," Ashley said, as she placed the drink in front of Nadia.

"Thanks," Nadia said, accepting the glass and taking a quick sip.

"It really doesn't matter," Vanity continued. "I won't be hearing from him again. I put him out, or should I say, he let himself out after he spoke his peace and left my kitchen a mess."

"Well, in other news, I met a guy who I'd like to bone, but I don't even know his name." Nadia slumped back in her chair, swirling the ice around in her drink, thinking about Mr. No-Name.

Vanity sat forward. "Oh, so names matter now, Nadia?"

"Hmm, not really, but it would be nice to know his. He looks like I'd actually call him back."

"Ladies, would you like another round of drinks?" Ashley asked.

"No, we're fine. Can you bring the check please?"

"Certainly. I'll be right back with the check."

"Okay, enough about these men. What about this party tonight, and where are we going to get something to wear?" Nadia asked.

Vanity chimed in, "I'm so excited that you're finally available on the night of one of my events! Since this will be your first time at one of my events, I don't want to tell you too much. However, these parties can get really wild, but they're all organized. The people that hire me to organize these events make sure security is strictly enforced, bouncers are in place, and of course I'll be there watching you and Kensi's back tonight, so don't worry. The theme is masquerade. Nadia, with this being your first time, it's a good thing the theme is masquerade, because just in case you never want to attend another party nobody will know your identity. However, I kind of hate that you won't get to see everyone with their masks off. You'd be quite surprised who goes to these parties. Not to mention, it's going to be at a mansion in Beverly Hills. But that's all for now. I'll clue you in on the rest when we get there. That way you'll have a visual of the place, and I'll be able to better explain to you what's going on."

Nadia's eyes grew wide with excitement. "Where are we going to get this masquerade stuff from?"

"Hollywood Boulevard of course." Vanity said, finishing off her second Bloody Mary.

They paid the check and headed to Hollywood to get the attire for the night. After hours of searching, they each found the perfect mask. Vanity texted the address of the mansion to Nadia and Kensi's phone as promised. The agreement was to go home, get dressed for the event, and then meet up at the mansion. They had a long eventful night ahead of them.

Diary Entry #7

Nothing like playing dress up and getting paid to do it. I really wish I could be an active participant in tonight's events, but I'm hosting. So, I guess watching will have to do for tonight, which sucks because I've become a fan of wearing masks when engaging in sexual activities. I've been blindfolded several times during sex, and I've done it in pitch-black rooms. Not being able to see anything can make the sex more amazing. All my senses were heightened, and I reached my climax in record time. Sex that allows you to focus purely on sensation can be the best sex, hands down. V.C.

Chapter Thirteen

Kensington waited in the valet line in front of the mansion, and it was beautiful. Lights stretched from two blocks away, tall crème-colored columns stood in the front, rose beds lined up and down the driveway, and well-dressed valet men rushed to the elegant cars that pulled up front. There were Lamborghinis, Ferraris, Vipers, Teslas, and she even spotted a white Bugatti with red striping. Kensi smiled as she thought back to the orgasm she'd chased in one of those going two hundred miles per hour and wondered if the same guy she was chasing it with was here tonight. Maybe he was the one who'd left the invitation on her car window. The address Vanity texted her was the same as the address of the invitation. Kensi was nervous about tonight, but not because of the event. She'd been to several before, but this time there was the lingering mystery of who'd sent her a personalized invite. After a few minutes, Kensi pulled to the front of the line, and one of the valet men opened her door and greeted her.

"Good evening, miss," the young man said, reaching for her hand and helping her out of her car. "My associate will park your car. Have a wonderful evening."

"Thanks." Kensi got out of the car and headed toward the main entrance of the house.

She was then stopped by a young woman. "Good evening and welcome. May I have your name and identification please?"

"Kensington Dumas," she stated, handing the young woman her driver's license.

The young woman smiled and checked the guest list for Kensington's name. She then handed Kensi back her license. "Enjoy your night."

"I plan to," Kensi said, heading into the mansion.

The inside of the home was beautiful. Extravagant paintings graced the walls; there were waiters in black pants, white tuxedo jackets, and gold masquerade masks carrying champagne flutes and sterling silver trays with different appetizers. The marble floors sparkled from the crystal chandelier lights, and there Kensi stood in the grand entryway unsure of which direction she should be heading in. She decided to look around before meeting up with Vanity and Nadia, and she headed in the direction of the French double doors.

***

The night had just begun, and Vanity was already tired from greeting, mingling, and conversing with the guests. She'd had two shots of tequila to relax her and they were already wearing off. Her iPhone buzzed and she was just about to answer it when she felt a tap on her shoulder.

"Well, I've only just got here and already I've found the most attractive woman here," a man said. He was wearing a black medieval mask with bronze spiraling from the temple to the cheeks. He was dressed in a black tuxedo and he was wearing it very well.

"Well, seeing that you can't see my face, I'll have to say that your compliment holds no weight, but that it also doesn't go unnoticed," Vanity countered.

"Well, I'm glad it at least gets some notice. However, it's not always a woman's face that attracts a man. Her body, smile, and personality can be just as desirable."

Even with her mask on, it was obvious that Vanity was beautiful. She was fully covered in a black chiffon gown that showcased her red lingerie underneath. The front of the dress was cut low, showing those breasts that Nadia would've killed to have, and the sleeves tapered at the wrists. Her hair was pulled back in an elegant chignon. The dress was full length and stopped just short of her ankles, just high enough to see her toes painted red, identical to her fingernails. Her red mask only covered her eyes, and she was flashing her million-dollar smile.

"Are you here with anyone?" he asked.

"I'm here with everyone," Vanity answered while reaching for one of the champagne flutes the waiters were carrying, but she missed.

"Oh really. Care to elaborate?" he asked.

"I'm the hostess of this event tonight."

"Really" he replied, while grabbing a champagne flute from another waiter passing by. "Well, it's a pleasure to meet you, Miss . . ." He extended his hand and held out the champagne flute, obviously waiting for Vanity to tell him her name.

Vanity smiled and accepted the glass. "I'm Vanity, and thanks. For a second I thought I was going to have to chase one of the waiters across the room."

He smiled back. "I'm Martin Buchanan, and I'm pretty sure none of the waiters, or any man here for that matter, would mind being chased by you."

"Quite the charmer, aren't you?" Vanity took a sip of her champagne.

"Let's just say I'm sort of a collector of all things beautiful. Usually, those that have true beauty . . ." he said, circling around Vanity, "are like butterflies." He then lowered his voice and whispered in her ear. "Pretty to look at, but very hard to catch."

"Let me guess. You were hoping to add me to your collection?" Vanity took another sip of her champagne and waited for his reply, but it never came. She turned around, and he was gone. She stood on her tiptoes to try to spot him in the crowd, but it was a loss.

Oh great, the first guy I meet tonight who actually interests me turns out to be Houdini, she thought, pulling out her phone. She had three missed calls—two from Kensi and one from Nadia. Figuring Kensi could handle herself, she decided to call Nadia back first since it was the first time she'd been to an event.

***

Nadia had valet-parked her car and was wandering around the mansion. There was a St. Andrew's cross in the middle of what seemed to be the hearth room. A woman was bound to it, and people were gathered around watching as she was being kissed by a whip from her partner. There was erotic music playing in the background and several more scenes taking place around her, but the woman in the middle of the floor had caught Nadia's attention. She was beautiful. Her hands and feet were secured in manacles, her breasts were perky, her nipples were reddened from the clamps in place, and her face was covered with a blue-green mask with feathers and jewels. Her body was slick with sweat, and her skin was reddened across her stomach and thighs as if she was on fire, but the sounds she made each time the whip kissed her flesh told a different story. Nadia could hear it in her voice that it was all pleasure and not pain. And those moans quickly captured Nadia's attention.

"The whole point of a masquerade ball is the anonymity."

Nadia, taking her attention away from the woman on St. Andrew's cross, looked over at the man who was speaking to her. He was dressed in all black like many of the male guests, but with a Phantom of the Opera mask.

"Might I suggest you put on your mask instead of just holding it in your hand," he said.

Nadia had been so wrapped up in valeting the car, calling Vanity and Kensi, and observing the woman in front of her that she'd forgotten to put her mask on.

"Hold this please." She handed the man her silver clutch and walked over to the oversized mirror in the corner of the room. She eyeballed herself in the mirror and was happy with her decision in both dress and mask. She'd decided on a red bandage dress to hug her curves and sparkling silver C.L. red bottoms to match. Her mask was red with black gems down the bridge of her nose, and black and red feathers surrounded the outer edges of the mask. Another reason she'd chosen black and red was so that she could wear the five-karat red sapphire earrings from Tiffany's her parents had bought her for her birthday last year.

Struggling to hold her hair and put her mask on at the same time, the gentleman offered her his assistance. He stood behind her and rubbed his hand across the back of her neck. Then he reached over her shoulder and handed her the clutch in exchange for the mask. He carefully placed her mask on and then turned her around to face him.

Nadia smiled. "Thanks." She then stepped around him and walked back over to the crowd to finish watching the woman on the cross.

Not even two minutes had passed before he was standing right beside her.

"You're enjoying watching her," he said.

"Yes, actually I am. She looks beautiful up there," Nadia replied.

"Would you like to be her?"

Without hesitation, Nadia replied, "No." She looked over at him. "I don't really like to be the one on the receiving end, if you know what I mean. Nice mask though." Then she walked away from the scene, past all the other onlookers, and her eyes landed on Vanity. Vanity was across the room speaking with one of the guests when she spotted Nadia. She excused herself and walked over to where Nadia was standing.

"So, what do you think so far?" Vanity asked.

"Well, I think I should've come to one of these events of yours sooner. So far I like what I see. I was just propositioned to participate in one of the scenes. I almost said yes. Almost!" Nadia grinned and took another sip of champagne.

"I think you should. After all, that's what you're here for," Kensi said, approaching Vanity and Nadia. "Well, don't you two ladies look absolutely fabulous this evening."

"As do you," Vanity said. Turning her attention back to Nadia, she asked, "And why did you decide against participating?"

"Because he wanted me to be the submissive and that's not my thing. I'm more into giving the orders than getting ordered," Nadia replied.

"Let me just say this before I leave you two ladies to it. Tonight is a night of exploration and one of anonymity. Why don't both of you take a few steps outside of your comfort zone. Try something different. Besides, we're all wearing masks, and there's absolutely no better time than now. However, you cannot partake in sexual activities if you've consumed any alcohol. Those are the house rules. And at these events, it's usually how you can tell the voyeurs from the exhibitionists." Speaking her peace, Vanity walked away to finish greeting the guests.

"So, who propositioned you, Nadia?"

"Hell if I know. Some guy with a Phantom of the Opera mask. I was watching the woman in the center of the room on St. Andrew's cross, and he asked me if I wanted to be her."

"And?" Kensi asked.

"And . . . I said no, but for a second I wanted to tell him yes. I don't know. It was something in his voice and the way he rubbed his hands across my neck that made me consider letting him put me on display in front of everyone. It's almost as if I've met him before or something."

"What would it matter if you did know him?" Kensi countered.

Nadia thought about it for a moment, then said, "I don't think it would."

"Then go for it. I'll catch up with you later." Kensi smiled and walked away.

"Yeah. Later." Nadia stood there contemplating Vanity's words. *Vanity's right. It is only for one night.* And with that, she set out to find the guy with the Phantom mask. Why not switch sides . . . for one night?

Chapter Fourteen

Kensi had come to this party with the intentions of finding the person who'd left that invitation on her car, but she didn't know where to start, and it really didn't help that everyone was wearing a mask. She headed up the winding staircase, admiring the decor of the mansion. There were several rooms, some with doors open while others were closed. She stopped in front of a room with the door slightly cracked. She'd been so intrigued with the paintings on the wall, the crown molding, and the lighting that she hadn't realize she'd come to the end of the hall. The house was gorgeous and it had been decorated to the nines, there was no way she was going to leave without at least getting a look at one of the rooms. Without further delay, she pushed the door open.

When she stepped inside, Kensi was in awe. There was an elegant chair with the legs outlined in gold, a dark gray seat, and a black throw across the back. The Victorian-style bed was all black and situated against the far wall. There were flameless candles carefully aligned around the footboard of the bed and on the nightstands on both sides of the bed. A metal pole, from the floor all the way to the vaulted ceilings, stood in the middle of the bedroom. To her left, there was a rack on the wall. Walking over to investigate further, she realized the rack was holding whips, riding crops, and what appeared to be feather ticklers. Some were long and thick, while others short and thin. Kensi ran her hand across one of the riding crops, imagining the sting from it, but more importantly, the pleasure it could bring. She stepped back and moved on to the chest. It was antique in fashion to match the bed and faded ash gray in color. *Just a quick peek,* she thought, as she opened the top drawer. There were anal beads, flavored condoms, vibrating tongue rings, and cock rings all wrapped in plastic and aligned neatly in the velvet-lined drawer. She closed it and opened the next one. Rows of butterfly vibrators, strap-ons, blindfolds, sex dice, and even a black-and-white box that read "The Accommodator." The look of the accommodator peaked her interest. She sat her clutch on top of the chest and took the box out of the drawer. She examined it trying to imagine how it worked. From the illustration on the box, it looked promising. She placed it neatly back in place, closed the drawer, and turned toward the bed. The California king-size bed looked so soft, so welcoming, and she couldn't wait to see if it was as soft as it looked. Without further delay, Kensi jumped backward onto bed. It was heavenly, and the plush bedding just sucked her right in. She rolled over onto her stomach, kicking the pillow with her legs.

"Have you cured your curiosity yet?" a voice asked from the doorway.

Kensi immediately sat up. "It's not nice to sneak up on people," she said to the masked man leaning against the doorway with his arms folded. He was dressed in a fitted black turtleneck, expensive white slacks, all-white mask, and his arms were folded like the world was his to command.

"I wasn't. I was simply admiring the view. I've been watching the woman in the purple dress since she came through the door."

Kensi had spent a pretty penny on this dress a while back and had been waiting on a reason to wear it. The dress was deep purple, bandeau in style, tight fitting, with a split that went all the way up her thigh. Her mask was the same deep purple as her dress, with midnight blue and sea-green stones around the eyes and cheeks of the mask, and she'd put a slight curl at the end of her hair and left it down to fall around her shoulders. She hadn't forgotten her objective of finding out who'd sent her that invitation. Nothing about him sparked her memory, but that didn't mean a thing.

"And do we know each other?" Kensi asked while slowly getting off the bed. "Or were you just hoping we'd get to know each other."

"The latter." He pushed himself off the doorframe but still kept his arms folded. "I'd like a little more privacy." He took two steps into the room. "Would you mind if I closed the door?"

"No, not at all," she said.

He turned around, shut the door, and went back to his original stance. The masks were becoming an annoyance to Kensi. She wanted to see his face. Not that his body wasn't something to look at, but facial features would've been nice. She figured it wouldn't hurt to ask.

"The door is closed. I think it's safe for us to remove our masks now," Kensi said, anticipating his response.

He took a few steps to the right in front of the chair, and then had a seat. "I'd like to keep them on. Mystery makes things more interesting, but if it would make you more comfortable, feel free to take yours off."

Kensi thought about being ballsy and taking off her mask just to show him she didn't care if he knew her or not, but she decided against it. From the neck down, he looked sexy as hell, and as long as he fucked as well as he looked then everything was all good. "I'll only show you mine if you show me yours," she said cleverly.

"That's where you're wrong. You're going to show me yours anyway."

"Oh. I am, am I?" Kensi asked.

"Yes. Starting with that dress. Don't get me wrong, it's beautiful, but I have a feeling it doesn't do your body any justice," he replied nonchalantly, crossing one leg over the other.

Kensi stood there. She was racking her brain trying to come up with a quick reply, but she couldn't. Her best reply was to undress. She turned around in her heels and reached behind to unzip the dress, but it was stuck.

Trying her best to remain sexy, she looked over her shoulder at him and asked, "Can you help me please?"

"No. Do what you would do if I wasn't here," he ordered.

"But you are here, and this is an eight-hundred-dollar dress," Kensi said.

He got up from the chair and stood behind her. "Send me the bill," and then he grabbed the back of the dress and ripped it off her. He threw the dress across the room and turned her around to face him.

He took a minute to admire her. The womanly curves, how soft her lips looked, and her brown eyes. With his finger, he drew a line from her wrist up to her chin. Then he tipped her head up toward him with his finger and his thumb. "Dance for me." Then he dropped his hand, walked back over to the chair, and sat down.

Kensi stood there in her Victoria's Secret half-bra and matching thong set. Contemplating her next move, she thought back to all those pole-dancing classes Vanity had dragged her to. She grabbed her clutch off the chest and took out her phone. Opening her iTunes app, Kensi chose Beyoncé's "Rocket," turning the volume all the way up. She looked over at him sitting there anticipating her next move. Taking her eyes off him and getting into stripper mode, she walked over to pole.

Kensi grabbed the pole with her left hand and wide-stepped around in front of it. With her legs still spread, she grabbed the pole with her right hand and dropped all the way to the floor. Then, she came back up slowly, bending over, and giving him a good look at her ass. While working her hips in a circular motion, she threw her hair over her shoulder and snuck a look at him. He was still cool and calmly enjoying the show, so she kicked it up a notch. She wrapped her right leg around the pole, then she jumped up and used her left leg to secure herself in place. Using her hands and legs, she climbed up the pole, and then she let her hands go and fell backwards with both legs still wrapped against the pole. She had an upside-down view of him; he was now sitting at the edge of the chair with both elbows resting on his knees and his hands interlocked. Kensi smiled to herself knowing she'd brought him to the end of his seat. Her confidence in herself was now through the roof. She was also silently thanking Vanity for dragging her to those classes. She reached behind her back and undid her bra; she slowly took it off and tossed it at him. He caught it and then threw it across the room on the floor with the remains of her dress. Using her upper-body strength, she brought herself back up and grabbed the pole with both hands. She swung around to face him and released her legs from the pole; she held them outward and spread wide while she slowly slid down the pole with her hands. As soon as her feet touched the floor, she spun away from the pole and dropped down to the floor again. She threw her head back, sexily scattering her hair over her back and shoulders. Then, she snatched off her mask, throwing it over her shoulder, and crawled toward him. When she reached the chair, she looked up at his still-masked face, rocked backward on her heels, and starting singing along with the song. "Punish me," she said. She slowly stood up and stepped back, and asked, "Did you like that?"

He didn't say a word. He stood up from the chair, snatched her off her feet, grabbing both of her thighs. He rushed her over to the bed and threw her onto it, landing softly on top of her. "You're beautiful," he whispered. Kensi didn't reply; she just stared into his sea-green eyes, bit her lip, and wondered what was going to happen next.

He abruptly got off the bed and walked over to the dresser. He opened the second drawer and took out two boxes. He opened the first one and removed the contents. It was a blindfold. "Sit up," he commanded. When she did, he reached behind her and tried to tie the blindfold.

Kensi grabbed his wrist. "You asked me to take off my mask just to cover my face with another one?"

"Shhh. Trust is how this works. Just trust me."

Kensi dropped her hand and let him tie the blindfold behind her eyes. Then he gently lowered her back onto the bed and opened the second box. "I saw you curiously studying this box. Perhaps I should show you how it works." He took the plastic wrapping off the accommodator. He strapped it around his chin and then slowly worked his way up her body. He placed kisses around her naval and drew imaginary circles on her thighs and stomach with his hand. Moving further down, he ran his tongue across her panties. Kensi moaned and squirmed. He knew what she wanted. Then he grabbed her thong with his teeth and dragged them down her thighs slowly. He removed them and spread her legs, and by this time, she was soaking wet and the anticipation was killing her. He lowered his head between her legs and slowly inserted the accommodator. Then he pulled it out a little and inserted it again.

"Yes!" Kensi's back bowed all the way off the bed, and that was all the indication he needed to know that she was enjoying it. He slid it all the way out again, and then without warning he slid all the way in and used his tongue to tease her clit. Still having two free hands, he used one hand to reach behind and grab her ass to hold her in place and the other hand reached up and pinched her nipple.

"Oh my gawd! That feels amazing." His tongue was moving faster than the speed of light, and Kensi's moans were barely able to keep up with all the sensations. "I'm gonna . . . I'm . . . I'm gonna come." With the accommodator penetrating her constantly, and his tongue soaking up every drop of her wetness, it wasn't long before she came.

Kensi exploded from the inside out. Her body quivered from all the different sensations she was feeling at one time. She'd been on the receiving end of oral sex plenty of times. But his tongue, the penetration, and his hands made her orgasm amazing. She was lying on the bed still trying to catch her breath. Carefully taking off her blindfold, he looked into her eyes. Then he kissed her cheek and headed toward the door. She wanted him and was anticipating him penetrating her. He'd lit a fire inside of her, and now he was going to leave before he put it all the way out.

"What the hell! That's it?"

He stopped at the door, but he didn't turn around. "I'll be in touch," he said, and then he walked out of the room, leaving Kensi on the bed in a state of confusion.

Kensi looked up at the ceiling, trying to put together everything that took place, "What in the hell just happened here?"

Chapter Fifteen

Nadia was secured on the cross and was as nervous as she'd ever been. She knew why the no-alcohol rule was existent, but she was also in total disagreement with it right now. A few shots of patron would totally put her at ease right now. She'd found the man with the Phantom mask and convinced herself to "step out of her comfort zone," as Vanity had suggested. But she was re-thinking everything right now. Not being too fond of being the submissive, she couldn't help but think of how glad she was to be wearing both the mask and the blindfold. She was glad that she couldn't see their faces and that they couldn't see hers.

"Just relax and let me take care of you," he whispered softly in her ear to put her at ease. He gently rubbed his hand across Nadia's bare back. Going down further, he cupped her cheek and gripped her thong.

As soon as he touched her, Nadia went from tense to relaxed. She was waiting on the first moment when he would strike her with the whip, or paddle, or crop. She wanted to look and feel like the woman who had been up there before her. Nadia licked her lips when he ran his thumb across her nipple, but that wasn't what she was up here for. Just as quick as his touch came, it went. She wondered what he was doing and just what the fuck he was waiting on.

Without any warning, Nadia felt several light stings across her back followed by the gentle caress of his hand. "Ohhhhhhhh," she said while thinking to herself that it was not a regular whip. It was a cat o' nine tails. "Again," she said, awaiting the next sting.

"You don't give the orders here. I do. Do you understand?"

Nadia said, "Yes, but please."

It pleased him to know she liked it, but it displeased him that she was still trying to give the orders.

"Who's giving the orders here?" he asked, but Nadia didn't reply.

He stuck his hands between her legs, massaging her clit. He was toying with her. He thought he was punishing her for not answering, but little did he know, she liked every minute of it.

"I'll ask again, who's giving the orders here?"

Nadia, still too brass to give in, didn't say a word, but she was secretly hoping he'd keep toying with her so she could catch the orgasm she knew was coming. She wiggled, but being secured to the cross made it difficult for her to maneuver. As soon as she'd gotten his hand in the right spot, he pulled it away.

Frustrated, Nadia asked, "What are you doing?"

"You don't give the orders here, I do. Therefore, you don't get to orgasm until, or should I say, unless I say so." He whispered in her ear, "You don't think I recognized what you were doing? Sweetheart, this is not my first rodeo."

He stepped back and struck her three times with the CO9T. Right cheek, left cheek, and then both cheeks, followed by his hand gently smoothing away the sting. He asked again, "Who gives the orders?"

Chasing her breath but still trying to hold her own, Nadia answered, "You . . . for now."

Smiling, he whispered in her ear, "Fair enough."

Chapter Sixteen

"Tough one, isn't she?"

Vanity took her eyes off watching Nadia, and turned to the man who had pulled a disappearing act on her earlier. "Ah, Mr. Buchanan. How nice of you to re-appear."

"Please, call me Martin, and a man can hardly stay away from someone as beautiful as you," he replied.

"Well, if I'm as beautiful to you as you say, then you wouldn't have vanished to begin with."

"My apologies. Perhaps you'll allow me to make it up to you sometime?"

Taking her eyes off him, she looked back at Nadia. Her chocolate skin made it difficult to see where she'd been whip-kissed, but all the other signs were there. She was slick with sweat, her hair had fallen, her breaths were heavy, she was licking her lips, and she'd all but threw in the towel. Nadia was defeated, but she still was not giving up. Looking at Nadia made Vanity wish she wasn't hosting or had any drinks so she could participate tonight. She was horny as hell and the champagne hadn't made it any better.

She looked back over at the gentleman standing next to her and said, "As a matter of fact you can, Martin Buchanan, and there's no better time than now. Follow me."

Vanity walked out of the room where half the party had gathered to watch Nadia. She and Martin went through the double doors and up the stairs. Going into the first bedroom with the door open, she snatched Martin's hand and pulled him in the room. Not bothering to turn on the lights, Vanity walked over to the bed and pushed him down, straddling him. She reached over to the nightstand and pulled a gold-wrapped condom from the drawer. Then she kicked off her heels and pulled down her panties. She was going to make this quick because she had to get back to the party, but she was going to enjoy every minute of it.

Without warning, she pulled down his pants and briefs. He was already erect and ready. *Perfect*, Vanity thought, because she didn't have time to resort to other tactics to get him hard. She slid the condom down and straddled him very slowly. Originally she was sliding down slowly to tease him, but midway down it became quite difficult to adjust and accommodate his size. The fullness itself was mind-blowing. She lifted herself all the way up and then back down again several times, keeping a steady pace. He grabbed her hips to slow her movements even more, but she wasn't having it. She came up here chasing an orgasm and she was going to get just that.

"Shhhhhhhhhhhitttt," he moaned, obviously enjoying Vanity's efforts.

"I hope you're almost there," Vanity said, because she was just about there.

Vanity lifted herself all the way up to the very tip of his penis, and then slammed down. She cried out in pleasure, as he grabbed her hips, lifting her up and dropping her on his length. He lifted her once more and he moaned in pure satisfaction.

Vanity caught her breath and then climbed off the bed. She grabbed her panties off the floor and slipped her feet back in her shoes.

"Hey," Martin said, but she walked out and closed the door.

She heard Martin say something, but if she couldn't meet a guy who was going to be no-strings-attached, then she was going to create her own circumstances. Besides, he'd already pulled a disappearing act earlier, so it was only right that she return the favor.

Vanity headed down the hall to find another vacant room that had a bathroom in it when she heard her name being called. At the end of the hall, Kensi was sticking her head out of the room. Vanity quickened her steps. Kensi opened the door, ushered Vanity inside the room quickly, and shut the door.

"What the hell are you doing in here?" Vanity asked.

"Doing what you told me. What does it look like?"

"Kensi, I told you to step outside of your comfort zone, not to get naked and go to a room and play with yourself. Hell, you could've done that at home. And where the hell are your clothes?"

"For your information, I was in here with someone earlier."

"Really? You mean to tell me you got so wild you ran the man off?" Vanity smiled.

"Ha-ha, very funny, Vanity. No. He ripped my damn clothes off, I did a strip tease for him, and then he laid me down and gave me incredible head using that thing." Kensi said pointing to the accommodator. "Then left me in here to get dressed, but I don't have a dress anymore. He tore it straight down the middle. It's basically in shreds over there on the floor."

"Damn, I wish I wasn't hosting tonight!"

Kensi looked at Vanity's hand and smiled. "Well, from the looks of it, I'd say you hosting hasn't stopped a damn thing."

Vanity looked down at her hand, where her panties were balled up in her fist. "It was only a quickie. Not much to talk about, but right now we need to get you something to wear. Where's your mask, or did he shred that too?"

"No, smart ass. I still have it," Kensi said.

"Okay, get your mask and pull yourself together. Get your dress, put in on as best as you can, and I'm going to go find you something to wear. I'll be right back."

Vanity headed back down the hall to find Kensi something to wear. But first she needed to stop by a bathroom.

Chapter Seventeen

Nadia was sitting on the edge of the bed in a room that appeared to be the master suite. She was in subspace. She felt hypnotic, euphoric, like she was floating. It was calming, and she'd felt so sexy, so desired, so cared for. But she couldn't get comfortable with those feelings. Her head was swimming with both welcomed and unwelcomed thoughts. She knew how it went, and she knew she was supposed to wait for him to come in, check on her, and make sure she was okay. But she was naturally a dominant. She didn't need some man to come check on her.

Nadia grabbed her clothes and quickly got dressed. She wasn't the type to sit around waiting on a man, and she wasn't going to let the fact that she'd switched sides on the whip for one night change that.

She gave herself a quick look-over in the floor-to-ceiling mirror. She looked like she did when she'd first arrived. When she stepped closer to the mirror, she saw that one of her earrings was missing. She immediately searched the room from top to bottom. She looked all over the floor, under the bed, she'd tossed pillows around, and still couldn't find it.

Having felt she'd wasted enough time looking for it, she opened the door and walked out of the room. She walked through the hearth room and glanced at the woman who was now in the spotlight of where she'd just been less than fifteen minutes ago. Without missing a step, she headed out of the front door and summoned one of the valet men to retrieve her car. She had to get home to get her head together.

***

Vanity had stopped by the bathroom, gotten Kensi something to wear from one of the playrooms, and was headed toward the stairs when she saw Nadia flying out the front door. "Hey," she yelled at one of the waiters passing by. He stopped, and Vanity took the tray from his hand and replaced it with the outfit she'd gotten for Kensi.

"Listen to me very carefully. Take this with you. Go up the stairs to the last door at the end of the hall. A woman will answer the door. Give that to her and tell her to meet me by the bar in ten minutes, okay?"

He nodded and turned quickly to deliver the items as instructed. Vanity was headed toward the front door to see where Nadia was going and why she was leaving so soon. She sat the tray she'd taken from the waiter on the table in the entryway next to one of the oversized flower arrangements and rushed outside just in time enough to see Nadia's taillights. She pulled out her phone to call her and saw that she had a notification from a group text. It was from Nadia to both her and Kensi.

Nadia: *Had to cut out early. Will call you both tomorrow.*

Vanity quickly texted back: *The party is over at 1am. I'll call you as soon as I wrap things up here!*

Vanity turned around and headed back into the house, and went in search of her boss.

***

"Alex, I was just about to call you. The woman you were with earlier, what happened?" Vanity asked.

"I'm not sure. I left her in the suite to go get a few things, and when I came back, she was gone. I was just heading up the stairs to see if she was in one of the private rooms."

"Well, don't bother. I tried to catch her, but she's already gone. I'll call her as soon as I wrap things up here," Vanity replied.

"So, you know her?" he asked.

"Yes, and I can assure you she'll be okay."

"I didn't even get the chance to tell her my name, who I was, or anything," Alex said, running his hand through his hair.

"And why is this all so important?" Vanity asked.

"Because I—"

"Alexander, I was wondering when I would get to speak with you tonight," Martin said, approaching them.

"Martin, nice to see you, man. I'd like you to meet the woman responsible for planning all of my events."

"Vanity," Martin said, interrupting Alex again.

Vanity casually shook Martin's hand as if she hadn't just had a quickie with him upstairs. "Mr. Buchanan, so nice to see you again. Alex, we'll continue this later. Gentlemen, if you'll excuse me." Vanity stepped away from the men and sneaked into an empty room.

Nadia was gone and Kensi was supposed to meet her at the bar. The night was coming to a close, and if anyone was ready for it to be over it was Vanity.

Chapter Eighteen

Kensi heard the knock at the door. She'd tried to figure out how she could put the dress on well enough to make it out of the party, but it was a total loss. She opened the door and was shocked to see one of the masked waiters.

"Yes?" she asked.

"I was told to bring you these," he said.

"Oh, thanks." She grabbed the clothes out of his hands and closed the door. She didn't know what the hell Vanity had sent her to wear. It was a leather shorts cat suit with slits down each side and looked like she'd need a bottle of baby oil to slide into it. She held it up and let it unfold, and something dropped to the floor. It was another envelope with her name on it. She ran to the door and opened it, looking for the waiter who had just brought her the clothes, but there was no sign of him. Kensi closed the door and ripped open the envelope. It was different from the invite she'd received; it was a white card with almost perfect handwriting in black pen.

It was instant gratification watching you arrive at this event.

But the sounds of you being pleasured were the most satisfying.

It's my fantasy to give you orgasms like that repeatedly.

And when fantasies become a reality then pleasure is certain.

Whatever, Kensi thought as she put on the silly leather suit. She shook her head at her outfit. She grabbed the note and envelope off the bed and put them both in her clutch. She still didn't know who was sending the notes, but she wasn't going to stand here any longer thinking about it. Kensi opened the door and headed to the bar.

When Kensi got to the bar, Vanity was waiting for her.

"Really, Vanity? The only thing you could find for me to wear was a boy-short Catwoman outfit?"

"Look around you, Kensi. We're not exactly at Neiman Marcus."

"Where's Nadia?"

"Don't you read your texts? She left about ten minutes ago."

"Why?"

"I don't know. I told her I'll call her after I finish things up here. She just ran out of here. You should have seen her, and without an explanation might I add."

"Well, judging from your tone, you're clueless as to why she left, so there's no need in me asking. Perhaps you can help me with this." Kensi handed Vanity the note.

Vanity read it, and then looked up at Kensi. "Who in the hell is leaving you love notes at a friggin' sex party?"

"Oh, that's the second one. The first one was an invitation to the party. Then, whomever you sent to the room to bring me this tasteless getup brought this with them."

"One of the waiters?"

"Yeah, but by the time I saw the envelope he was already gone."

Vanity turned around and looked out at the crowd of people. It was swarming with both guests and waiters. She'd told one of them to take the clothes up to the room, but she didn't know which one. All of them were wearing the same thing and everyone had on a mask.

She felt bad that she didn't have more information for Kensi. "I'm sorry, but I have no earthly idea which waiter I asked to bring you those clothes, but what I can do is get you a list of all their names. We have to do in-depth background checks, and everyone has to sign confidentiality agreements—the whole nine yards. Maybe you'll recognize one of the names on there."

"Then what? You going to make a love connection for me, Vanity?"

"You know, for someone who could have a potential stalker you sure are calm," Vanity countered.

"I think it's this outfit." Kensi looked down at the skintight leather cat suit. "I'm dressed like a badass, so I might as well act like one. Besides, my dress is upstairs in ruins and I'm still floating a little. I'm going to go home, jump in the shower, and then pass out."

"Well, I still have to finish up here before I can go or I'd be walking right out of the door with you."

"Do your thing here and I will see you later, girl," Kensi said, then headed toward the exit.

Vanity wished she were leaving, but she had too much to do, and finding out what the hell happened between Alex and Nadia was at the top of her list. She'd get that list of names to Kensi later, but this couldn't wait; she was sure Alex was just as anxious to talk to her as she was to talk to him.

It was 12:30, and she was glad this party was almost over. The crowd had thinned out but only a little. People were leaving randomly, some with people they knew, some with people they just met, the usual. Vanity thought about getting another drink but decided against it. She wanted to be fully alert and oriented when she spoke with her boss, Alex. Leaving the bar, she set out once again to look for him

Vanity found Alex in the master suite twirling something between his fingers. "Alex," she said.

Taking his focus from what he was doing, Alex stood up from the bed and looked Vanity square in the eye. "I need her address. I'm going to go check on her. You can handle things here, can't you?" Assuming Vanity was going to roll over and do as he said, he started readying himself to go.

"I can't give that to you," Vanity said.

Alex stopped what he was doing. "Come again?"

Vanity crossed her arms and gave him the same menacing glare he was giving her. "She's a friend—one of my best friends to be exact—and I'm not going to offer up her address to you for your own personal needs."

"You know as well as I do that the last thing a submissive should be right now is alone. I'm going to her house, so you can either give me the address yourself, or I'll get it from the database. I was just hoping you could save me the trouble," Alex countered.

"Well, Nadia is not a submissive. She was just stepping outside of her comfort zone. Secondly, you won't find her address in the database."

A look of confusion briefly passed his face before he asked the next question. "You did not invite a woman to this party without clearing her. And surely you didn't invite a woman *and* allow her to participate in tonight's events without running her through the system. Did you, Van?"

Vanity just stood there. "No." Alex stared at her like she was slowly putting together a puzzle he was anxious to have solved. Vanity looked around the room. "I let two women in." Alex walked toward the window and put his hand across his mouth in total disbelief of what he was hearing. "But they are both my closest friends, and I know them very, very well. And why are you getting all bent out of shape over this? I've seen you be a lot calmer about much more trivial issues," Vanity said.

"I've met her before," he said. Vanity stood there patiently waiting for him to elaborate. "Remember when I told you that I co-owned a bar in Studio City?"

Vanity's forehead wrinkled as she tried to recall him telling her that. Alex owned so much in LA and had his hand in so many different things it was very difficult to keep up with all of his endeavors.

"She was there, at the Blue Flame earlier this week. She was at the bar, and I offered to buy her a drink. We didn't exchange numbers or anything." Alex stopped and ran his fingers through his hair. "Hell, we didn't even exchange names. I made small talk, and then I left her to enjoy the rest of the night alone, but I haven't stopped thinking about her since that night. It was like seeing a dream come true when I saw her here tonight. She wasn't even wearing her mask; it was as if it was meant for me to see her or something."

"So now that she knows who you are, what's your plan?" Vanity asked.

Alex looked up at Vanity. "Well, we didn't actually get to that part. My plan was to take off my mask and let her see my face, but when I got back to the room she was gone. And you say she's your best friend?"

"One of them, yes," Vanity said with a look of concern on her face. *Just what was he getting at?*

"I'd like to be the one to tell her. Not you. Me," Alex said.

Vanity raised her hand. "Whoa, whoa, whoa. So, what you're saying is you want me to lie to my best friend? Because make no mistake about it, we will discuss tonight. She will inquire about who you are, and I will tell her."

"No, you won't, Van. Strict confidentiality applies to everyone, even you and I. I know that she's your best friend. I'm not asking you to lie. I'm just asking that you omit some particulars."

Vanity opened her mouth to object, but Alex interrupted. "I'll expect you to do me this courtesy in exchange for me forgetting the fact that there were active participants here tonight who had not been pre-screened."

Vanity stood there processing what Alex was saying.

"And I'll still need her address too." Vanity was just about to object when Alex added, "Not to stop by personally, but to return this to her." He held up the red sapphire diamond earring.

Vanity just shook her head at the predicament Alex was putting her in. "I'll see what I can do. Is there anything else we need to discuss?"

"Yes, two things actually. I'll be expecting both of your 'friends' files to be completed ASAP. Secondly, Martin would like for you to collaborate with him on the next event. He seemed very pleased with your work here tonight."

Oh, just fucking great, Vanity thought. Just when she'd thought she found the no-strings-attached situation-ship she was looking for, her boss attached the strings himself. "Yes, Mr. Buchanan, the gentleman from earlier. No problem, it would be my pleasure."

"Good, because he's very eager to work with you . . . almost too eager," Alex said, staring Vanity in the eyes.

Vanity knew where Alex was going with this, but she chose to shy away from the obvious. "What do you mean?"

"It means, I didn't get this far by not paying attention to details. Martin is a man of many means. There can only be one reason why he himself would choose to personally work with you on the next event. He made it clear that he won't be sending a representative, and that you will report and work directly with him." Alex stepped closer to Vanity. "Watch yourself around him, Van. I'm expecting one hundred percent professionalism on this project. We clear?"

"Crystal." Vanity turned on her heels and headed back to the party. It was time to bring the night to an end.

Chapter Nineteen

Diary Entry #8

I can still feel the burn on my skin. I keep touching myself in the places that were kissed with the whip and it takes me back to last night at the party. I've been lying here in bed trying to figure out what it was that I liked so much. I mean, I'm a woman and there's no better touch than from the hands of a man. But this . . . this was different. It was more than just sexually satisfying. I've been riding an euphoric wave since the CO9T first struck me, and I don't want to get off. There was also that man, the mysterious one who touched more than just my body. He ignited something in me that I didn't know existed. I have to find this man who has been invading my mind since last night, and I know just who to ask. N.H.

***

Vanity lay in the bed, looking at the ceiling, and recalling all of last night's events. The Alex and Nadia situation, Kensi having a potential stalker, and also the upcoming project with Martin. What did he look like without that mask? She ran her hands across the top of her panties. Just before she could touch herself, the phone rang.

"What's up? I missed your call last night. I fell asleep," Nadia said.

"What happened, Nadia? You ran out of there like the house was on fire, and before I could catch up you were gone."

"Nothing happened."

"Oh, something happened."

"What I mean is that nothing bad happened. I just didn't want to stay like some needy girl waiting on a man to come and coddle her until she came back down from her high. I can hold my own. I don't need that."

"Well, you could've at least stopped to see me before you left. I was worried."

"Yeah, I guess I could've done a little better than a text message."

"Damn right you could have."

"Why don't you get dressed and let's go have a drink. My treat. I really need to get out of the house and I really need to talk."

"Oh God. Are you serious?" Vanity said, not wanting to leave the comfort of her bed.

"Yes, come on, Vanity. Get your ass up and meet me at the Blue Flame. Have you eaten anything yet?"

"No, not yet."

"Okay, then it's settled. Get dressed, and I'll meet you there in an hour. We'll have drinks, food, and more drinks."

"An hour, Nadia? Are you for real? It'll take an hour to get there. How about two hours?"

"Okay, two hours it is. If I get there before you I'll go ahead and get the table."

"All right," Vanity agreed.

They both hung up the phone, but Vanity had no intention of leaving her bed. She dialed Alex right after. If he had any intentions of telling Nadia who he was, now was his chance.

★★★

Nadia arrived at the Blue Flame and was sitting at the bar, casually sipping her drink. She'd texted Vanity to let her know she arrived, but Vanity hadn't replied. She summoned the bartender over to where she was sitting.

"Excuse me. I'll have another French connection please," Nadia said.

"Sure, right away," the bartender replied.

"No more Midori sours?" a voice whispered in her ear.

A smile slowly spread across her face, and then he came into view. "Ah, Mr. No-Name, what a pleasant surprise. And no, I'm straying away from the Midori sour today. I've actually grown quite fond of the French connection."

Smiling himself, he flagged the bartender and held up two fingers so he could bring him one as well. "Alexander."

"Excuse me?"

"Here you are. If you need anything else please let me know." The bartender placed their drinks in front of them.

"Thanks," Nadia said.

"Alexander. My name is Alexander."

"So Mr. No-Name has a name after all," Nadia said, taking a sip.

"Yes. I was hoping you had one also."

Nadia looked at him for a second. "You know, there's something very familiar about your eyes."

"Is there? Or are you just avoiding my question?" he asked.

"Yes, there is, and my name is Nadia."

"Nadia, huh? I wouldn't be surprised if there was a lot of promise in the first half of that name," he said, smirking.

Nadia turned her bar stool to face Alex and slowly crossed her legs. "Wouldn't you like to know?"

"I may already have somewhat of an idea," Alex said, swirling his drink around in his glass. "Do you believe in magic?"

"Why? Are you a magician?"

Alex reached into his pocket, pulled something out, then held out both hands. "Pay close attention." There was a quarter in his right hand and his left hand was empty. He closed both hands and then reopened them, and both hands were empty this time.

Nadia sat there with a look of minimal amusement on her face. "You'll have to do better than that, Alexander."

Alex closed his hands again. With his right hand, he reached behind her ear. He held his closed hands out toward Nadia.

"Let me guess, you found the quarter behind my ear."

Alex smiled. "No, but I did find this." He opened his hand and there was Nadia's red sapphire diamond earring.

"Oh my God!" Nadia exclaimed, making half of the bar turn around to look at her.

"Just an earring, people. Nothing to see here," Alex said.

She picked up the earring and looked at it. "You," she said, staring right at Alex. "Those eyes. It was you last night, wasn't it?"

"Yes, it was," Alex said, finishing his drink.

Nadia just shook her head. *That damned Vanity has some explaining to do.* She looked at the earring again and then closed her fist around it tightly. "I truly appreciate you returning this. It means a great deal to me." Then she stood and grabbed her purse. She got as close as possible to him and pressed her body against his. "However, this is not what you think it is. Last night was a one-time thing. But, if you ever want to know what it's like to kneel before a real woman, feel free to find me."

Just before she could turn to leave, Alex grabbed her wrist and pulled her close. With her chest pressed up against his, he stared into her eyes and said, "And if you ever want to re-live last night, relinquish all control over to me, or just learn what it feels like to have me deep inside you, then feel free to find me."

Nadia didn't say a word. She smiled, turned around, and headed toward the door. She stopped by the hostess and told her she'd had a change of plans and to cancel her table. Her heart was beating a mile a minute and she could barely catch her breath.

As soon as she was in the car, she pulled out her cell phone and called Vanity. It rang several times, but she didn't get an answer, so she left a voicemail.

"Hey, Vanity, it's me. I just cancelled our fake dinner date that I'm almost certain you had no intention of showing up to anyway. On another note, I did have the pleasure of meeting Mr. Alexander. I'm sure you know whom I'm speaking of, and I'd be willing to bet my earring on it. Call me when you get this message."

She hung up the phone and stared at the red earring that she had been sure was lost forever. She looked out the window at the Blue Flame and smiled again. He would call her. She was almost certain of that.

Chapter Twenty

Diary Entry #9

I still didn't find the person who sent the invitation, but I guess I can blame that on the wonderful distraction I'd had. Last night a stranger ripped off my clothes, and then he watched as I danced for him exotically. Being watched was an aphrodisiac, and my sexual desire increased more when he touched me. I don't know why I didn't require him to remove his mask. I'd give anything to know who he was. He said to send him the bill for my dress, but how the hell do I send someone a bill if I don't know who or where they are? K.D.

Kensi had already rolled out of bed, showered, gotten dressed, and was sitting in traffic on her way to her dad's house. The drive to Santa Barbara was an hour and a half away, but it was beautiful and well worth the drive. She figured her dad would like the surprise, and she was looking forward to seeing him and Maddie. Her stepbrother and stepmother not so much. Kensi's iPhone was programmed to play randomly from her iTunes and was completely in sync with her current state of mind. She sang along with Taylor Swift and Jhene Aiko. When the Queen Bey came on, she immediately catapulted back to last night. She'd made a mental note to herself to take a drive to Secret Desires and purchase her own accommodator. She'd also made a note to find out who the man was behind the mask, for both her own personal interests and so she could get reimbursed for the dress he'd ruined in the heat of the moment.

Before she knew it, the beautiful drive along Pacific Coast Highway had come to an end. Kensi pulled into the driveway of her dad's house and killed the engine. She hadn't been home for months, but the house was exactly the same, thanks to Maddie no doubt. The yard was perfectly manicured, the flowerbeds were flawless, and nothing was out of place. Kensi got out of the car and walked up the brick stairway, but before she could knock on the glass door, it swung open.

"Maddie!"

"Oh, get over here and give me a hug. You look just as gorgeous as the last time I saw you, and you're glowing." Madeline stepped back to look at Kensi. "You have a boyfriend?"

"I wish, but no, it's still just me."

"Girl, I practically raised you. Just you, my ass. We'll talk later."

"You're glowing yourself, Maddie. Do you have a man you'd like to tell me about?"

Before she could reply, there was this annoying voice that vibrated off the walls like screeches from hell's angels.

"Kensington, is that you?"

"Yes, Sara, just thought I'd drop in for a visit," Kensi replied, not taking her eyes from Maddie's.

"I'll get your father," Maddie said and squeezed Kensi's hand.

"Well, you look nice. That dress, is that Tahari's new fall collection?"

Kensi had to give credit where credit was due. Her step-monster knew fashion, but whether or not she knew all her ABCs was still questionable.

"Yeah, it is."

"Nice, and Louboutins too I see. The platform of your shoes match that new pretty red BMW you parked in the drive. I'm guessing your father's still sending you a monthly allowance," Sara insinuated. The two just stood there eyeing each other. They had nothing to say to each other, and they both knew it. Cordial with each other was all they ever were and all they would ever be. However, asking about her finances and monetary arrangements with her father was strictly off limits!

"Kensi, baby girl!" Kensi's dad always had perfect timing.

"Dad!" she said, walking right past Sara into her dad's arms.

"How's my little girl doing?"

"Dad, I'm not a little girl anymore. But I'm fine, I'm actually here to check on you. How are you doing?"

"You'll always be his little girl, Kensi. No matter how well you fill out that dress or how high those heels get, young lady," Madeline said.

"She's right. You'll always be my little girl."

"Kensington, you should join us for dinner," Sara said just when everyone was forgetting about her presence. "Madeline was just about to set the table. She's cooked her famous roast beef."

Kensi hated when she dismissed Madeline as if she was just the housekeeper. Maddie was more of a mother figure to her than Sara ever was.

Sara cleared her throat. "That'll be all, Madeline."

But Madeline didn't move an inch.

"Kensi. I'll put your jacket and purse in your old room. David, will you be needing anything else?" Madeline asked.

"No, Maddie, I'm fine. Kensi, are you hungry?"

Kensi was standing there trying to analyze what was happening. Maddie subtly dismissing Sara and calling her dad by his first name. Her dad called her "Maddie" instead of "Madaline." Her dad hadn't used "Maddie" instead if "Madaline" since Sara forbid it. Sara claimed it was too personal for her liking so he'd stopped using "Maddie" to respect Sara's wishes. But it seems like Sara's wishes weren't holding any weight anymore. She didn't know what the hell was going on, but she'd definitely be sticking around for dinner. Without further delay, Kensi said, "I'm starving, and roast beef sounds wonderful."

"Great. Dinner will be ready in five."

"Thanks, Maddie. Kensi, come with me to the study. Your old man needs a drink."

"I think I'll have one too, Dad."

"Sure, honey, there's plenty of bottled water," he replied, and headed toward the study.

Kensi rolled her eyes and followed her dad into the study. She was getting a glass of wine, the hell with water. She stepped into the study and slid the doors closed. "So, what's new?"

"For starters, this Frapin cuvée 1888 cognac. Bought for me by my lovely wife," he said, turning toward Kensi. "With my own money, of course. Everyday I'm beginning to forget what I ever saw in that woman."

"Dad," Kensi said in a tone she preserved only for her father. "You want to talk about it?"

"Baby girl, I haven't seen you in forever. The last thing I want to talk about is Sara. Tell me what's new in the big city. New job, new car, new wardrobe."

Kensi looked down at her dress and her shoes.

"You know, your mother used to wear shoes like that all the time. Not that high, but there were wall-to-wall pairs of shoes, clothes, and purses.

And anytime I got ready to take her out somewhere she'd always say the same thing."

"I don't have anything to wear," they both said at the same time.

"It's amazing. All these years have passed and I still miss her."

Kensi walked over, put her hand on her dad's shoulder, and rested her head on it. "I think about her too, Dad. She's watching over us all the time you know."

"Well, I hope not all the time," he said, chuckling.

"Come on. Dinner is ready, you two." They hadn't even realized the doors had opened. Madeline smiled at them both before heading toward the dining room.

"I don't know what we would've done without, Maddie," Kensi said.

"Me either, baby girl. Me either." He kissed Kensi on the top of her head. "Come on. Let's go eat."

***

"Kensi, would you like some more wine?" Madeline offered.

"Yes, please."

Kensi's dad looked over his glass and said, "You're spending the night, young lady."

"Dad, that was sort of the plan anyway."

"Good. Maddie, why don't you sit down. Join us."

"Actually, I—"

"I'm sure Madeline has other duties to attend to around the house," Sara interrupted.

"Actually, I'd love to sit down and chat but— "

"But, I'm sure she agrees that's not very appropriate. After all, this is a family dinner," Sara said, interrupting Madeline again.

"And Madeline is family," Mr. Dumas interjected, staring at Sara. "Maddie, please have a seat," he said, not taking his eyes from Sara's.

Kensi looked at Maddie as she sat down at the table across from her. Her father was clearly starting something that was not about to end well. Sara was dabbing both sides of her mouth with a napkin. Her face was almost as red as the color on her lips. *What the hell is going on around here?* Kensi thought. "Where's Blake? I thought he was on fall break," Kensi asked, not really giving a damn where Blake was, but changing the subject couldn't hurt at this point.

"That makes two of us, Kensi," her father said.

"He was here, but he's gone now. He left just this morning," Sara added.

Maddie smiled. "Kensi, do you remember when you were kids and you two used to pick the oranges from the tree in the neighbor's yard. Then you'd go hide out in your playhouse and peel them. You'd come back in the house all sticky and I'd ask you two—"

"Yes, we all remember, Madeline," Sara snapped. "I've had enough to eat. You can take my plate away now."

"You're being very rude, Sara," Mr. Dumas said. His eyes were cutting into Sara as if he was cutting into his roast.

"I'm not the one cozying up to the help, am I?"

"Enough, Sara! You will not speak to or about Madeline that way." Mr. Dumas threw his napkin on top of the table.

"Don't you mean, Maddie?" Sara chuckled. "Oranges, really? Ha, give me a break."

"Well, I'm sure Blake will be seeing plenty of orange where he's going, right, Sara?" Mr. Dumas said, loosening his tie. Kensi sat there wide-eyed.

Sara stood up from the table, leaned forward, and placed her hands on the edges. "You can sit here casually with the help and discuss oranges and any other mediocrities you wish. However, I won't dignify this with my presence."

Sara left the dining room. Kensi, Madeline, and her dad sat there in silence for a minute or two.

"I'll clear the table," Madeline said. Mr. Dumas didn't say a word. He pushed back from the table, swirling his drink in his hand, and had a look that suggested how highly pissed off he was.

Not sure of what else to do, Kensi volunteered to help Madeline.

"May I take your plate, David?" Madeline asked.

"Sure. Thanks," he said, then got up from the table and left the dining room.

Kensi and Madeline finished clearing the table in silence.

Madeline hummed as she and Kensi cleaned the kitchen. Kensi had always found her humming to be soothing, and it was something she had gotten used to hearing as a child. She'd remembered that Madeline hummed while she was cleaning, but she'd also remembered that she hummed when something was bothering her.

"Maddie?"

"Yes, Kensi?"

Kensi dried her hands with the kitchen towel and turned toward Madeline. "What was all that about?"

Madeline stopped wiping the counters. She stood there for a second, not knowing where to begin. She grabbed the unfinished bottle of wine off the counter and said, "Get us two wine glasses from the cabinet, grab that tray of fruit in the fridge, and follow me."

Kensi followed Madeline out onto the patio. She poured them two glasses of wine and waited to be filled in on what the hell had just happened at the dinner table.

"Things have not been right between your father and Sara for quite some time now," said Madeline, taking a sip of wine. "There have been some arguments. Some very heated arguments."

"They have always argued, Maddie. What's so different now?"

"Your father suspects Sara has been sneaking around with another man, and she has made the same assumptions about him."

"And you? What do you think?"

"You know I don't get into all that, Kensi. I steer clear of all that drama, just as I always have."

Kensi sat her glass down on the patio table. "Maddie, you're the eyes and ears of this house, and whether you like it or not, you're also the glue that's been holding it together. If anyone knows anything about what goes on at this house it's you."

"I do, and I think I've said enough about Sara and your father's affairs. Any other questions you have, I think you should ask your father yourself."

"Okay, but what was all the talk about there being plenty of orange where Blake is going?"

"Now that is another issue in itself. Sara had been taking large sums of money from their joint account, leading your father to believe she was giving it to Blake for college."

"Oh my God, was she giving it to a man?"

"No, the money was for Blake. It just wasn't for college. Apparently, he had been accused of assaulting a young lady on campus, and your stepmother had been paying for the young lady's silence. Sara refused to give her any more money and the young lady went to the police. Both of them had to come clean to your father yesterday. FYI, your father and the district attorney went to college together."

"And Sara needs my father to call in a favor to help her son."

"You got it, but that's not all. The school is also threatening to expel him. He's suspended pending investigation."

"So he's home indefinitely, not on a fall break?"

"Yes, and your father is livid. Blake, your father, and Sara all got into an argument this morning at the breakfast table. Blake left afterwards. I wish he'd taken Sara with him."

"Me too, Maddie, me too. When Blake and I were kids we were so close. Remember Maddie?"

"I remember. The two of you were inseparable."

"Yeah we were. But when we became teenagers I couldn't stand to be around him. He started hanging with a different crowd at school, and getting into trouble all the time. It had gotten to a point where I would literally go out of my way to avoid him. He just turned into a totally different person. I even stopped showering when he was at home. The way he'd look at me when we'd cross paths in the bathroom gave me the creeps. I just steered clear of him at home and at school. I was so relieved when he went off to college."

Maddie grabbed Kensi by her chin and turned her face toward her, "Kensi bear, I had no idea he made you uncomfortable. Why didn't you ever say anything?"

"I don't know. I had gotten so good at avoiding Blake. I figured why say anything at all. I guess I just didn't want to cause anymore drama between Sara and dad."

"You'd obviously mastered avoiding him, because I had no idea. And you know I don't miss much."

Kensi thought back to all the times Maddie had caught her sneaking back into the house after curfew and smiled, "No, you don't." Kensi drank the last few drops of wine from her glass, "I think we're going to need another bottle of wine."

Madeline raised her glass. "I'll drink to that."

Kensi giggled at Madeline and headed back to the kitchen to fetch another bottle, still trying to process all the new information.

Chapter Twenty One

When Vanity woke up the next day, sunrays were beaming brightly through her curtains. She reached over to her nightstand and grabbed her phone. She'd slept the rest of Sunday and wasn't ready for the day to begin, but Monday had arrived and there was work to be done. Dreading it, she grabbed her iPhone and looked at the screen. Seven missed calls, three voicemails, and one text message. Before she could listen to the first message, her phone vibrated in her hand. Even though she hadn't programmed it in her phone, it hadn't been long enough for her to forget the number. Red or green was the debate she was having with herself. "Answer or don't answer," she asked herself. Before she could make a decision, the phone stopped ringing.

Vanity fell backward onto her bed and closed her eyes. Spa day was the first thing that registered in her mind. After this weekend, she'd need a full day of relaxation. Her phone vibrated again in her hand. It now read four voicemails. *I need a secretary*, Vanity thought, swinging her legs over the side of the bed. She sat up, braced herself, put her iPhone on speaker, and started listening to her voicemails:

"Vanity it's me, Paul. I . . . umm . . . probably shouldn't have walked out like that. Maybe I shouldn't have walked out at all. I was just wondering if we could talk, or if we could meet up somewhere for a drink maybe. You've got the number, call me."

"Hey, Vanity, it's me. I just cancelled our fake dinner date that I'm almost certain you had no intention of showing up to anyway. On another note, I did have the pleasure of meeting Mr. Alexander. I'm sure you know whom I'm speaking of, and I'd be willing to bet my earring on it. Call me when you get this message."

"Hey, girl, it's Gianna. I'll be in LA soon and we have to link up when I get there. Call me back at this number when you get this message."

"Vanity, Martin Buchanan speaking. I trust my colleague Alexander has spoken with you. The sooner we get started on this next event the better. You were sent a phone number via text message. Contact me at that phone number tomorrow no later than nine o'clock."

Vanity looked at the clock. It was only eight a.m. and she was already exhausted. She got up and headed to the bathroom. She was going to at least shower, brush her teeth, and gather her thoughts before she officially started her day.

Diary Entry #10

Who in the hell does he think he is barking specifics at me on my voicemail? Nine o'clock, my ass. Out of all the men at that damn party, I had to sleep with one of Alex's business associates whom I just learned I'll be collaborating with on the next event. The next few weeks will be quite interesting. And what the hell is Paul talking about? Go get a drink? What part of "I only want to fuck" does he not get? I should get a sign for my entryway that says, "This is a sex-only zone. Leave your feelings at the door." I really wish we as women could take different characteristics and personalities of different men and put them together to create the guy who's perfect for us. It'd make life sooooooo much easier. V.C.

***

By the time Vanity finished primping it was a quarter to ten. She'd thought long and hard about calling Paul back. Actually, the thoughts of him being "long" and "hard" were why she was considering calling back at all. Deciding against returning his call, she opened the text message she'd received with Martin Buchanan's information. She called him and took a deep breath while the phone rang.

Vanity was just about to hang up when Martin answered, "Ah, Vanity, I was beginning to think you couldn't tell time. It'd be such a shame for you to be all beauty and no brains."

"Perhaps you can provide me with a Cartier La Dona so I can be more punctual," she countered.

Martin laughed. "Ms. Carter, I do look forward to working with you. I'm sure there won't be any dull moments."

"Speaking of which, Alex informed me that you would like for me to coordinate an upcoming event. However, he was unable to provide me any details. Care to enlighten me?"

"I'd like to do more than just enlighten you, Vanity." Before Vanity could respond to his coy remarks, he continued, "But unfortunately, I'm heading into another meeting. I'll have my assistant send over some details." Then he disconnected the call.

Vanity looked at the phone as if it had grown a head. She was leaning toward calling him back and telling him to shove the details up his ass, but she thought that might make his day so she called Gianna back instead. When there was no answer, Vanity left a message for her to call when she got into town. Scrolling through her other missed calls, she stopped when she got to a familiar number. Vanity couldn't help but consider calling Paul back. Refusing to give into her impulses, Vanity called Nadia instead. She leaned back in her oversized chair, put her feet up onto the ottoman, and waited on the earful Nadia was about to give her.

Chapter Twenty Two

"Dad?" Kensi opened her eyes to see her father sitting across from her in a chair. He had the same look of weariness on his face as he did last night at dinner.

"Good morning," he said, taking a sip of his coffee.

"What time is it?"

"It's almost noon."

"Didn't you have to be at work this morning?" Kensi asked.

"Took the day off. Figured you may want to talk after everything that happened last night."

"Yes, actually I would." Kensi sat upright in the bed and brushed her hair from her face. "What's going on between you and Sara? Last night's dinner was pretty intense. I was expecting for food to start flying at any minute."

"Things haven't been going so well between your stepmother and I. We're arguing more and more, and there are large sums of money unaccounted for. Hell, I don't even know where she is half the time."

It pained Kensi to see her dad so unhappy. "So, do you think she's having an affair?"

"I think so, yes. But, can I prove it? No, I can't."

With a little hesitation, she said, "Dad? What about you? Are you having an affair?"

He looked over at Kensi with a facial expression she was unable to read. " Sara and I haven't been in a good place for a long time now. She doesn't know, but I've actually gone to see a divorce lawyer. I haven't filed yet, but I wanted to know what my options were and what kind of a fight I'd be facing. It's going to be an ugly battle, and with me not having any proof that she's cheating, it may be a costly one too. But I've grown so tired of the arguments, the lies, the blatant disrespect, and now this thing with Blake. I want out. I'm miserable with her, and I'm going to change that no matter the cost. I'm going to end this."

Kensi placed her hand on his shoulder. "Do what you have to, and whatever you decide I support it."

"Thanks, baby girl. What do you say you get dressed and let your old dad take you out for some lunch."

"That sounds great, but I'm scheduled to work tonight. I kind of need to be heading home as we speak. Can I take a raincheck on that?"

"Feel free to cash it in at any time." He stood up and kissed Kensi on the forehead. "I'll go see if Maddie can whip you up something before you hit the road."

"Thanks, Dad."

When her father shut the door, Kensi sat there for a few moments looking around her old room. There were still pictures of her and her high school friends surrounding the mirror on the dresser. Her reading nook still had all her old stuffed animals, and the books were in the same place she'd left them on the shelves. The posters she'd tacked up of Justin Timberlake, Beyoncé, and Carrie Underwood were fading and beginning to fold at the edges. Everything was still exactly as she'd left it. The sheets even smelled of fresh lavender, as if they'd just been washed. She was sure that was Maddie's doing. If it were up to Sara, she'd probably knock down the wall and turn her room into extra closet space. She cringed at the mere thought of that happening. It was almost noon and she had a road trip and a twelve-hour shift ahead. Throwing the covers off, she got up and got moving.

Chapter Twenty Three

Three and a half hours later, Vanity still hadn't heard anything from Martin's assistant. She was awaiting info on the event, figuring the quicker she began the sooner she'd be done. He'd been a jackass earlier and hung up in her face, so there was no way in hell she was calling him back. So, she'd just have to wait patiently, and patience was not a virtue of hers.

Nadia had talked her into going to lunch. Feeling guilty about technically standing her up yesterday, Vanity didn't argue with her. She simply obliged and put spa day on the backburner. She'd put on a short but simple khaki dress by Hayden with her high-heeled Guiseppi Zanottis, and her matching Berkin bag. Vanity dressed to kill even when she was attempting to keep it simple. After she finished admiring herself in the mirror, she grabbed her keys and headed for her front door.

When she opened the door, she was staring into the face of a woman who looked to be in her late thirties but with the face and body of a super model. Vanity eyeballed the woman from head to toe. High cheekbones, high brows, serene green eyes, reddish-brown hair, slender, but taller than average. The Kurt Geiger shoes, Hermes handbag, and Chanel jacket told Vanity she was well kept. For a moment, Vanity thought the woman looked almost as good as she did . . . almost.

"Ms. Vanity Carter?"

"Yes, how may I help you?"

The woman gave her a warm smile. "Good afternoon. I'm Felicity, Martin Buchanan's assistant," she said, reaching down into that handbag

Vanity would've sold her left thumb to have. "Martin asked that I stop by and bring you this." She handed Vanity a white box and a white envelope.

"What's this?" Vanity asked.

"It's from Martin. His instructions were very clear, Vanity. He said to only give you the box and the envelope."

Vanity looked down at the box and the envelope and then back at Felicity. "Well, then I guess your work here is done."

Felicity smiled. "I guess it is. Have a good day, Ms. Carter. Oh, and cute dress."

Vanity closed the door and sat her keys and purse on the table in the foyer. She walked into the living room, sat down on her sofa, and opened the letter first.

Ms. Vanity Carter,

I'm delighted to know you've accepted my request to assist me on the next event. I'll be by to retrieve you from your home at eleven tonight. You'll receive several visitors beginning at four o'clock in preparation for tonight. Feel free to invite a friend over to indulge in these preparations—whatever makes this experience more enjoyable for you. Consider today's activities as part of the compensation for your assistance. You've already received the first gift. I hope it's to your liking.

M.B.

Vanity looked down at the white box. She didn't know what Martin was up to, but she would be lying if she said she wasn't a little excited. She placed the letter on her end table and opened the white box. She pulled out the small card and read it aloud:

Perhaps this will assist you with being more punctual.

If anything further is needed for you to perform your job duties, please feel free to let me know.

M.B.

Vanity folded back the tissue paper and saw a red box with the Cartier gold lettering. Grinning from ear to ear, she pulled the small red box out and opened it. She was speechless. He'd made a comment earlier about not returning his call on time, and she'd suggested he buy her a watch, but she was only kidding. She took the watch out of the box for closer examining. It wasn't the La Dona she'd asked for, it was the Ballon Blanc. She'd admired this watch a thousand times. She loved the dazzling face, the white gold, the dial that was mother of pearl, and the solitaire diamond in the curve of the dial. The only thing she didn't like about it was the price tag. Fifty thousand dollars was too much for her to spend just to tell time, but it seemed as if it was only pocket change for Martin. Vanity was so wrapped up in her new accessory that she didn't hear her phone ringing. She quickly answered.

"Hey, Vanity, I'm headed out the door now," Nadia said. "I couldn't decide on what shoes to wear and then I couldn't find my mascara."

"There's been a change of plans. Meet me at my house."

"Why? What's going on at your house?"

"I don't know, but I have a feeling that we're going to like it."

"Well, give me about forty-five minutes and I'll be there."

"See you then," Vanity said, and hung up. *I'm not even going to pretend like I'm going to give this back,* she thought as she stared at her new time piece. It was such an expensive gift, but who was she kidding? Vanity knew she was the shit. If you asked her, she'd say she deserved that watch, the world, and much, much more.

Chapter Twenty Four

"Can I have my Dilaudid, Benadryl, Phenergan, and Ativan please? And the doctor said he was going to order some Ambien because I have trouble getting to sleep. So, can you bring that in too? Oh, and the Benadryl and Phenergan are IV, right?"

Kensi looked up at the clock in the room and knew it was going to be a long night. It was only nine-fifteen, and this patient had brought her to her wits' end. Being a nurse was always a struggle between the kind of nurse you wanted to be and the kind you were forced to be.

"No, I can't give you all of those together, and you don't have anything due right now," Kensi said. "I'm tied up with something else at the moment, but as soon as it's time for you to have something I'll come in and we'll see what meds take priority, okay?"

When her patient didn't respond, she just closed the door. She didn't have time for the bullshit tonight. There was too much on her mind. Her potential stalker, the great sex she'd had with the mystery man, and now her father's situation. Why didn't she just go with her first instincts and call in sick from the parking lot? She needed some stress relief, and she needed it fast. As if he could hear her thoughts, she looked up and saw Dr. Randahl walking toward her. Kensi tried to look preoccupied, but it was difficult to take her eyes away from him and that confident walk.

Without breaking eye contact, Dr. Randahl walked right up to Kensi, but he didn't say a word. He just stood there staring down at her. Kensi was trying to think of something clever to say, but her mind had drawn a complete blank. Just when she was about to ask him what the hell he was looking at, he said, "Meet me, doctors' lounge, midnight." Kensi opened her mouth to say something, but he placed his finger over her lips. "Don't say anything, just meet me," and then he confidently walked away.

Kensi stood there speechless, wondering if she was going to meet him later tonight. Just when she was about to decide against the meet with Dr. Randahl, the call light went off, adding to her irritation. It was the same patient whose room she'd just left. Kensi heard the intercom click, but before the secretary Ms. Gwen could say anything, Kensi cut her off and let her know she was on top of it. She wasn't going to be at the doctors' lounge at midnight; she was going to be there at 11:59.

Chapter Twenty Five

After an evening filled with pedicures, manicures, waxing, facials, and massages, Nadia and Vanity were both exhausted.

"I feel like a new woman," Nadia said, looking at herself in Vanity's floor-length mirror. "But I'm also drained. I don't even want to drive home."

"You can stay here tonight if you want. I don't know when I'll get back home," Vanity said from inside her walk-in closet.

"He's going out of his way to please you. I think this is beyond business. Expensive gifts, personal spa treatments at your home, what's next? A beach house in Malibu and your own personal Alfred?" Nadia said as she plopped down on Vanity's bed and fell backward. "Oh, this bed feels so good."

"Nadia, this is strictly a business relationship. I'm sure all of this is part of a compensation package for the event I'll be coordinating for him. Alex specifically warned me away from anything else."

"Well, I don't really see how what you and Martin do is any of his business. And FYI, I'm still mad at you for not telling me who Alex was."

"I thought today's activities would make up for all that. Was I wrong?"

"The apology is accepted, but I still can't believe you didn't tell me. But getting back to Martin, you already gave him a sample of your goodies at the party. You really think you'll be able to back him off after that?"

Vanity emerged from her closet wearing the skintight dress Martin had a stylist bring over for her to wear to tonight's event. "I can back anyone off. This dress may make it a little bit difficult though."

Nadia sat up on the bed to get a look at Vanity. "Yeah, I can see where you may run into some trouble. You look hot!"

Vanity was wearing a Herve Leger black sequined dress. It stopped mid-thigh, showing off her gorgeous stems, and had a plunging neckline that showed just enough cleavage to make a man salivate. To say the very least, she was wearing the dress quite well.

"Thanks," Vanity said while turning every which way in the mirror to get a full look at herself. "I don't really like the shoes the stylist brought. I think I'll wear my leather Tom Fords instead."

"If you mean the ones with the ankle strap and the lock, then I think that's an excellent choice. You might also consider a light jacket; it's going to be cool outside tonight."

"Jacket. Right," she said, walking back into her closet.

"I wonder if Alex will be there tonight."

"You should come with me and find out."

"No, thank you. I have a date with your bed and that pint of Chunky Monkey I saw in your freezer."

The doorbell rang, and Nadia hopped off the bed and headed to the front door. "I'll get it, you finish getting ready."

When Nadia got to the door and opened it, she wasn't surprised at all. Martin could've easily been mistaken for George Clooney's twin.

Martin held out his hand for Nadia to shake. "Good evening. Martin Buchanan. It's a pleasure to meet you. Nadia, right?"

"Yes, hi. Please, come in. Vanity's still getting dressed. How did you know my name?"

"I asked for a detailed report on how today's events went. My staff informed me that both Vanity and her guest, Nadia, appeared to have enjoyed the day of pampering. Oh, and before I forget, " Martin said, handing Nadia a single white rose, "this is for you."

"Thank you. It'd be my guess that the rest are for Vanity."

"Yes, they are."

"Your staff, huh?"

"Yes, I co-own a chain of spas in LA."

"Really? Well, you're staff was very impressive. Thanks for your hospitality. Vanity's in her bedroom getting ready. Would you like something while you wait?"

"Unless you're going to give me permission to go watch, then I think I'm fine."

Nadia shook her head. Backing Martin off was sure to make for an interesting challenge, one that she couldn't wait to hear all about. "I'll go and see if she's ready. Living room is to your right, so make yourself at home."

When Nadia walked back into the room, it looked like a tornado had hit. "What the hell happened in here? I was gone for like two minutes and you've got shit thrown all over the place."

"I can't decide on what jacket to wear."

Nadia looked at the jackets thrown over the top of Vanity's closet door, the several piled on top of the bed, the one barely clinging to the hanger on the door, and the one she had on. They were all black. "I'd say go with the black one."

"Very funny, Nadia. I need help picking one."

"You need help period, possibly reverse retail therapy."

"Nadia, seriously, which one?"

"The one you have on looks fine. Besides, it's not like you're going to have it on very long anyway."

Vanity smiled. "You're right, he probably won't last five minutes."

"You either. He looks hot in that suit he's wearing. I personally wouldn't mind tying his ass up and making him beg for mercy."

Vanity grabbed her purse and iPhone off her dresser. "I'd pay good money to see that."

"You can use that watch as a down payment," Nadia said, following right behind Vanity.

Vanity walked into the living room and halted. Martin was quite handsome. Standing there in his tailored suit, Ferragamos, and crisp white shirt with a hint of gray at his temple, he looked gorgeous. *Keep it together, Vanity. He's just a man. You can get through this night without sex.* Obviously, her brain and vagina were having a disagreement.

"Vanity!" Nadia said, nudging her. She'd been so wrapped up in admiring how handsome Martin was that she hadn't noticed the roses he was trying to give to her.

"What, oh yes. Thank you. They're beautiful."

"Shall we?" Martin said, offering Vanity his arm.

"Put these in water for me please," Vanity asked Nadia.

"Sure. I got this."

"Nadia, it was a pleasure meeting you."

"You two have a nice night. Do everything you know I would do."

Vanity rolled her eyes at Nadia's remark as she stepped out into the cool air, thankful she'd listened to her and grabbed a jacket. Martin led her to a black town car with the door being held open by the driver. Once they were in the car and settled, Vanity didn't waste any time rolling out the questions.

"Care to tell me what all this is about? Where are we headed?"

"You look beautiful tonight. Not the shoes I picked, but still lovely."

"Thank you. Now where are we headed?"

Martin smiled. "We are headed to a party tonight for a colleague of mine. I truly apologize for the late hour. I would have loved to have taken you out first for dinner and a cocktail, but I had some business that had to be attended to."

"Let's get something straight. The watch, the spa treatment, this dress . . . all of this is very flattering, and I appreciate your hospitality. However, the time we'll be spending together organizing this event will be strictly professional. What happened at the Masquerade Ball cannot happen again, understood?"

Martin put his hands up in defensive. "Understood."

"Great." Vanity felt better having got her little speech out of the way. She just hoped it hadn't fallen on deaf ears.

Chapter Twenty Six

Kensi was in the elevator trying not to talk herself out of forgetting this whole thing. She couldn't and wouldn't give Dr. Randahl the satisfaction of not showing up. She stepped off the elevator and headed straight for the doctors' lounge. The door was wedged open slightly with a wooden stopper. She looked around to see if anyone else was watching. Noticing it was all clear, she pushed the door open and pulled it shut behind her.

"Well, I'll be damned," Kensi said as she walked through, giving herself a tour of the lounge. The main room had the setting of a banquet hall, with a buffet against the right wall and a hall to the left. Kensi grabbed a strawberry off the buffet table and then headed toward the hall. The hallways had several keycard access doors. Deciding against screaming his name down the hall, Kensi figured it would be better just to check the rooms.

She looked through the square glass window of the first door, but it was all lockers with a push cart filled with surgical scrubs. Kensi looked through the second door and it was filled with gym equipment. *A gym. They can't make sure we're properly staffed on the floor, but the doctors have a friggin' gym.* When she got to the last door, she gasped. It was a sauna, but it wasn't the sauna that had made her lose her breath.

Dr. Randahl was lying across one of the benches in the sauna wearing nothing but a towel around his waist and a towel across his face. Sure that her keycard didn't authorize her to be down here, she didn't bother to swipe it. Instead, Kensi pulled on the handle, hoping it was open, but it wasn't. However, the jiggling of the handle got Dr. Randahl's attention. He pulled the towel from his face, slowly got up from the bench, and walked over to the door.

He stopped right in front of the window and made eye contact with her again, just as he had done earlier on the floor. He opened his mouth and mouthed, "You're late." Kensi didn't reply. She stood there looking through the little glass window waiting on Dr. Randahl to make his next move, and that he did.

He pulled his towel off and held it up to the window before dropping it to the floor. He backed away from the door slowly, never breaking eye contact, and giving Kensi a full view of him naked. How she'd pictured him naked didn't do the real thing any justice. It was as if someone had taken an ivory statue and chiseled it to perfection. Dr. Randahl was all muscle. Biceps, triceps, and abs formed down to his pelvis in a V cut. Kensi stood there fantasizing about wrapping her limbs around the right places so she could climb the tree of man before her.

Still not taking his eyes from hers, Dr. Randahl fisted his cock. *Oh dear God . . .* Kensi broke eye contact and looked around the door to see if there was any way she could get in. Hopeless, she looked back into the small window of the door to the sauna. He was still staring at her, stroking his length back and forth. There was an intense ache between her legs, and her heart raced a mile a minute. Dr. Randahl was the one inside of the sauna, but Kensi was the one who was burning up. Before she could stop herself, she licked her lips, which was an obvious turn on for him, because he began pleasuring himself faster. Completely turned on by the mere sight of him, Kensi's eyes went back and forth between his cock and his intense gaze. Just when she thought the show couldn't get any better, the muscles is his abdomen clenched, his forehead wrinkled, and then he broke eye contact, throwing his head back and letting out a primal growl. Kensi was no amateur; she'd seen men come plenty of times before, but she'd never seen something so hot, so animalistic, so sexy in her life.

She stood there staring at him when he looked into her eyes. He walked up to the door and didn't say a word. He picked up the towel up that he'd shed earlier and wrapped it back around his waist. He walked back over to the bench and stretched out in the same position he was in earlier, tossing his arm across his face.

Kensi turned away from the door and walked down the hall toward the banquet area. The journey back seemed much longer. She spent the entire walk back to the elevator replaying the images of Dr. Randahl in her head. She checked her watch to see how much time she had. She'd need at least ten minutes to stop by the clean utility room and grab a bar of soap and a pair of mesh panties. Kensi might not have been the one to orgasm, but he'd definitely gotten her faucet running. She needed to freshen up before her break was over.

Chapter Twenty Seven

When Vanity and Martin arrived at their destination, it was nothing like she'd expected. She'd tried to get more information about tonight's plan from him, but she was unsuccessful. The conversation on the way there had been so strained after Vanity's outburst that she just stopped trying to make small talk altogether and decided to stare out of the window and enjoy the view of city lights.

When Vanity's car door opened, she stepped out into the cool air, wondering what they were doing here. They weren't in an upscale area of LA. The buildings were old and rundown, with windows that were partially shattered. The air smelled of stale smoke, old garbage, and spoiled fruit. The concrete was uneven, and Vanity found herself walking unsteady and trying to keep her heels from sinking in the cracks. Vanity miss-stepped and almost took a nosedive onto the pavement, when Martin grabbed her by her waist. "Hold onto my arm. This area is obviously not well paved."

"Obviously," she said, looking up at Martin. She hesitated, then grabbed onto the arm he'd held out for her, deciding it would be better than falling and ruining her dress or scarring her legs she'd worked so hard to keep flawless. Arm in arm with Martin, they came to what appeared to be the entrance of an abandoned warehouse. Vanity halted and asked, "Martin, what are we doing here?"

"Research. Pay attention," was all he said.

Standing six feet tall and at least three hundred pounds, a gentleman with a stance similar to the men of the Secret Service guarded the door. His all-black attire and lack of people skills made it clear that he was there to send the message that disruptiveness would not be tolerated. Vanity smiled at the man as he opened the door to let her and Martin in, and as she suspected, he didn't smile back. But he also didn't look at her twice. If she wasn't almost certain that not socializing with the guests was part of his job requirements, her ego would have been a little bruised.

The inside of this place was incongruous with the outside. The air smelled of leather, and the sexual energy was palpable. Martin led the way while Vanity surveyed the surroundings. The walls were deep gray, almost black, with dim red lighting. The music was instrumental—not to fast, not to slow, but just the right rhythm to put her in a sexual trance. There were stations of play everywhere complete with crosses, benches, chains, whips, cuffs, and more. Each station was occupied with exhibitionists who were so deep into pleasure they'd completely tuned out the voyeurs with lust and envy in their eyes.

It was a large crowd of people, but it wasn't crowded. Most of the people who were still wearing clothes were dressed as Martin and Vanity were. Those who were not were either dressed erotically or naked and engaging in acts of pleasure. Vanity noticed one woman dressed in an outfit similar to the one she'd given Kensi to wear the night of the masquerade party. The woman was blonde, tall, and her body looked as if she'd never skipped the gym a day in her life. There was a handsome male with a collar around his neck and a chain connected to it that she held in her hand. She walked right past Vanity and Martin, with the young man crawling right behind her with a look of worship in his eyes that Vanity was very familiar with. She'd never follow a man around or be collared by anyone, but she knew the look of desire and lust when she saw it.

"See something you like?" Martin asked, snapping Vanity from her thoughts.

"Not particularly, no," Vanity replied. "You said research. What exactly are we researching? So far I haven't seen anything that I haven't seen before."

"That's because you're looking at things from an entertainment perspective."

They took a seat on a plush sofa centered in the middle of the room. Vanity wouldn't have been surprised if the chair was reserved strictly for Martin. There was a perfect view of the entire floor from where they were sitting. Martin had released her arm from his, and Vanity got comfortable and removed her jacket. He sat comfortably in his suit, leaning back on the sofa, with one leg crossed over his knee.

Patience not being one of Vanity's qualities, she turned and faced Martin. "Okay, enough with the bullshit. What is it that I'm supposed to be looking at?"

"Don't look at those participating. Look at the ones who are not." He turned Vanity's face toward the crowd and they sat in silence for a few moments. Vanity re-surveyed the party. Taking his left hand, he rubbed his thumb on her back slowly in a circular motion. "Tell me what you see, Vanity."

"I see people watching the different play stations. Look at this couple right here," Vanity said, referring to the woman dressed in a skintight purple dress and a man who had his arm wrapped securely around her waist. The couple was watching the man and woman from earlier that were walking past them when they first entered. The mistress was dressed in all leather and standing over her submissive whom she'd bent over a leather bench. She was striking him slowly across the back with a red suede leather whip and metal handle. She worked her wrist like a pro, holding the whip in one hand and the chain from his collar in her other hand.

"She wants to be her," Vanity said, referring to the girl in the purple dress. "Every time her wrists releases that whip and meets his flesh, she gets excited."

"And how do you know that? How can you tell it's excitement? It could be that she's terrified,"

Martin said, earning a give-me-a-break facial expression from Vanity.

"Look at her face," Vanity answered. "Each time the mistress raises her hand, the woman in purple gets a look of lust in her eyes. Sort of like a twinkle. Then, upon impact, you can see her shifting her weight on her heels and squeezing her thighs together. She's aroused by the entire scene."

"Good observation," Martin said, still rubbing calming circles at the small of Vanity's back. "But why do you think she's just watching and not participating?"

"Maybe she doesn't want to? Not everyone wants to participate, Martin. Some people enjoy watching."

"I agree, and in some cases that's true." Martin pulled Vanity's hair back and whispered in her ear, "But my question is, do you think she only wants to watch? Her body language, that look you say she has in her eyes. Look closer." He placed a few soft, intimate kisses at the base of her neck. Vanity was trying to pretend she didn't enjoy his closeness, but it was getting more and more difficult by the minute. Martin held Vanity's hair back with one hand and slowly ran his other hand down her shoulder. "Can you see that what she really wants is to be the woman holding the whip? Can you see that she's fantasizing about being in her position? Being the one to pleasure her submissive?"

Vanity turned to Martin. "That doesn't make sense. If she wanted to participate, she could. That's the whole point of this atmosphere, to provide an environment that's comfortable and welcoming. When people feel comfortable, it lowers their inhibitions and allows them to explore their inner desires."

"Another good observation, but again you're looking but you're still not seeing."

Vanity reached down and cupped Martin's crotch in her hands. "Well then, stop it with the kisses and the caressing. Take your hands off me and let's get on with why we're here," Vanity said with unmistakable impatience coloring her words. "The woman in the purple dress . . . who is she?"

"You have so much fire in you, Vanity. I like that," he said, smiling. Clearly amused by Vanity's eagerness, Martin removed his hands from Vanity as requested. "The young woman in the purple dress is Bethany Mildred. Name ring any bells?"

"Mildred, as in Thomas Mildred? Attorney General Thomas Mildred's daughter?"

"That would be him, and that young woman in the purple dress would be his daughter."

"Damn! She doesn't look anything like the conservative pictures they show of her on TV and the Internet."

"They never do."

"What the hell is she doing in LA and here at this party?"

"Ah, now you're asking the right questions." Martin sat forward and pulled on the lapels of his suit jacket. "What she's doing is watching—like we're watching her, but there's a difference. If I strap a collar around your neck and please you until your sex spasms for everyone else to see, nobody is going to think twice about it. However, if she were the woman doing the things she appears to so desperately want to partake in, then it would be on every website, blog, news station, paper, and social media site before the sun comes up tomorrow."

"And you want to be the one she indulges in this fantasy with?"

"Ha, not in this lifetime, sweetheart. What I want is to provide an event that's provides the opportunity to play publicly and or privately."

Vanity sat there with a look of understanding, but her facial expression then turned to one of confusion. "We already have that. Each event I've hosted, planned, or been a participant at has offered private rooms. So, what is it that you want to provide that would be different?"

"I want a restricted event at a restricted location. Enough variety for people to find what they're looking for, but enough privacy that everyone feels comfortable enough to engage in their wildest fantasy. I know you have plenty of contacts, I have a lot of contacts, so does Alex, and those contacts have contacts who are all interested in these events that we throw. But," Martin said in a business-like tone, "they're more concerned about their personal interests affecting their professional lives. I'm sure your patients aren't privy to knowing that when you're not saving lives, you're wearing seductive attire and hosting the types of events that would probably be the cause of someone's heart attack."

Vanity didn't take light to Martin's comments. "While that was probably meant to be a joke, let me be clear. My patients and I are very similar. I don't know what they go home to and do unless they volunteer that information, which most don't, and they don't know what I go home and do because I don't volunteer that information at all. They expect me to come to work and do my job to the best of my ability, and I expect them to allow me to do so. Whom I tease, please, pleasure, fuck, and anything else I choose to do is none of their business. Which I guess would make you have something in common with them as well, being that it's none of your damn business either. Now, as much as I have enjoyed your company, I think it's best we go. That is, unless you have something else you'd like to show me or if you'd planned on participating."

"Is that an offer?" he asked. Vanity gave Martin a cold glare to shut down any thoughts or hopes he had of engaging in any sexual activity with her. "I guess not." He stood and held out his hand. "Shall we?"

Vanity took Martin's hand and stood, and then secured her arm around his as they both headed past Bethany Mildred and out of the party.

***

Martin insisted on walking Vanity to her door and seeing that she went inside safely. When they arrived at the door, Vanity turned to Martin, and before she could say anything, he pulled her into him and kissed her. She placed both hands on his chest with intentions of pushing him away, but found her hands moving to his hair and pulling him in closer instead. The kiss was rough and passionate, their tongues tangled and danced. Martin held Vanity by the waist as close as he could get her, and Vanity was losing all the restraint she had left to keep from taking him inside and fucking him right then and there. Vanity finally pulled back, breaking the kiss. She straightened herself, and Martin stood there with a look of pure promise in his eyes that told her if she invited him in she wouldn't regret it. She thought about saying the hell with it and inviting him in. Instead, she said, "That cannot happen again. Understood?"

"Yeah. Yeah, I understand. I don't know what came over me I just . . . never mind. Call me when you're ready to run some ideas by me."

"Good, and I will. Goodnight, Martin." Vanity went inside and shut the door. She put her keys on the small table by the door, threw her jacket across the back of her chaise, and quickly unstrapped her Tom Fords. Heading into the kitchen, she grabbed a glass flute out of the cabinet and a bottle of Belaire Rosé. Staring at the bottle, the sparkling wine made her think of the night she'd met Paul. She'd wanted to try something different, and Paul recommended she try the Rosé instead. They'd talked and laughed until closing time, and several glasses later he refused to let Vanity drive herself home. He had been the perfect gentleman that night. Vanity was the one who initiated the sex, assuring him she was in her right mind and knew exactly what she was doing. That night was amazing, much like the last night they'd shared. She poured the remnants in a crystal decanter, grabbed her cell from the small table, and then headed upstairs to her bedroom.

A few sips in and her nerves were calming down, but her sex drive was going the opposite direction. Vanity's thoughts bounced back and forth between Martin and Paul. Paul's tongue, Martin's hands, Paul's huge cock, fucking Martin at the masquerade party, fucking Paul right there in her bed . . . She grabbed her cell phone and scrolled through her contacts to Paul's name. She sat there and stared at his name and number, and stared some more. Finally, she tossed the phone onto her nightstand and threw back the rest of her wine. Vanity refused to have a weak moment and dial Paul, especially when she knew he wanted to talk about "them" and all she wanted was a one-night stand. She reached into her top drawer and pulled out Jackson, her B.O.B. She just needed an orgasm, and she could take care of that herself without all the extra emotional bullshit.

Chapter Twenty Eight

Diary Entry #11

I want to fuck Dr. Randahl. I can still picture him staring at me with those eyes, so intense and primal. Watching his gorgeous body all slick with sweat while stroking himself back and forth had me wanting to break the door off the fucking hinges to get to him. He's definitely the type of man who has women falling all over him, but not me. I like how he gives me orders at work, and I can't wait to see how he'll order me around in the bedroom. But I'll be damned if I'm the first to give in on this little game we're playing. He put on a show—a hell of a show—but I'm Kensington Dumas and I can put on one that's ten times better. K.D.

"Vanity, wake up," Kensi said into the phone.

"Kensi, it's seven forty-five in the morning. What the hell?"

"Oh, whatever, you only work one damn day a week anyway."

"Correction, I work one day a week at the hospital. I have more than one hustle, Kensi. Therefore, I work more than one day a week."

"Well, listen, this is important. I just got off work, and there was another damned note on my car."

"What?" Vanity replied.

"Focus, Vanity. Another note was on my car again this morning."

"From whom? What did it say?"

"It says that I'm beautiful, and that if they could look at me every day all day they would blah, blah, blah."

"Really, Kensi, you woke me up 'cause some guy, who clearly wants to get into your pants, is leaving you more love notes?"

"I don't know who it is, and it's weird. Do you have the list of names you said you'd give to me, because I need to figure out who this is."

"Yes. I just need to compile the names and get them to you. I'll have it by the end of the day."

"Okay. You want to go get breakfast?"

"Goodbye, Kensi," she said, and hung up.

"Guess not," Kensi said, putting her phone back on the car charger.

Kensi put on her seatbelt and powered on her music system. Throwing the car in reverse, she put her arm behind the headrest on the passenger side and began to back out, but came to an immediate halt. Dr. Randahl had stopped right behind her car. He stood there a few seconds before walking around to the driver-side window.

What the hell does he want? Kensi rolled down the window.

"Kensington, I was hoping to catch you before you left, but when I went to the floor they told me you'd already left."

"How may I help you, Dr. Randahl?"

"I wanted to ask you over for dinner. Are you by any chance free this weekend? Friday perhaps?"

"I'm sorry, not Friday," she said just to see his facial expression when he was rejected. To her disappointment, he displayed nothing. *Damn him.* "I am free Saturday though. That is, if Saturday works for you."

"Actually, I'm free on Saturday. Can we exchange numbers, and I'll call you with the details?"

After exchanging phone numbers, Kensi sat in her car smiling, but not because he'd asked her over for dinner. She was smiling because her mind had already begun to construct a plan for seducing him that evening.

Chapter Twenty Nine

Nadia stood in the mirror looking at her rack. In three more weeks, she'd have bigger breasts and she couldn't wait to show them off. Cupping her breasts in the mirror, she thought of the shopping she'd need to do. Nadia was prepared to spend a great amount of money on new bras, panties, and lingerie from Agent Provocateur and La Perla. Her thoughts halted when she heard her cell phone ring. She grabbed her phone and answered, still admiring herself in the mirror.

"This is Nadia."

"So, have you thought any more about my proposal?"

Nadia didn't even pretend to not recognize the voice on the other end of the phone, nor did she feel like pretending like she didn't know how he'd gotten her number. "Alexander. And what proposal might that be?"

"Well, seeing that I've only propositioned you once, I'm pretty sure you know which proposal I'm referring to."

"Cut the shit, okay? We both know you want me to submit. We also both know that's not going to happen. So, unless this phone call ends with you confessing your desire to submit to me then I'm afraid we're both wasting each other's time."

"Straight to the point—I like that about you, Nadia. However, me submitting to a woman is not my style. However, I do have another confession to make."

"I'm listening," Nadia said, stepping away from the mirror and taking a seat on the edge of her bed.

"Despite our disagreement on sexual submission. I do enjoy talking with you, and I'd like to see that beautiful smile of yours again."

"Maybe that can be arranged . . . maybe."

"I'm opening a new club this Friday night. Maybe you'd like to come and check it out? Who knows, maybe you'll have a good time."

"This Friday? Oh, I don't know. I'll have to check my calendar, but maybe I can work something out."

" I'll keep my fingers crossed."

"Legs and toes too."

Alex laughed. "Yes, legs and toes too. Have a good night at work, Nadia."

"Until next time, Alex." Nadia disconnected the call and fell backward onto her bed, staring at the ceiling.

Diary Entry #12

Just like a man—give them an inch and they want a foot. What happened at the Masquerade Ball was a one-time thing. I was just experimenting, trying something new, stepping outside of my comfort zone. Submitting to a man was not something I'd planned on doing, and submitting to Alex was definitely not something I planned on continuing. I'm a natural dominatrix, but Alexander wants me to completely change up and give all control over to him. There's no way I can fully submit to him, is there? I'll be at that damned opening Friday night. And I will be the baddest bitch in the building. N.H.

Chapter Thirty

Unable to go back to sleep, Vanity decided to get up and get started on planning. Martin had already e-mailed her the date, along with a few ideas he had for the event. Vanity spent hours at her computer researching possible venues. She toggled between websites, viewing the photos, and comparing the pros and cons. The biggest concern was privacy. The location would need to be somewhere that was secluded but not creepy. Easy to find, but still difficult for the paparazzi to access should they get wind of the event. Vanity had gone back to the drawing board several times before choosing the venue. She'd called and booked the location, but there was still much more to be done.

The guest list was the next thing on Vanity's to-do list. She'd need an estimated head count before she could even begin to do the staffing, book caterers, plan the station preparation, book adequate security, etcetera. She and Martin had discussed merging their contacts, but he hadn't provided her with any yet. She thought of calling him but decided against it. Instead, Vanity chose to reply to the e-mail he'd sent her earlier, thinking it'd be easier to read his thoughts than it would be to hear his voice. Martin's voice slid over her body and undressed her, and if she wanted to stay focused on the task at hand, she'd have to avoid making that phone call. Vanity replied to his email.

Martin,

After careful selection, I managed to secure a location this morning. The next order of business would be to construct the guest list and send out invites urging everyone to RSVP as soon as possible. Last time we spoke, we discussed merging the contacts of you, Alex, and myself. I already have access to Alex's contacts, but I will need you to provide me with yours. I understand the level of discretion needed in reference to the contacts you hold. Therefore, I think it would be wise not to send the list via e-mail. The sooner you get them to me the better, so that I can continue to work diligently on this project.

Warmest regards,

Vanity Carter

Though she'd proofread the e-mail several times before sending it, Vanity re-read it once more to make sure there were no grammatical errors. Before she could close out her e-mail, it chimed to let her know she'd received a new message. It was from Martin.

Vanity,

It would bring me much pleasure to take time out of my schedule and deliver the contacts to you personally. However, I will be in meetings all day and unable to do so. I'll have Felicity get the list to you within the hour.

Even warmer regards,

M.B.

Vanity just sat there and stared at his e-mail. She wanted to reply and tell him to come over. She wanted to reply and tell him she'd pick up the contacts, and that he was more than welcome to spread her across the desk in his office. She wanted to tell him all those things, but she didn't. Instead, she got back to work. There was plenty to be done.

***

It's all hands, lips, legs, soft bites, and rough kisses. He's all over me and I can't get enough of him. My flesh is damp from sweat, but the rising of the temperature in the room doesn't bother me as long as he doesn't stop. As long as he doesn't stop placing kisses in all the places that I dab with perfume. As long as he keeps his chest pressed against mine as if he's trying to fuse our bodies together. As long as he doesn't take his hands from under my ass where he's holding me open to him. As long as he doesn't stop pushing into me so hard that I think he's going to split me in two. I take a minute to catch my breath and admire his facial features—that handsome face. But his eyes bore so deeply into my soul that I quickly look away, fearing that he might see something I wasn't prepared for him to discover about me. Then there's loud thumping that fills my ears. I'm so close to orgasm, but the thumping is distracting. His thrusts are getting rougher and rougher, and the thumping is now louder and louder, but I'm almost there. I grab on tighter with one hand and dig my fingernails into his back with the other. My head flies back and I can hear him commanding me to come, but the thumping is now a loud knocking that I can no longer ignore . . .

Vanity lifted her head from the desk and looked around the room. She was trying to bring herself out of her sex-filled haze when she heard the loud thumping again. But it wasn't the headboard making thunderous sounds as a result from love-making. No, the loud knocking was from someone rapping on her front door. She got up and headed toward the front of the house.

Vanity swung the door open, and there was Felicity standing there. Felicity was wearing expensive attire, not one hair was out of place, and she flashed her perfect teeth through a cheerful, bright smile. "Good afternoon, Vanity. I'm so sorry to disturb you, but Martin asked that I get these contacts to you right away."

Vanity didn't say a word; she just stood there staring at the woman who could have been mistaken for a high-fashion mannequin had her mouth not been moving.

Felicity handed Vanity the envelope. "That's everyone. I'm sure I don't have to tell you the level of confidentiality that is to be expected in the handling of this file."

Vanity stood there without saying a word, and asking Felicity if she'd like to come in wasn't at all an option.

Felicity continued on, not seeming to be the least bit bothered by Vanity's silence. "Well, if you need anything else, don't hesitate to contact me or Martin, whichever your preference, and have a great rest of the day." Then she turned around and left.

Vanity closed the door. She had no reason to dislike Felicity, but she had no reason to like her either. Maybe Felicity was a great asset to Martin, but Vanity had the feeling that her simple existence was going to be annoying. *Have a great rest of the day,* Vanity mocked as she tossed the envelope onto her desk and plopped back down in her chair.

Chapter Thirty One

Vanity, Kensi, and Nadia all sat around the break room table chatting it up. It had been a while since they'd all worked together, but when they did, it never felt like they were at work. The three of them together turned a twelve-hour shift from stressful and dragging to a fun-filled night of all laughter.

"I've already started working on the next event, which will be in three weeks. Actually, two weeks from this upcoming Saturday, to be exact. It'll be at the old police precinct in Montebello. Of course you two are invited," Vanity said.

"Well, likewise, my dear, because Alex is opening his club this Friday night and he's invited me to come. I haven't made up my mind yet, but if I decide to go I want you and Kensi to come with me," Nadia said.

"You haven't made your mind up yet, or you have made up your mind you just don't want him to know you're definitely coming yet?" Vanity asked.

"Both. I don't know how tired I'll be by the time Friday gets here. And when I do decide, I'm not going to let him know until the last minute. You know, keep him guessing."

"Oh, I see. You're still trying to play hard to get?"

"Something like that. But getting back to this event. A police station? Really?"

"Yes, really," Vanity said, leaning in closer and lowering her voice. "This won't be just another event where people come to mingle and explore fantasies. We've had exclusive guests before at our events, but these guests are a bit of a step up from our usual patrons. Privacy and security will be a top priority at this event. What place is based on being more secure than an actual police precinct? Also, the old police precinct has interrogation rooms, cells, and offices, all of which I plan to use to my advantage when decorating. The decor for this event will be astounding, possibly my best yet."

"Damn, I don't get my breast implants until the Monday after the party," Nadia said. "I wish I was getting them the week before, that way I'd be able to show them off at this event. It sounds like it'll be a lot of potential there."

"Oh yes, plenty of potential, but you needn't worry about that because you won't be able to shake Alex long enough to participate in a damn thing anyway," Vanity said, giggling. She looked over at Kensi, who just sat there in silence. "Hello? Earth to Kensi. You mind telling us what's going on in that head of yours?"

Kensi told them what had happened with Dr. Randahl in very vivid detail. Vanity and Nadia were completely fascinated by Kensi's encounter with the doctor. "Now he's asked me over to his house for what I assume is a date, and I accepted. I'm going to get him back for that stunt he pulled in the sauna. I want my counter-attack on him to be as primitive as his was. "

"You know he asked me out on a date?" Vanity said, earning all eyes to be on her. "I turned him down, of course." She opened a bag of pretzels. "Plus, I don't know if you ladies are familiar with the saying, 'Don't shit where you eat,' but it's one I hold near and dear to my heart."

"Oh really?" Nadia chimed. "So, did you learn that phrase before or after you met Martin?"

Vanity threw a pretzel at Nadia and another at Kensi for laughing. "For your information, Martin and I had an encounter before I knew who he was. Secondly, now that I'm working with him on a project, our relationship is now strictly professional."

"So, Dr. Randahl hit on you too. I'm not surprised men can be such whores, but it doesn't matter. I just want him one time anyway. Just to see how good he actually is in bed. As far as the Martin situation, I can't wait to see how that goes Vanity." Kensi said. She finished off her Red Bull and got up from the table to throw it in the trash.

"Yes. You will see. Besides, he's got a little assistant. I guess she's his right-hand man and errand girl. Very, very attractive. I wouldn't be surprised if they had something going on."

"Attractive, huh? Sounds like competition." Kensi plopped back down in her chair.

"You guys, I already told you. Our relationship is a strictly professional one, so there are no worries on my end. But, getting back to you and Dr. Randahl . . . tell us more about this counter-attack your planning."

Nadia reached across the table and grabbed a handful of Vanity's pretzels. "Yeah, Kensi. What are you planning to do? Cater to him and then tip over into a deep abyss of love and hope he jumps in after you?"

"I don't know what I'm going to do exactly, but whatever I decide is going to be epic."

"Sounds like a plan." Vanity looked at her watch and sighed. "Well, ladies, duty calls. Let's get back to saving lives."

With smiles on their faces, the three friends headed out of the break room and went back to work.

Chapter Thirty Two

Nadia pulled in front of Neiman Marcus to valet her car. She was giving herself a once-over in the rearview mirror when the gentleman opened her car door.

"Thank you," Nadia said. She'd worked the night before, only had four hours of sleep, and hadn't eaten anything. However, when she exited the car, she looked like a million dollars. She liked to dress simple when going shopping. For her, the key to an easy day of shopping was wearing something sexy so she already felt beautiful, but it also needed to be something that was easy to get out of. Nadia accomplished that in her cap-sleeved abstract-print sheath dress and black suede Jimmy Choos that came over the knee.

"You're very welcome," the young man responded with a grin.

Nadia strolled into Neiman Marcus like she owned the place. The sales women were on her in a heartbeat.

"Welcome to Neiman Marcus. Are you looking for anything in particular?"

Nadia turned to the young woman and looked her over. Light makeup, petite, and a warm smile. She looked to be no more than eighteen.

"Yes, actually. A friend of mine has invited me to a grand opening and I need a dress."

"Oh, how fun. Well, the great thing about shopping here with us is that we have something for all occasions, which brings me to my next question. What type of grand opening? Is it a restaurant, or a—"

"It's a nightclub," Nadia cut in. "And it's tomorrow night, so I definitely have to leave here with something, and it has to be gorgeous."

"Got it. Right this way."

Nadia followed the young woman. They spent an hour browsing through dresses, and another hour and a half trying the dresses on before Nadia found the perfect one. She emerged from the fitting room wearing a blue evening dress by David Helwani. The knee-length long-sleeved dress, with the plunge illusion neckline and leather side panels, was breathtaking on her.

"Nice dress."

Nadia turned from the mirrors and saw a woman she didn't recognize but in no way could ignore. "Thanks," Nadia replied, unable to tear her gaze from the woman's distinctive eyes. Nadia waited on the woman to look away, but she didn't. It was as if they were staring each other down, trying to read each other's thoughts.

"I'm sorry, but do I know you?" Nadia asked, breaking the silence.

"No, you don't. I'm sorry I didn't mean to stare. It's just that . . . well, that's a very nice dress and you wear it really well. I'm not sure how many others you've tried on, but it would be a shame for you not to get it."

Nadia turned back around to face the mirrors. "Thanks." She smoothed her hands down the dress and turned from side to side to get a look from different angles. "Actually, this may just be the one I go with."

"So, you like it, huh?" the saleswoman asked. "I have the perfect pair of Rebecca Minkoff booties to go with it. I'll be right back."

Nadia looked around, but the beautiful woman was nowhere to be found. She stood there staring in the mirror waiting on the supposedly matching shoes, she wasn't thinking of the dress. She was thinking of the woman who'd complimented her on the dress. Blonde hair with dark roots, distinctively piercing green eyes, pouty lips, flawless makeup, and dressed to kill. She reminded her of Vanity and what Vanity would look like in fifteen years.

"Here you go. As you can see, they match perfectly. Try them on."

"No need, I'm sure they'll do just fine. Go ahead and box them for me please, and I'll be taking this also. Just give me a minute to get out of it," Nadia said, as she headed back into her fitting room. She felt on top of the world.

Chapter Thirty Three

"I'm just glad everything is okay, and I'm glad you went with him to tell the doctor all the things my dad would 'accidentally' forget. I told him I'd go with him, but he never called to tell me when the appointment was going to be," Kensi said, rolling her eyes.

"Yes, you know your father," Maddie replied. "The doctor started to ask questions, and your father was just sitting there like everything was fine and dandy. By the time your father got done saying how great everything was and how good he felt, the doctor had this look on his face like, well, what the hell are you here for'? But of course I chimed in. They had us at the office for some hours checking everything out, but according to the doctor everything is okay."

"I'm glad to hear the old man is still in good shape."

"Yes, still kicking."

"And I'm glad you were there with him. Thanks, Maddie."

"You don't have to thank me. Personally, I don't know what I would do without him. I'm just as glad as you to know that everything is okay."

"How about things with Sara?"

"For lack of better words, I'm expecting the shit to hit the fan any minute now."

"Do me a favor, Maddie. Call me when it does. Dad's always been there for me. I'd like to be there to support him whenever it does hit the fan."

"You'll be my first call."

"Thanks, Maddie. Love you. Give Dad a hug for me."

"Take care. We love you too. Come and visit us again soon."

"Will do," Kensi said before disconnecting the call.

Knowing that her father was okay was a load off Kensi's mind. However, her thoughts were still occupied by Dr. Randahl. He'd called earlier to confirm that they were still on for Saturday night. She assured him they were, which wasn't a lie. She'd made up her mind to go, but what he didn't know was that she planned on getting him back for being such a tease. Then, the doorbell rang, snapping her from her thoughts.

"Just a minute," Kensi said, grabbing her bathrobe and heading to the door. "Who is it?"

"Nordstrom delivery."

Nordstrom? Kensi opened the door.

"Delivery for a Ms. Kensington Dumas," said the deliveryman.

"Yes, that's me."

"If you'll please sign here for me," he said, pointing to his small clipboard, and then handing Kensi the gift-wrapped box. "Enjoy, ma'am."

"Thanks," Kensi said, looking puzzled as she carried the perfectly wrapped box into her bedroom.

She hesitantly pulled the card from the box, fearing that the sender was the same person that had been leaving her notes. Flipping over the card, Kensi's smile lit up the room when she read the message on the back.

It's not the exact dress, but I'm sure it will be beautiful on you. Can't wait to see you dance for me in it.

The guy from the party that ripped my dress. How the hell did he find me? Kensi wondered, as she set the card to the side and pulled back the tissue paper. "Beautiful indeed." She pulled the dress by its straps from the box. It was a black sequined matte-shift dress. She walked over to the mirror and held the dress up. It was short, and standing on her tip toes, Kensi figured it would come mid-thigh with heels on. The dress would be perfect for the grand opening tomorrow night. Just then, her phone pinged with an alert of a text. She picked up her phone and saw a group text.

Nadia: *We'll all meet up at my house. Alex managed to find us transportation. Even though it's last minute. :)*

Vanity: *Excuse me? You have me to thank for that. Alex couldn't find his ass with both hands in his back pocket.*

Kensi: *LOL! And okay Nadia how's 9ish?*

Nadia: *Well, in case I forget to tell you later, thanks for all you do, Vanity. And yes, Kensi, 9ish is fine.*

Vanity: *You're very welcome. I do try my best, and 9ish it is. That'll give us enough time for last-minute primping before the car arrives.*

Chapter Thirty Four

It was five minutes until midnight and the bass could be heard thumping from two blocks away, which was probably where the line to get in came to an end. Kensington, Nadia, and Vanity arrived in style, via stretch Bentley. The club was an impressive three-story building that looked to have a high-fashion dress code judging by the line of patrons outside and a larger-than-life sign that read CLUB PANDEMONIUM. All three exited the Bentley dressed to kill. Nadia's plan to be the sexiest in the building was so far going accordingly. The hostess was petite, with a punk-rock look, complemented by her pixie-style hairdo that was the color of cotton candy. She escorted the three through the crowd and upstairs to the third floor to their VIP booth.

Nadia turned to Vanity and asked, "Did you help decorate this place?"

"I only helped with the layout of things, like the DJ booth, the VIP sections, the bars, and things like that. We have this guy named Dylan, and he does the actual color schemes, patterns, arrangement of furniture, etcetera."

"Well, this is impressive." Nadia said, turning her attention back to the club. The VIP section was roped off and plush, with crimson red leather on the half-moon-shaped sofa, a low-sitting two-dimensional glass table outlined in the same crimson red, and black marble on the floors that twinkled from the fluorescent lighting.

"I was instructed to escort you ladies to your section. This is Infinity," the cotton-candy-haired girl said, pointing to the long-legged redhead standing next to her. "She'll be taking care of anything you ladies need tonight, and I hope you enjoy your evening."

"As she said, I'm Infinity and I'll be at your service tonight. What can I get you ladies to drink?"

"Champagne. Ace of Spades if you have it, and don't let our glasses go dry," Kensi said with no hesitation.

Vanity and Nadia nodded.

"Champagne it is. Anything else?" Infinity asked.

"Yes, some strawberries if you have them. I'm sure it's a busy night for him, but if you see Alex, could you tell him to stop by when he's able?" Nadia asked.

"Strawberries and champagne coming right out, and if I run into the boss I'll tell him to head over here to greet you ladies."

"Thanks." When their personal hostess was gone, Vanity asked, "Kensi, you got something you want to talk about?"

Kensi casually answered, "No, I'm just ready to get the party started, that's all."

Before they could ask Kensi any more questions, a voice Vanity recognized chimed in. "Well don't you ladies look beautiful tonight. Vanity, how are you?"

Vanity pasted a smile on her face—one that didn't look fake but it didn't look real either. "I'm great, thanks for asking. Nadia, Kensi, this is Martin's assistant, Felicity."

Felicity extended her hand and shook both Kensi and Nadia's hand. "Alex said this booth was secured for all of us. I hope that's okay."

Kensi and Nadia both looked over at Vanity, who was still wearing the fake smile.

"Sure, no problem at all. There's plenty of room. We just ordered champagne. I hope that's okay?" Vanity replied, scooting over in the booth to make room for Felicity.

"Perfect," Felicity replied, and that was exactly how she looked. She wore a bright red bandage dress cut low enough to show her amazing rack, and cut short enough to show how flawless her legs were. Her dress was completed with red bottom heels and a jumbo Hermes clutch bag. Vanity instantly wondered how much Martin was paying her, and if providing him with sexual favors was part of her job requirements.

"Here you ladies are," Infinity said, snapping Vanity from her thoughts. She'd brought three bottles of Ace of Spades to the table in a bucket of ice along with disposable champagne flutes.

"Well, looks like I'm late to the party." Amber said walking up to the VIP booth.

"Heeeeeeeey, Amber. What are you doing here?" said Nadia.

"I was off tonight from the Blue Flame, so Alex invited me to come to his grand opening. He said I'd be sharing a VIP booth with very close friends of his, whom I'm guessing are you ladies, since this is where the pink-haired lady directed me to," Amber answered.

"Looks that way. You guys, this is Amber," Nadia said, as Amber waved to the ladies. "Amber, these are my friends, Vanity and Kensi, and Vanity's friend Felicity." Vanity shot Nadia a look that could kill. Kensi just took a sip of her champagne and gestured for Amber to come have a seat. "Amber is a hostess at Blue Flame."

"Yes, I believe we have met before. Wow, I didn't recognize you outside of your work attire. Nice to see you again, Amber," Vanity said after coming to the realization that she and Amber had met before on several occasions.

"Yes. You're the one who throws the extravagant events for Alex, right?"

"Guilty," Vanity said. "You should come and check one of them out."

"Maybe you can invite her to the one you're planning for Martin. I'm sure she'll enjoy that," Felicity chimed in, prompting Vanity to slip her fake smile back into place.

"I'd like that," Amber said, smiling.

"Okay, ladies," Kensi said, interrupting the conversation. "Each of you raise your glass." She held her champagne flute in the air as if it was some sort of torch. "We are here. We are dressed to kill. And if I must say so myself, we are the baddest bitches in the building. So, here's to a fun-filled night of laughter, alcohol, and dancing."

"Whoooooooooooooo hoooooooooooo," they all cheered in unison. It was time to get the night started.

***

Nadia, Vanity, Kensi, Felicity, and Amber all made small talk over the first two bottles of champagne. By the third bottle, Kensi and Amber were ready to dance.

"I'm going to go to the ladies' room and then I'm hitting the dance floor. Anyone care to join me?" Kensi asked.

"Sure. I was just about to go myself," Amber answered.

Amber and Kensi headed off toward the restroom. Nadia, Felicity, and Vanity were left in the booth chatting and sipping champagne.

"So, how long have you worked for Martin?" Nadia asked Felicity, causing Vanity to sit up, because she wanted to know the answer herself.

"I've been with Martin almost five years now."

Been with him? What the hell does she mean by been with him? She cleared her throat and said, "Five years is a long time."

"Yes, it is. I've gotten acquainted with the majority of his contacts, acquired some contacts of my own—the exposure to the different types of things is priceless. Working with him has been a rewarding experience in itself. Martin is really a great boss."

Boss? Hmmmm. So are they fucking or not? Vanity thought.

"Wait. You said boss? So, you and Martin aren't like an item?" Nadia asked, reading Vanity's facial expression.

"Oh God, no!" Felicity answered, almost choking on her champagne.

Nadia giggled and took another sip of champagne. "Well, you said been together, so I thought maybe there was an intimate relationship there. You know, a more intimate and rewarding experience."

Felicity laughed at Nadia's candid comments. "You say what you're thinking, and you ask instead of assuming. I like that."

Vanity threw back her drink and excused herself as best she could. "Well, I'll leave you ladies to it. I'm going to head off to check on Alex and see if he needs anything."

"Tell him I'm saving a dance for him," Nadia said, prompting Vanity to roll her eyes again.

"What about you?" Felicity asked Nadia. "You and Alexander have something serious going on?"

"No. Well, not really. We just met, and he invited me to his grand opening. Nothing serious."

"Well, I'm glad. Maybe that means there's still a chance you and I can get to know each other better," Felicity said while scooting closer to Nadia.

"I'm not sure what you mean," Nadia said, wanting Felicity to elaborate. She'd never been with a woman before, but she was bi-curious and Felicity was very attractive.

Felicity put her hand on Nadia's thigh, careful not to break eye contact with her. "It means just what it sounds like."

Nadia took another sip of her champagne. This was going to be a very interesting night.

Chapter Thirty Five

The club was much larger than it looked. With three floors, three dance floors, several bars, dance cages, and a grand performance stage on the main floor, finding Alex was very difficult. Vanity had been looking for Alex when she bumped into a familiar face.

"Good evening, Vanity."

Vanity had to give the man in front of her a thorough look-over before she realized who he was. "Good evening yourself, Dr. Randahl. What brings you out tonight?"

"Well, I'm new to the area and I heard a couple of people I know talking about this place opening tonight. So, I thought I'd come check it out and see what all the hype was about."

Vanity half heard what Dr. Randahl was saying. Looking over his shoulder, she'd spotted Martin at the bar talking to some woman in a cheap spandex dress and frazzled blonde hair. As if he could feel her eyes on him, Martin looked up toward Vanity, and she immediately looked away. "So, what do you think so far? Was it worth you coming out tonight?" Vanity asked, leaning into Dr. Randahl, making an attempt to look more interested than she actually was.

"It's not that bad. I'm actually glad I came out tonight. I'd be even more pleased if you said you'd dance with me."

Vanity snuck another look at Martin out of her peripheral to see if he was still watching her. He was, so she answered, "I'd love to."

"Lead the way," Dr. Randahl said. Vanity grabbed his hand and they headed to the dance floor. She could feel Martin's gaze burning a hole in her from across the room, but she didn't give a damn. He was flirting with someone. Why couldn't she? Besides, it wasn't like they were dating. It wasn't like she was jealous or anything, was she?

***

"I'm going to the bar to get another drink. You want something?" Kensi asked Amber. They'd been dancing for a while now, and the buzz they'd gotten from the champagne earlier was wearing off.

"No, actually I think I'm going to go back to the booth. Or I can go with you to the bar if you want," Amber said.

"No, I'm fine. Let me grab a drink and then I'll be right over too. I need to give my feet a rest. These are not dance-all-night shoes." Kensi pointed to her four-inch Giuseppe Zanotti heels.

"Yeah, these are killing me too," Amber said, pointing to her five-inch stilettos. "But they go perfect with my dress."

They both laughed and headed off in opposite directions—Kensi to the bar and Amber back to the booth. The bar was crowded, which was to be expected. After maneuvering her way to the front, Kensi practically had to scream over the music to get the bartender to fix her an amaretto sour. She was standing at the bar when she heard a somewhat familiar voice standing next to her ordering a drink. "Whisky straight, please." Kensi looked up and stared into a pair of breathtaking sea-green eyes that belonged to a man who could only be described as impressive. Wearing loose-fitting jeans and a white V-neck T-shirt with what appeared to be a pair of Ferragamos, Kensi was growing more and more impressed by the second. So lost in her own thoughts, she hadn't noticed she was staring. When she did realize it, she had no choice but to speak.

"Hi," was all that came out, but it wasn't nearly all she wanted to say.

"Hi yourself," he responded.

"I didn't mean to stare. I just thought they had a dress code that was strictly enforced."

"They do. But the owner is my cousin, so I just slipped right in."

Owner is his cousin. Kensi made a mental note to herself.

"Amaretto sour for the lady and whiskey straight up for the gentleman," the bartender said, handing them their drinks.

"Oh no, please allow me," he said, pulling out his Amex to pay for the drinks, all the while smiling at Kensi. He signed the receipt and turned his attention back to her. He killed his drink as quickly as he picked it up from the bar.

"Damn. You better slow down before one of these women sees you and decides to get you home and take advantage of you."

He smiled and it was boyish, and so damn sexy. "What about you?"

"What about me?" Kensi asked, taking another sip of her drink.

"Perhaps you'd like to be the one to get me home and take advantage of me."

Blushing, she answered, "You don't even know me."

"Is that so? What can I do to get to know you?"

"You can start by asking me to dance?"

"All right. Dance for me."

"No."

He laughed and the sound made her toes curl. "No? You just said to ask you to dance."

"I meant dance *with* you, not *for* you." Kensi gulped down the rest of her drink, moved around in front of him, and held out her hand. "Kensi. Kensi Dumas."

He grabbed her hand and said, "Julien Walters."

Kensi yanked him toward her. "Okay, now let's dance."

All eyes were on them as they parted the crowd heading onto the dance floor. A small smiled tickled the corner of Kensi's mouth as she was sure all the women were in envy of the eye candy she was about to dance with. By this time the club was packed, each dance floor was filled, and people were a mess of hands, legs, sweat, alcohol, and grinding to Nicki Minaj and Beyoncé's "Feeling Myself."

Kensi didn't waste any time getting to it on the dance floor. She came to an abrupt stop, causing Julien to slam right into her backside. Taking advantage of that, she started grinding her ass into him right then and there. Reaching behind her, Kensi grabbed his hands and placed them on her hips as she swayed from side to side to the music. Julien was completely taken aback by Kensi, but that didn't stop him from falling into movement with her. He had his hands on her hips, waist, and even her thighs when she raised her leg over his hip and he dipped her, making the crowd hoot and whistle. She'd sucked him into her trance, and he was completely mesmerized by her.

"You look beautiful in this dress," he said. Kensi just smiled, but she was taken by him too. The defined muscles in his arms was an indication of what lay beneath his clothing. His smile was sexy, with dimples that Kensi was sure melted away many pairs of underwear. Wrapping her arms around his neck, Kensi slowed her movements to match the beat of August Alsina's "I luv This Shit" remix. They we're completely in sync with each other. The dance floor was a sea of people, but they could only see each other. She could feel him hardening against her, and that just made her grind against him even harder.

"So, Julien. Do you plan on taking me home tonight?"

"Hadn't planned on it, but plans change all the time."

"Is that so? What makes you think I'll let you take me home? I thought we already went over the fact that I don't know you."

"And I thought this dance was our way of becoming more acquainted."

"True, but I still haven't decided that I know you well enough. Besides, you're so cute I'd hate for you to disappoint me."

"Baby," Julien said, taking her arms from around his neck and spinning Kensi around so that his front was now digging into her backside. He pulled her arms back, gripped her wrists, bent her forward, and grinded into her on the dance floor in front of everyone. Some people hooted, hollered, and catcalled, while others rolled their eyes. Kensi wasn't the least bit bothered by the attention, wearing a smile the entire time. He pulled her back up toward him. "It'll be just like the song says . . . you'll love this shit." With that, he spun Kensi back around to face him. She was ready to go anywhere he was willing to take her in that moment.

***

"What the hell are you two over here discussing?" Amber asked, sliding her way back into the booth with Nadia and Felicity.

"Nothing," Nadia answered. "Where's Kensi?"

"She went to the bar to grab a drink, but when I looked back at the bar, she was leading some sexy guy onto the dance floor."

Nadia grinned. "Yep. That sounds like her."

There was complete silence for a moment. Then Felicity said, "Well, ladies, I think it's about time I hit the dance floor, and I just spotted my boss. So, I guess I'll be polite and go over and speak. Anyone want to join me?"

"I'm going to wait here and see if Alex comes over," Nadia said.

"And I need to give my feet a rest," Amber said, looking back down at her feet.

"Suit yourself," Felicity said, heading off into the massive crowd of people.

"Well, she seemed nice," Amber said. "I'm sorry if I interrupted a private conversation."

Nadia almost choked on her champagne. "No, no, no. Not at all. No worries."

"So, Alex still hasn't shown his mug yet, huh?"

"No, not yet," Nadia said a little irritated that she hadn't seen him yet.

"It's the first night. So many things go wrong on the first night of a grand opening people wouldn't even believe." Amber poured herself another flute of champagne. "The grand opening night of Blue Flame, the head chef quit, two waitresses were carpooling and were in a car accident so that left us short, and there was a fire in the kitchen."

"Really? All in one night?"

Amber nodded. "Yep, all in one night. We made it through. Alex even rolled up his sleeves and came out of the office to help serve. First time I've ever seen an owner do something like that."

Nadia smiled at the thought of Alex rolling up his sleeves to help out his team. "Wow. So you said you've been there since the grand opening of Blue Flame. Is that how long you've known Alex?"

"Yep, two years."

"And you've never been to one of his parties?"

"Never."

"Why not?"

"You want my honest opinion?"

"Yes. I would really like to know."

"I always thought they would be packed with snotty, posh people, passing around trays of caviar and fancy saltines discussing things that are far beyond my comprehension."

Nadia just sat there listening.

Amber looked over at Nadia's face and instantly began to elaborate. "No, offense. Not that my boss is stuck up or anything, but I know he deals with very well-rounded people. I just didn't want to show up and stick out like a sore thumb."

"Well, the next event is one that Vanity is planning. The atmosphere is definitely different from anything you can imagine. I do not have all the details yet, but I can say that we'll all be there. I think you should come and check it out. Take a few steps outside your comfort zone. You might like it," Nadia said, using the same words Vanity had used on her the night she met Alex.

"Well, well, well. I see you ladies are enjoying yourselves. Numerous bottles of our best champagne," Alex said, picking up a bottle and looking it over before placing it back in the bucket. "Strawberries, too, I see. Guess I'm late to the party."

"As a matter of fact you are," Nadia said, not taking her eyes from Alex. "However, I know you're the boss, so I'll let your rudeness of not coming over to speak sooner slide this time."

"Alex, thanks for the compliment, the champagne, and the strawberries, but the DJ is playing my song, so I'm just going to excuse myself," Amber said while sliding out of the booth.

"Sure, sure. Go enjoy yourself. Glad to see someone is having a good time," Alex said, not taking his eyes from Nadia's face.

"I'll join you in a minute," Nadia said looking toward Amber, who was already being swallowed up by the crowd.

Nadia threw back the rest of her champagne and grabbed a strawberry. She slowly brought it up to her mouth before biting it, knowing Alex was watching her every move.

Alex grabbed her arm, pulled her hand toward his mouth, and bit the strawberry. Then he slowly licked the juice from her fingers and began a trail of soft kisses from her hand to her wrist and up her arm. "You're the guest of honor tonight. I hope you know that. "

Nadia rolled her eyes, but she couldn't hide her facial expression from him. He continued the slow kisses all the way to the nape of her neck.

"Okay, okay, okay, enough. We are in a public place you know."

Alex pulled back and gave Nadia a look that said every bit of "who cares"? He rested his hand on Nadia's thigh and started rubbing slow circles. Probably innocent, but Nadia was feeling everything but innocent in that moment. "Are you not enjoying yourself?" he asked. "I haven't seen you get up since you came in."

"You've been watching me?" Nadia asked, curious to know his answer.

"Guilty," Alex said. Then he pointed to the cameras in the ceiling. "They rotate at three hundred sixty degrees, if needed. Even though I haven't been sitting here with you physically, I've still had my eyes on you all night."

"Is that a fact?" Nadia said. *I wonder if he saw the part where Felicity had her hand on that same thigh he's rubbing circles into.*

"Yes, all facts. You can't truly get the full Pandemonium experience sitting here in a VIP booth."

"Is that so? I'm actually quite comfortable."

"I have no doubt you are. However, I'd like to show you around the club and possibly steal a dance from you while everything is still calm around here. I'd hate for someone else to get the pleasure of dancing with you first in my club."

"You mean before a fire breaks out, or you have to roll up your sleeves and get your hands dirty?" Nadia said, eliciting a smile from Alex.

"That's exactly what I mean." Alex stood up and held out his hand to Nadia. "Shall we?

"We shall." Nadia gave him her hand and was immediately pulled to her feet and pressed against his chest. Their noses were within an inch of each other.

"Just in case I forget to tell you later, I hate your dress."

"Really? I'm actually quite fond of my choice of attire. It's a shame you don't find it appealing."

"Oh, I find it very appealing indeed. However, it's the other men in here who will also find it appealing that I have an issue with."

"Ah, jealous much?" Nadia teased.

"Madly," Alex answered without hesitation. They smiled from ear to ear at each other before venturing out for Nadia's tour of the establishment.

***

Vanity had spotted Martin earlier talking to some young woman at the bar, but now he was dancing with Felicity. Carefully watching from the second floor, Vanity could no longer hear anything Dr. Randahl was saying to her. She was too busy staring down at the first floor at Felicity and Martin. To the average onlooker, they appeared to be having a good time. To Vanity, he looked to be having too much of a good time.

"Dr. Randahl," Vanity said, "I see something right now that I'm not so happy about. You'll have to excuse me."

Before he could respond, Vanity was already making her way through the crowd and down the stairs to the first floor. The first floor was much more congested. It seemed like it took an eternity to fight her way through the crowd, but eventually she made it over to Felicity and Martin. Tapping Felicity's shoulder, Vanity said, "Excuse me, but I think I'll cut in, if that's okay with Martin." She gave Martin a look that said he'd better not say anything less than "it's okay."

"Well, it's okay with me. I was just going to the bar to get a drink. He's all yours," Felicity replied, removing herself from the equation.

Vanity and Martin stood there staring at each other for a few seconds, and then Justin Timberlake's "Suit and Tie" blasted over the speakers. Martin snatched Vanity from her trance and said, "You said dance, so let's get to it."

Martin pushed Vanity toward the middle of the dance floor and got her moving to the music. However, it wasn't long before he began dancing circles around her. Vanity was grooving to the music, but Martin was the one causing a scene. Before they knew it, everyone on the dance floor was crowded around them. Martin was dancing as if he did the choreography for the "Suit and Tie" video. His feet were moving rapidly, his arms were swinging, his jacket flying, and the entire crowd was clapping. Vanity, not at all disturbed by his boldness, was determined not to look taken aback by his performance. She started stepping too, swinging her hips, and getting low. She could see Martin was amused and that only encouraged her. Halfway through the song everyone was watching, from other floors, standing on the bar, and some women were even being lifted by their boyfriends so they could get a glimpse of the show. When the song ended, everyone in the house was clapping, and Vanity and Martin were laughing as they exited the dance floor.

"I thought all physical contact was out of the question?" Martin asked Vanity while they waited to be served at the bar.

"Oh, it is. That was just a harmless dance."

Martin raised his eyebrows in question at Vanity's remark. "Oh, okay."

Nadia and Alex approached them. "That was fantastic, you guys. Where'd you two learn to dance like that?" Nadia said.

"I was just moving to the music. However, I think my dance partner over there may have taken some lessons," Vanity said.

"Lessons from who? J.T. himself?" Nadia asked.

"You hear these two, Alex?" Martin asked.

"I'm inclined to agree with them. I didn't know you could dance like that, my man." Alex slapped Martin on the arm. "I'm sure that show you just put on will be great publicity for the club."

"Hey, anything to help a friend," Martin replied.

Vanity just stood there grinning, happy to see a softer more playful side to Martin. Her concentration was soon shattered when the bartender asked if they'd been helped. Vanity almost swallowed her tongue. *Paul? Holy fucking shit. He's every damn where, and he looks good enough to eat.*

"No, I'll have a French connection," Martin said.

"Two French connections," Alex said, looking over the Nadia to inquire what she was having. She only raised her eyebrows and smiled. "Make that three French connections."

"All right. And for you, miss?" The bartender asked, directing his attention to Vanity.

Miss? Oh, so he's not going to acknowledge me? Two can play that game. "I'll have a slow comfortable screw, please, extra on the 'slow.'"

"Coming right up." *Damn him.*

All of a sudden, glass shattered behind the two double-swinging doors next to the bar. "What the hell?" Alex said. "I'll be right back," and then he headed off through the double doors.

Martin stood there admiring Vanity, who was not returning his interest in the slightest. She'd been thrown off her rocker by the sight of Paul.

"Here you are. Three French connections and a slow comfortable screw, extra on the slow," he said, and without saying another word or offering another look in Vanity's direction, he moved on to serve the next customer. *Maybe, he thinks if he says something to me he'll lose his job. Maybe he thinks I'm here on a date with Martin.* Vanity was going over a list of reasons why Paul could have been giving her the cold shoulder . . . heavy on the cold.

"Are you okay, Vanity?" Martin asked, snapping her from her thoughts.

"Yeah, you look like you've seen a ghost," Nadia chimed in.

"I'm fine. Just got a little hot is all. I'm going to go to the restroom."

"You want me to come with you?" Nadia offered.

"No, you stay here and wait for Alex. I'll be fine."

Nadia and Martin stood there looking at each other while Vanity headed into the crowd to the restroom. Without an exchange of words, Martin threw back the rest of his drink and then took off behind Vanity. Nadia stood at the bar watching the patrons. The two next to her were engaged in a lip locking that looked like it would take a chisel and a hammer to pry them apart. When they did come up for air, they spotted Nadia staring. The female, obviously disgusted by Nadia's boldness of watching, grabbed the guy by the hand he'd planted on her ass and led him away from the bar. Nadia immediately snatched the free bar stool and had a seat. She hadn't taken a swig of her drink yet. She was waiting on Alex to re-appear.

"I see you bought the dress after all."

Nadia spun her stool around. The woman standing before her looked familiar, but she couldn't place her face.

"I saw you in Neiman Marcus when you were trying the dress on. I told you it would be a shame if you didn't get it."

"Oh, yeah. Yes, I decided to go with this one," Nadia said, looking at the woman carefully.

"Scarlett," she said, holding out her hand toward Nadia.

"Nadia. Nice to meet you."

"Likewise," Scarlett said. Breaking eye contact, she looked out at the crowd. "Wow, look at this place. Nice, huh? Great turnout for the first night, don't you think?"

"I'd have to concur. Were you invited?" Nadia asked boldly, trying to gauge exactly who the hell this woman was, and why she'd seen her twice within the same week.

"Yes, actually I was. I'm here with friends. They have a VIP booth. I snuck away for a moment to really get a look at the place. Impressive."

"Oh," Nadia said, getting a little comfort from knowing she was invited by friends and not by Alexander. "I'm glad to see you're enjoying yourself."

"It's not something I do often. Clubs are not my thing. I'm more of a 'mixer at the house' type of gal. But I like the atmosphere here. I also enjoyed the little show on the dance floor. Delightfully entertaining."

"I agree," Nadia said. She looked in the direction of the double doors, but still no signs of Alex. She was sure the woman was only being nice, but she'd had enough of the small talk and wanted to know where and what the hell was taking Alex so long. He'd invited her here and spent a handful of minutes with her since she'd arrived.

"Well, I'm going to get back to my booth," Scarlett said. "It was nice running into you again, Nadia."

"Likewise, Scarlett." Something didn't sit well with Nadia about the woman, but she couldn't put her finger on what it was.

"Hope I didn't keep you too long," Alex said, sneaking up beside Nadia.

"As a matter of fact you did. I thought I was going to have to drink both of these myself," she said, gesturing toward their drinks.

"Well, I'm glad to see you decided against it." Alex grabbed both drinks and placed one in Nadia's hand. "May I propose a toast?"

"You may," Nadia obliged.

Alex and Nadia both raised their drinks. "Here's to wishes coming true, especially when you keep your fingers, legs, and toes crossed." Alex knocked back his drink, and Nadia took a sip of hers.

"I need to run upstairs to my office. Care to join me?" Alex offered Nadia his arm and she accepted.

They walked through the crowd. They only got a few steps each time before someone stopped to congratulate Alex on the opening, or tell him what a great time they were having.

Martin and Vanity were back on the dance floor, but they weren't drawing a crowd this time. They were swaying to Lorde's "Royals" in complete sync with each other. Amber and Felicity were both sandwiching some guy who had an uncanny resemblance to Dr. Randahl. Nadia had spotted everyone but Kensi. Alex was leading her through the crowd by hand, but he halted when he realized some resistance in Nadia's pace.

"Is everything okay?" he asked.

"Yeah, it's just hard to spot anyone. It's such a big crowd."

"Looking for anyone in particular?"

"Yeah, Kensi. I haven't seen her in a while, and I don't see her anywhere."

"I have plenty of eyes in the sky, remember? Once we get to my office I'm sure you'll be able to spot her."

"Okay," Nadia answered, following Alex's fluid movements up the stairs. He led Nadia through the crowd, up the stairs, and behind the bar on the third floor. When they got behind the bar, he entered a code into the keypad on the wall and then a door unlocked, sliding backward and to the side, revealing an office.

"After you," Alex said, gesturing for Nadia to enter.

"You're office is just as plush as the club. Not that I'd expect anything less from you," Nadia said, taking a few steps into the office.

"Are you hot?" Alex asked, removing his suit jacket.

"No, I'm fine," Nadia answered, still admiring his stylish office. The floor was black marble, with a large black-and-white desk in front of the windows that looked out into the club, and to the right of the desk was a wall of cameras. There was a matching black-and-white checkerboard couch on the opposite wall with a glass table, similar to the one in the VIP booth minus the red trim. There was also a small bar in the corner of the room with tumblers all filled with amber liquid. Nadia could use another drink, but she needed to look at the cameras first to see if she could spot Kensi.

"These windows give you a great view of the club, so why the need for cameras?" she asked.

"You can't see everything from one standpoint. You have to be able to move around and see things from different angles. Secondly, I'm not in here all the time. Third, just in case I need to rewind and look at something I can always play the footage back. Damn. I am really hot."

"Maybe you should take your shirt off too," Nadia suggested before turning her attention back to the cameras. Nadia hadn't laid eyes on Kensi in a while and with the letters she'd been getting recently, Nadia just wanted to make sure she was okay. *Come on, Kensi, show that pretty face of yours. Where the hell are you?* On the screen that overlooked the VIP section, she spotted Kensi and a very attractive man having casual conversation in the booth.

"You should get buddy trackers. You know, the little things they give out to groups of friends at clubs, resorts, and large events so people know where their partners are. More and more people are investing in them," Nadia said.

Nadia was still looking at the cameras. The club was amazing, and she could tell both Alex and his team had put a lot of work into the place. Nadia moved over toward the windows overlooking the club. "This is very nice,

Alexander. Job well done." She turned around to find Alex on the couch with his arm folded across his forehead. "Oh, come on! You can't open a night club and then get exhausted in the middle of the grand opening. Alex?" Nadia walked over toward the couch.

"Oh Alexaaaaaaanderrrrrrr," she said, singing his name while standing over him.

"Alex, I know you hear me," Nadia said again, knocking his arm out of the way. Alex lay there still, pale as a ghost, and clearly unconscious.

Chapter Thirty Six

Despite Martin, Julien, and Dr. Randahl's requests to accompany the ladies home, Nadia, Kensi, Vanity, Felicity, and Amber all stayed together in the ER waiting area. Luckily, Alex had passed out in front of Nadia. If he'd gone back to his office by himself, he probably wouldn't have made it. Vanity found Dr. Randahl using the cameras in Alex's office, and Nadia, Vanity, Kensi, and Dr. Randahl all worked together as a team and managed to get Alex to open his eyes before the ambulance came. The ER doctor had been out only once to give them an update; Alex was stable, but they didn't know what had caused him to pass out. That was two hours ago.

Julien paced back and forward in the waiting area. "They don't know shit yet. Damn, how long does this usually take?"

"As long as it takes," Nadia, Vanity, and Kensi all answered in unison.

"This is ridiculous," Julien said still pacing back and forth.

"We hear it all the time, sir," the ER doctor said. "Mr. McCoy is resting in bed. We'll be keeping him overnight for observation."

"Do you know what caused him to just blackout like that?" Nadia asked.

"And you are?" The ER doc was awaiting her response, as was everyone else.

"She's his girlfriend," Vanity said without hesitation. Nadia didn't correct her. If her being his girlfriend was going to get them information, then she'd happily pose as the girlfriend.

"Oh, well his lab work shows that he was drugged with Ketamine. It's an anesthetic that was used about fifty years ago. Now people are using it in powder form as a date-rape drug."

What the hell? Nadia thought.

"Can we go back and see him now?" Julien asked.

"Yes, but only one of you for now. He's still very groggy. We're waiting for him to be assigned a bed and then he'll go up to the floor where he'll be able to have more visitors."

"You go ahead and see him, Julien. We'll wait out here," Vanity said, knowing that his actual family should go back and see him first.

Julien followed the ER doctor through the automatic doors.

Nadia took a seat in one of the chairs next to the vending machines, and Kensi and Vanity grabbed a seat by her side.

"Nadia, you're way too pretty to be slipping poor, defenseless men mickeys. Got us all in the ER in the wee hours of the morning," Kensi said, grinning from ear to ear.

"I did no such damn thing. I was with him, and then he just passed out on me. Maybe he slipped it to himself."

"Thinking it was ginseng or Viagra so he could keep up with your sexual appetite maybe." Vanity nudged Nadia with her elbow.

Vanity and Kensi were joking, but Nadia didn't find it funny at all.

"You guys, this isn't funny," Nadia said barely able to keep from laughing at Vanity's comments. "Seriously though, someone did slip him something. It could have been anyone in the club, and it could have happened to anyone in the club. It could have been one of us lying in the hospital bed or worse."

"We know. The security cameras were working fine. If I know Alex, he'll get it all sorted out as soon as he's back on his feet. He'll find out who did this and then he'll have their ass. I guarantee it," Vanity said with the utmost confidence.

"Thank goodness you were there, Nadia," Kensi said.

"Thank goodness we were all there. I panicked when he didn't respond. I could barely find the strength to call you and Vanity. If it weren't for you two, I'm not sure what condition Alex would be in."

"Yeah, and where the hell did Dr. Randahl come from?" Kensi asked.

"I'd danced with him earlier that night. He said he'd heard people talking about the club, so he came out to check it out," Vanity answered.

"Well, I'm glad he did. I thought I saw someone who looked like him dancing with Felicity and Amber earlier, but I wasn't sure," Nadia said.

" I spotted Paul, and it wasn't a case of mistaken identity. It was definitely Paul," Vanity said.

Kensi and Nadia just sat there looking at Vanity.

"Paul. *The* Paul," Vanity said, trying to jog their memory.

Kensi and Nadia furrowed their brows in confusion.

"Make-love-to-you-and-then-get-up-and-cook-you-breakfast   Paul," Vanity huffed.

"Oh, the guy with the body like a Greek God who serviced you to perfection and then wanted to feed you after the fuck. Him?"

"Yes," Vanity answered tight-lipped. "That Paul. He acted as if I didn't exist."

"Can you blame him? The guy cooked you breakfast and you put him out. I'm sure that wasn't the response he was expecting. Honestly, if a guy did to me what you did to Paul, I wouldn't acknowledge him either if I saw him out," Kensi said.

Vanity didn't say anything. She knew on some level that Kensi was right, but she didn't want what Paul wanted. It wasn't that the sex wasn't great, or that making breakfast wasn't a sweet gesture. Vanity was focusing all her energy into her nursing career, and her side business as a professional sex event planner. Being serious with someone was just not on her to-do list, and neither was leading someone on.

"But come on. Not even speak to me though?" Vanity asked.

"Well, did you speak to him?" Nadia asked.

"Point taken," Vanity said. She looked over at Martin and wondered if she'd end up in the same predicament with him once she finished planning his event. She was daydreaming about what it would be like to be in a relationship with Martin. Just when she was letting her imagination run away with her, Martin jumped up from his seat and headed toward the unit secretary.

"Hello. My name is Martin Buchanan. Me and several of my colleagues make multiple donations to this hospital, and right now I have a friend who is in one of your rooms waiting to be admitted. Not only do I demand to see him, but I am also requesting that you expedite his admission. The sooner he gets a room, the better. You got that Ms . . ." Martin looked down at the woman's name tag. "Margerie? Or do I need to speak with one of your superiors?"

"I'll see what I can do?" The older woman got up from the desk and headed to the back. There was no doubt that Martin's message was about to be relayed to her superiors. Martin buttoned his jacket and re-claimed his seat.

Felicity walked over to the vending machine. Looking down at Nadia, she said, "I knew it wouldn't be long before Martin utilized his clout. The man is very impatient."

"I see. We deal with people like him all the time. I guess it's kind of different when it's your loved one your waiting to hear news about." Nadia said. "I also wanted you to know I didn't lie when I said Alex and I are not together."

"Oh, no worries. I'm just glad you were there with him. It could have been a lot worse. I'm going to wait here with you guys until we have a chance to see him, which, with Martin's bank of patience now being depleted, won't be long. Then, I'm going to get Martin to give me a ride home."

Vanity looked up at the mention of Felicity saying that Martin was taking her home. Felicity pushed a button on the vending machine and waited for her purchase. She bent down and retrieved her Cheetos. "Gosh, haven't had these in forever. Girl's gotta watch her figure." She then walked back over and took a seat with Dr. Randahl and Amber.

"Ya know, for someone who claims that they aren't fucking, she sure does need a lot of attention from him," Vanity said, prompting Nadia and Kensi to snap their gazes in her direction.

Nadia started laughing, and laughing, and laughing. "I'm not the smartest person in the world, but I don't think it's Martin she's interested in."

"Meaning what?" Vanity asked.

"Felicity hit on me tonight at Pandemonium. I didn't mistake her gesture. I'm not hallucinating, and yes, I'm sure. She definitely hit on me."

"Oh. Since your boyfriend is hospitalized, are you going to venture over to the other side? You know, cure your bi-curiosity?" Vanity asked.

"You are just full of shit tonight, aren't you?" Nadia asked.

"McCoy family?"

"Right here," Martin said, jumping up from his seat along with everyone else.

"Hello, Mr. Buchanan. I'm Jeff, one of the house supervisors here. Mr. McCoy is being moved to his room as we speak. He'll be in room 3104 on our observation unit. If you follow me I can walk you over."

Everyone followed behind the man as he led the way through the hospital to Alex's room. Martin, always the gentleman, held all the doors, and then he caught up to Vanity to keep his hand at the small of her back as they walked through the hospital. Vanity didn't miss his kind gesture. She also didn't miss Dr. Randahl and Amber chatting it up. *For him to be so attractive, he's very whore-monger-ish. First Kensi, then me, now Amber.* When they arrived to Alex's room, the transporter, the nurse, and Julien were all helping to transfer Alex from the stretcher to the bed.

"They're getting him all set up. If I could just get you all to wait out here, we'll let you come in as soon as he's settled."

"Sure, no problem," Martin said.

Then Jeff turned his attention to Martin. "On behalf of myself and the hospital, thanks so much for your contributions. They really mean a lot to us."

"You're very welcome," Martin replied, standing there all cool and collected with his hands in his pockets.

The unit was not the most well-decorated place, but it was cozy enough for one night.

After a few minutes, the nurse came out of the room. "Hi, I'm Pierre. I'll be the nurse for Mr. McCoy—"

"It's Alex," Alex called from inside the room.

"I stand corrected. I'll be Alex's nurse for tonight. I'm going to put his information in the computer, check his orders, and if you all need anything just push the call light and let us know how we can help."

"Thanks, Pierre."

When they entered the room, Alex was lying in bed, and Julien was standing at the bedside talking with him. He'd regained some color in his face, but not much.

"Damn it, Alex. I hope you know I'm going to have to miss my beauty shop appointment today behind this stunt you pulled," Vanity said.

All heads turned to Vanity. Alex just smiled at her comment. "I'm okay, Van."

"Glad to hear that." Vanity grabbed his hand and squeezed it.

"You've all heard it from the horse's mouth. Now you can all go home and get some rest. Martin, you son of a bitch, did you do this to me?"

"Nah, my man. Not this time. Besides, if it was me, you would've left with the coroner not in an ambulance."

"Touché," Alex replied. He winced as he tried to reposition himself in the bed.

"Let me help you," Nadia said, rushing to maneuver the pillows behind Alex's back. "There, is that better?"

"Perfect." Alex reached for Nadia's hand. "Sorry for passing out on you like that. I was with it one moment and then . . . who the hell are you?"

All heads whipped in the direction of Dr. Randahl.

"That's Dr. Randahl. He was at your club. When you passed out, I called Kensi and Vanity and then she found Dr. Randahl."

"This is the guy responsible for saving my life, huh?" Alex held out his hand for Dr. Randahl to shake. "I'm sure you already know by now, but I'm Alex McCoy."

"Nice to meet you, Mr. McCoy. I'm Dr. Kenneth Randahl, and these ladies already had everything under control by the time I got to you. It's them you owe the thanks to."

"Well, thank you too for being there for me, for them, and for waiting. Consider yourself welcome at the club anytime."

"Thanks, man, I appreciate that. I'm going to go ahead and get out of here. Take it easy, and get well soon."

"Alex." Amber approached the head of the bed and gave Alex a mild squeeze of a hug. "Glad to see you're all right, boss. I'm going to head home too. Kenneth said he would give me a ride."

Kensi's head snapped in her direction, but she didn't say anything. Not with everyone paying attention, and she definitely wasn't going to say a word in front of Julien. However, she did make a note that he and Amber were apparently on a first-name basis.

"Thanks. Be safe. The rest of you all need to go home and rest. I'm fine. I am a man made of steel."

"Well, man of steel, I guess I'll head home too. Nadia, take care of my cousin. Don't let him give you any shit."

"Oh, don't worry, I won't."

"Kensi, if you need a ride I can drop you on my way," Julien said.

"Well, I planned on staying a little longer," Kensi said.

"No, no, no, go ahead and go home. They're just going to keep me for observation and then I'm going home," Alex said.

Kensi looked up at Nadia for her assurance that she'd be okay. Nadia gave her a nod, letting her know they'd be fine.

"Sure, Julien, where do you live?" Kensi said.

"Why? You planning to come to my house instead."

Oohs and ahhs spread throughout the room, and then an outburst of laughter with the exception of Dr. Randahl. He wasn't laughing at all.

"You guys chill out," Kensi said, barely able to control the blush spreading across her face. "And the answer is no. I just didn't want you to go out of your way."

"It won't be out of the way at all," Julien replied, flashing his playboy smile.

"Four down, four more to send home," Alex said.

"Well, make that two more. I think Felicity and I are going to head out. I stayed around to see if you'd be taking a trip to the morgue. Now that you have disappointed me, I guess I'll head home," Martin joked.

"Sorry to disappoint. I'll try harder next time around," Alex said.

They all laughed and were happy to see that Alex was okay. Dr. Randahl, Martin, Julien, Amber, Felicity, and Kensi all said their good-byes. Alex made several attempts to persuade Vanity and Nadia to go home and get some rest in their own beds. After his last attempt failed, he gave up. Nadia had curled up in the chair in the corner with a pillow and blanket and dozed off to sleep. Alex and Vanity were wide-awake. Though instructed to relax, Alex refused and instead gave Vanity a list of things he needed done. He sneaked glances over at Nadia every now and again.

"You really are taken by Nadia?" Vanity said.

"Yes, I guess I am. Tell me about her."

"Oh no you don't, Alex."

"What? I just said tell me more about her."

"And I will be doing no such thing. Whatever you want to know ask her. Nobody can tell you better about Nadia than she can."

"Van, Van, Van."

"Alex, Alex, Alex," Vanity countered with a look on her face that showed she was not budging.

"Are you this protective when people ask you questions about me?"

Vanity leaned over the bed railing and said, "Alex, you may find this hard to believe, but nobody asks jack shit about you. Contrary to your beliefs, you are not Mr. Millennium."

He replied, "Girl, I got women drugging me trying to get these goods."

Vanity smiled and grabbed his hand. "You're so arrogant. And I am beyond glad that you are okay."

"Me to, Van. Me too."

Vanity got up from the chair and grabbed her blanket and pillow "Alright Alex. Seriously, it's time to get some rest."

"You read my mind."

Vanity pulled up the blankets for Alex and let the head of the bed down. "Sweet dreams," she whispered, but he was already drifting. She then hit the lights and snuggled in her chair with her pillow and blanket. What a night.

Chapter Thirty Seven

Julien and Kensi were sitting in the car outside of her house. The conversation carried on for an hour before Kensi went ahead and asked him the question she'd been wondering since they left the hospital.

"How did you know where I lived?"

"Seriously?"

"Yes. Seriously."

"I just figured I had the right address since you were wearing the dress I sent you."

Kensi just sat in the passenger seat and stared. A slow smile crept across her face. "You smug bastard."

Julien didn't respond. He sat there staring at Kensi and watching her facial expression as she put everything together.

"The card."

"What about it?"

"It's not the exact dress. Can't wait to see you dance for me in it. Those were the exact words you wrote on the card that came with the dress."

"And you are just now coming to the conclusion that it was me?" he asked. Kensi remained silent, wanting Julien to continue.

"Did you send me the other cards too?" she asked.

Julien gave Kensi a look of confusion, "What other cards?"

"Nevermind. It's nothing."

"Wow. Must be a lot of guys sending you expensive presents all the time."

"No. Not really, " Kensi answered. Not wanting to go into detail. "So, at the club when you asked me to dance for you—"

"I wanted to see you dance just like you did the first night I met you."

Kensi eyes widened. "Oh my gosh. We've already . . . I mean you . . . We . . ."

"Oh yeah," Julien said, wagging his eyebrows up and down, which caused Kensi to break out in a fit of laughter.

"You've got to be fucking kidding me?"

"Kid you not, baby. I've already tasted you." He reached over and rubbed his finger across Kensi's jaw. Kensi smacked his hand away and playfully punched him in the arm.

"What the hell is that for?"

"You left me hanging. I wanted you and you left me." *Smack, smack, smack.*

He grabbed her hands and held them. "Stop it with the hitting already." He looked into her chocolate eyes. "So, you admit that you want me?"

"Wanted. We're speaking of something that occurred in the past, remember?"

"Yes, I do remember. Vividly." Staring at her mouth, Julien pulled Kensi closer to him. "I want to taste you again, and I want to savor every moment." Kensi licked her lips and didn't resist when their mouths crashed together in a slow and sweet kiss. They sat there with their hands entwined and their mouths fused together for what seemed like the longest of time.

Then, Kensi broke the kiss. "There's nothing past tense about this. I want you right now. Get out of the car." Kensi reached for the door handle to get out, but Julien stopped her. She turned back to look at him, but he only shook his head.

"You don't want to?"

"Oh, believe me I want to. I'm a flesh-and-blood man. You're damn right I want to."

"Just not right now?"

"It's not the right time. You need to go in and get some rest."

"Oh, so now you're concerned about my beauty sleep?"

He pushed a strand of her hair out of her face, still staring into her eyes. "Baby, you could never sleep another day in your life and I'm certain it wouldn't make you any less beautiful than you are now."

Kensi blushed. "You can stop it with the sweet talk. I already invited you in . . . even though you declined." Her phone pinged with a text message, but she didn't dare to break eye contact with Julien to see who it was. It could wait.

"It'll happen." He leaned in and kissed Kensi on the lips again, soft and sweet. "And when it does, I'll need you well rested so that you're able to keep up."

Smiling, Kensi hopped out of the car and bent down to the passenger window. "You're right, it will happen, but it won't be me struggling to keep up." Without looking back, Kensi strolled up to her front door, leaving a grinning Julien behind in the car.

Diary Entry #13

I invited Julien in so that we could finish what we'd started at the Masquerade Ball, but he declined. Now I'm all hot, bothered, with nobody to jump on. That's okay though. Dr. Randahl texted me with a time and his address for tonight. What I didn't get from Julien I'll be sure and make up for tonight when I see Dr. Randahl. For some reason, I'm perfectly fine with Julien wanting to take his time with me. Dr. Randahl won't be afforded the same courtesy. It's about time that he and I dealt with the sexual tension building between us. K.D.

Chapter Thirty Eight

Vanity had been making phone calls all morning. She'd issued a press release that Alexander was okay, and that he merely fainted but was stable and expected to be home possibly today, no later than tomorrow. She'd left out the part where he was drugged, knowing that would have been bad for business. Between managing the media, contacting the managers of establishments he owned, and still working on planning the ultimate party, Vanity was exhausted. However, after two cups of coffee and a Starbucks refresher, she was restless. Sleep would have to wait until much later. Having made all business-related calls, it was one call she'd been wanting to make since last night. Paul not acknowledging Vanity at the club last night was not sitting well with her. Refusing to debate whether or not to call him any longer, she pulled out her phone and called. She was anxious, biting on a pen top, as the phone rang, and rang, and rang. She thought he'd picked up on the last ring, but it was only his voicemail. *Should I leave a message? Should I not? If so, what the hell should I say?*

"Hi Paul, it's Vanity. I've been busy working on some projects, but I wanted to return your call. I saw you called me not too long ago. Well, I've got your voicemail . . ." She stopped mid-sentence and pressed nine. After listening to the prompts, she erased the message and started again. And again. And again.

Deciding to finally go with, "Paul, it's me, Vanity, returning your voice-mail. Call me." When she was satisfied, she sent the message with normal delivery. For her it was urgent, but he didn't need to know that. Not wanting to waddle in her thoughts of Paul longer, she dialed Gianna hoping she'd answer the phone this time and put an end to their phone tag. And she did answer.

"Biiiiiiiiiiiiitch, I thought I was going to have to pop up on you. You're a hard woman to catch up with."

"As are you," Vanity replied. "So, what's up? What's new? How have you been?"

"What's up, you ask? Well, if you'd have called me fifteen minutes earlier I'd have said my skirt. You remember that fine-ass US marshall I met last Memorial Day weekend in Miami?"

"Yeah, what about him?"

"He just left. I didn't even have to ask him to leave. We fucked and then he left. I love it when they don't need instruction to get lost."

Vanity shook her head. Gianna was the same as she'd always been. One hundred percent raw and had been proving year after year that she was never changing, for anyone. "Yeah, I still consider that a trait to be held in high regard myself."

"Oh, really? Well, perhaps I should be asking you what's up?"

"Nothing. Or should I say everything."

"Well, which one is it, Vanity?"

"I'll take everything for six hundred, Alex. It's work, it's the event planning, it's the men in my life, it's everything."

"Okay, slow it down. One subject at a time."

Vanity filled Gianni in on everything that was going on with Paul, Martin, Alex, and the next event she was planning. She even confided in her about working at the hospital and how she thought it was time for a change, which was something she rarely discussed with other people.

"Well, Vanity, I've been telling you for almost a year now. All the event planning you're doing, you could be making a fortune. Sex sells. I'm sure Alexander pays you a very nice salary to handle his light work, but I'm also sure you could be making money hand over fist if you invested in yourself. Look at how much you know about the business already. All the contacts you've made, the knowledge you've gained, the business sense that I know you have. There's no damn reason you should still be working at the hospital. I know you went to school to be a nurse, and I know you said taking care of people was your calling, but what if your calling is to take care of people in a different way?"

"What do you mean?" Vanity was all ears.

"I mean that maybe nursing was a stepping stone for you. Perhaps it's meant for you to take care of the needs of people but in a different way. Maybe it's more of their sexual needs rather than medical that you should be attending to."

"I don't know, G, but it's something that I've been thinking a lot about. I can do so much more with myself, and watching other people chase their dreams has made me want so much more."

"As you should. Just think about it, Vanity. You're a nurse, so I know you're smart as hell. It takes brains to be able to save a life, and you've got to be amazing to stay focused and finish such a meticulous degree. The sky is the fucking limit for you. So, figure out how you want to venture out on your own and just do it. You only fail when you don't try."

"Aw, listen to you, sounding like my own personal motivational speaker."

"Uh-huh, and make sure that no matter what you decide to open that you create a position for me. I'd be great at whatever you needed me to excel at."

"I have no doubt about that. When are you coming to LA?"

"I'll be there within the next two to three weeks."

"Just in time for the event I'm planning. You have to come. It'll be an event like no other."

"I'm always down for a party. Count me in, baby. What do I need to do?"

Vanity filled Gianna in on everything. The event she was throwing for Martin was going to be exclusive. Each guest would be invited by invitation only, with an option to bring a plus one. If you came and enjoyed yourself, you'd have the option to become an official member on the guest list for future events. They ended the call on a positive note, but Vanity was a little uneasy. She'd always known what her next move was, but right now she wasn't so sure what she was going to do next.

Chapter Thirty Nine

Nadia waited until Alex dozed back to sleep before deciding to go home. Getting car service to the club left Nadia without her vehicle. She'd called car service, been home, showered, grabbed an overnight bag, and was back at the hospital within three hours. That was record time considering LA traffic. Nadia was trying her best to find her way back to the observation unit. She wished Alex had been taken to Ellerton Memorial, where she was more familiar with her surroundings and staff, but this hospital was the closest to Pandemonium. She'd already gotten turned around twice and was working on a third time. Realizing she was once again going in the wrong direction, she looked around for someone who worked at the hospital. Nadia headed toward one of the nurse stations when she spotted a familiar face.

"Dr. Kaleb, what are you doing here?"

Dr. Kaleb nervously looked around before managing to choke out a reply. "Nadia, I work here. What are you doing here?"

"I was visiting a friend. I was just about to ask someone to point me in the direction of the observation unit."

Dr. Kaleb didn't reply, nor did he offer his assistance. Nadia stood there watching him fiddle with his phone. His discomfiture prompted her to check out her surroundings. Nadia didn't see anything unusual, but just because she didn't see it didn't mean it wasn't there. *Maybe he's fucking one of the nurses at this hospital.* Nadia smiled and asked, "Is everything okay, Dr. Kaleb?"

"Yes, everything is fine."

" I'd really appreciate the help, if you know where it is."

"Where what is?"

What the fuck am I speaking, Cantonese? "Directions." Dr. Kaleb stood there with his eyebrows furrowed. "To the observation unit. "

"Oh." He pointed down the hall and said, "Go all the way to the end of the hall, past the first set of elevators. When you get to the second set of elevators go to the third floor and then follow the signs."

"Thanks," Nadia said, knowing that she didn't hear a word he said. She was much too busy trying to see what had him all shaken up.

"Listen, it was great seeing you, but I really have to run."

"Okay," Nadia said, but Dr. Kaleb had already walked away. She looked around again, but all she saw were nurses going about their routine—a routine she knew all too well. Trying to recall the directions Dr. Kaleb had just given her, Nadia headed in the direction he'd pointed her in.

After another ten minutes of wandering around, a transporter felt sorry for Nadia and escorted her over to the observation unit. She was hoping to come back to a resting Alex. That hope was soon crushed when she walked in and saw him sitting on the side of the bed, fully dressed, and talking on his cell phone.

"Alex, what in the hell do you think you're doing?"

"Well, in 1973, the first portable cell phone was created. This allowed people to be able to place calls—"

Nadia cut him off before he could finish. "I mean, what the hell are you doing dressed and out of bed, smart ass?"

"I was waiting for you."

Nadia sat her overnight bag and purse down in the chair and walked over to the bed with her hands on her hips. "Waiting on me for what? How did you know I was coming back? And more importantly, how are you feeling?"

Without warning, Alex snatched her down to the bed and pinned her hands above her head. "I feel fine. You don't seem like the type of woman to abandon someone in their time of need. And I would be feeling even better if you'd let me strap you down to this bed and give you the Alexander McCoy treatment."

"Well, as flattering as the 'Alexander McCoy treatment' may be, I'm more concerned about your health. I'm a nurse. I'd like to think I know what I'm talking about."

"That's just it; you're doing too much thinking. You should just surrender yourself to me and let me do the thinking for both of us. And as far as my health, baby, I'm the real McCoy. I'm as good as new."

Nadia lay there with her hands still pinned, shaking her head. A knock sounded at the door.

The day shift nurse walked in and her facial expression was priceless. "Oh! Excuse me Mr. and Mrs. McCoy. I was just—"

Alex interrupted the nurse before she could finish, "It's perfectly fine, Liya. My wife and I were just fooling around." Nadia's eyes widened and then narrowed. Last night she was his girlfriend and apparently she'd graduated to wife.

Nadia could not have been happier that she'd decided to go with wearing jeans, a T-shirt, and heels instead of a dress. If she had on the dress she'd contemplated wearing, the nurse probably would've walked in on more than Alex having her pinned to the bed. Determined to rectify the situation, Nadia opened her mouth to set the record straight. "Actually, I'm not—"

"She's not in the playing mood," Alex said. "Come on, babe, up you go." Alex pulled Nadia up from the bed in one swift movement and gave her a slight pinch on the ass before she could get out of reach.

Liya was still standing in the doorway with paperwork in her hand and blushing beet red. "I have your discharge instructions, Mr. McCoy. It's basically a packet of all the things we discussed earlier. Come back to the hospital immediately if there's any lightheadedness, dizziness, nausea, vomiting, anything out of the ordinary, okay?"

"Got it. Did you get that, baby?" Alex looked at Nadia, who was staring at him like he'd lost his damn mind.

"I already know what to look for. It's you who should be listening, pumpkin," she added, smiling.

"You will need to take it easy, at least for the first couple of days. Sometimes, people have delayed reactions when they're drugged. So, just try to take it easy. Be sure and follow up with your primary care physician within the week, and if I could get you to sign right here." The nurse pointed to the last page at the bottom.

Alex quickly signed his paperwork, obviously anxious to go home.

"Do either of you have any questions for me, Mr. and Mrs. McCoy?"

"Yes, I have one question," Alex said. "Sex. You said to take it easy, but what about sex? See my wife here can be somewhat insatiable at times, and I was wondering—"

"Okay, that's enough," Nadia said, getting up from her chair. "Thank you so much, Liya, but you don't have to answer that, because Alex won't be getting any anytime soon. Now, if there's nothing else, I'll be taking Alex's fresh-ass home now."

With both eyebrows raised, Liya said, "I'm just going to remove his IV and then he's free to go. All I have to do is call for him a wheelchair."

"Wheelchair? No, nope, no way in hell. I'm walking out of here as soon as you take this needle out of my arm."

"Well, someone has to escort you out, sir."

Nadia chimed in with a compromise before Alex could get all worked up about it. "Perhaps you could just walk with us downstairs and we can skip the whole wheelchair thing."

Liya looked back and forth between them and obliged. She removed his IV, gave him a copy of his paperwork, and thanked him for his previous contributions to the hospital. "I'm going to put this on your chart and I'll be right out at the front desk. Whenever you're ready, I'll escort you and your wife downstairs to the lobby myself."

"Thanks, Liya," they both said in unison.

As soon as she closed the door, Nadia stood in front of Alex and started in. "Baby? Wife? Insatiable? I can't figure out if you're crazy as hell, or if you're just trying to get a reaction out of me."

"Possibly a little bit of both." Nadia wasn't laughing. Alex put both of his hands on her hips and said, "I was just having a little fun."

"Yeah, at my expense," Nadia said with raised eyebrows. "And how much of a donation are you and Martin making to this place? When Martin told them who you were last night, they immediately got their asses in gear. You were moved to a room in less than an hour."

"Rightfully so. Let's just say it's enough for them to do a little butt kissing. The CEO and CFO were here about thirty minutes before you walked in."

"What did they want?"

"The usual. 'Thank you, Mr. McCoy. How has your stay been? How is the staff treating you?' The usual B.S. people do when they find out you have money."

"Well, I kind of wish I'd have stayed." Nadia looked over her shoulder at the chair with her overnight bag and purse. "I don't really need this overnight bag anymore."

Tightening his grip on her hips, Alex pulled Nadia back down to the bed again. Taking advantage of her hands not being pinned, Nadia reached up to grab ahold of his face. She ran her hand back and forth down Alex's chin. "Someone needs to shave."

"Seeing that I'm supposed to take it easy, I was hoping my in-house nurse for a couple of days could help me with that."

"In-house nurse?" Nadia stopped and looked at Alex, who was staring back at her with all seriousness. "In-house nurse? You're serious?"

"Only for a few days, and I'll pay you."

"You don't have to pay me, Alex, I'm not an escort. I'm a nurse, and a friend of a friend helping a friend."

"Just a few days. That's all I'm asking."

Nadia was finding it very hard to say no to the Carolina-blue eyes that were staring back at her. So instead of saying no, she gave a counter offer. "I'll go home with you and nurse you back to health." Alex's smile spread across his face faster than wildfire. "But under one condition." Alex's smile immediately faltered. "Don't look like that; you haven't even heard my proposal."

"I'm listening," he said, trying his best to remain optimistic.

"You and I both want to dominate each other, so I'll go home with you under the circumstance that both parties surrender their tastes."

"Meaning?"

"Meaning, I don't make any attempts to make you submit to me, and you promise to not do the same." Alex's eyebrows furrowed as if he was really contemplating her offer. "Do we have a deal, Mr. McCoy?"

"You drive a hard bargain, but yes, baby. I'd say you have yourself a deal. Are kisses okay?"

Now a smile spread across Nadia's face. "Why? Would you like to kiss me?"

Staring at her lips, Alex replied, "I think that would be a great start on my road to recovery."

"I thought you were already as good as new?"

"Shh," was all Alex said. He moved in slowly, his eyes darting back and forth between Nadia's hazel eyes and full lips. Alex planted a chaste kiss on her lips and then pulled back to steal another look into her eyes. Then he kissed her again, this time slowly working his tongue into her mouth, and Nadia melted right into the kiss. Her hands moved from his face to the back of his head, pulling him in closer and deepening the kiss. The feel of something now pressing into Nadia's thigh prompted Alex to break the kiss. Resting his forehead on Nadia's, he said, "I gotta get you out of here."

"You're still not getting any."

Alex's smile resurfaced, and Nadia couldn't get enough of it. "That's fine. But you already agreed that kissing was okay, and I can't wait to get you home and kiss you all day and night."

Chapter Forty

Kensi arrived at Dr. Randahl's house at nine o'clock. He'd texted that dinner was at eight-thirty, but given the events from the evening before, surely he'd understand her need for the extra time. The condo was nice with a red brick pathway leading to the front door, aligned with white flowers, and an inviting mahogany front door. Bottle of Chardonnay in hand, Kensi walked up to the door and knocked. She wasn't standing there long before the door swung open, and she got an eyeful of a more casual Dr. Randahl.

"Evening." Dr. Randahl was dressed in a blue- and white-checkerboard button-down with the sleeves rolled up, and a matching pair of distressed blue jeans. He looked good enough to fuck right there on the doorstep.

"Good evening." Kensi handed him the bottle of wine. "It's a 2008 Littorai Thieriot Vineyard Chardonnay. I was saving it for a special occasion."

He twisted the bottle around in his hand to look at the label. "And this is a special occasion?"

"Someone preparing a meal for me? Yes, I'd say that registers as special in my book."

"Uh-huh." He just stood there staring at Kensi.

"Are you going to invite me in? Or are we going to picnic outside on the lawn this evening?"

Dr. Randahl stepped back and held out his hand, gesturing for Kensi to come inside. He closed the door and sat the bottle of wine on the table against the wall. "Please, may I take your coat?"

"Sure." Kensi turned her back to him and undid the sash on the front of her burgundy trench coat. She pulled the coat slowly down her bare shoulders and let it slip down to the floor. With the exception of the jewelry and red bottoms she had on, she was naked as the day she was born.

Not bothering to pick up her coat, Kensi walked down the hall. "This is a nice place you have here," she said, admiring the earth-tone hues and multi-colored paintings hanging in the hall. She continued walking as if she was fully clothed. She desperately wanted to see Dr. Randahl's face, but she was fighting against the urge. She was completely comfortable in her skin, but she wanted to know what he was thinking. She got to the end of the hall, spun around on her heels, and turned to face him. "Which way?"

Dr. Randahl was still standing at the door when Kensi turned around, mouth agape, and eyes filled with promise. Kensi had on six-inch leopard-red bottoms, a long layered snake-chain necklace that was knotted at the end and fell perfectly between her breasts with earrings to match. She'd pinned up her curly hair so that he could see every inch of bare skin. Kensi had come to play and to win!

Dr. Randahl hurried down the hall toward her and pinned her to the wall. "I thought we'd agreed to have dinner."

Not wanting to miss the opportunity, she pressed her body into his and smirked. "Oh, we're going to eat. We're going to sit, drink wine, eat dinner, and talk. We're going to do everything you've planned this evening, and this is what I'll be wearing. Unless you have a problem with that." Kensi smirked at his jaw twitching. He was fighting hard to control himself and she was loving every minute of it. "Do you have a problem with that?"

Dr. Randahl backed up and put his hands into his jean pockets. "No, I don't think that'll be a problem at all."

"Great. So, point me into the direction of the dining room. I'm starving."

Dr. Randahl gestured to the left. "It's right in there. Table is already set. Make yourself at home."

"Oh, I plan on doing just that." Kensi headed in the direction he pointed, adding a little extra switch in her hips because she knew he was watching.

Dr. Randahl walked back toward the door and picked up Kensi's coat from where she'd dropped it. He placed it neatly on a hanger in the hall closet and retrieved the wine she'd brought from the table. He then disappeared into the kitchen and returned with the opened bottle of wine.

He came to an immediate stop as soon as he entered the room. Kensi was sitting in the chair at the head of the table with both legs crossed on the table, and her arms resting on the arms of the chair. She'd chosen to wear light makeup, not wanting anything to take away from her nakedness.

Dr. Randahl tapped one of her shoes. "Feet off my table. Where are your manners?" he asked, jokingly.

"Sorry, Kenneth," Kensi said. She uncrossed her legs and took one of her legs off the table, leaving her legs spread open for him to get a good look at her snatch. She then slowly pulled her other leg off the table. "It is okay if I call you Kenneth?"

Pulling his eyes from Kensi, he began pouring her a glass of wine. "How long am I going to have to suffer through this?"

"Ah, ah, ah, ah. I asked you a question first."

"Yes, Kenneth is fine. Now it's your turn."

Kensi ran her hand across one of her nipples and over to her necklace. She twirled the necklace around her fingers, hoping to draw his attention to her chest. It worked. "I've always thought my body was rather flattering without clothes on. I'm sorry if you find the sight of me unbearable."

He set the bottle of wine down on the table. "You're flattering period. Whether it's a pair of scrubs or a very short and tight dress for a nightclub. It's not the sight of you that's going to be unbearable tonight." He leaned down within an inch of Kensi's face. "It's remaining a gentleman, because you're really close to being thrown onto this table and being fucked. Hard."

Kensi licked her lips, squared her shoulders, and said, "Say you promise." They sat there staring at each, both refusing to look away first. "Are we going to eat or just stare at each other all night?"

Dr. Randahl ended the stare-off and headed into the kitchen to get the first course. This was payback for the show he'd put on in the sauna, and Kensi was trying her best to make him lose control.

Dr. Randahl returned from the kitchen and placed a bowl of baked fettuccine with Asiago in front of Kensi. "Mmm, smells delicious."

"Tastes even better." He winked and then headed back into the kitchen to grab his plate. He took a seat at the opposite end of the table and was making a terrible attempt to keep his eyes above Kensi's jawline during conversation. "So, how long have you been a nurse?"

"Not long. How long have you been a doctor?"

"Long enough."

"What made you want to become a doctor?" Kensi took another bite of her pasta. "This is really good by the way."

"Thanks," he said, picking up his glass.

"Really good. Almost better than sex."

His glass stopped midway to his mouth. He was looking at Kensi over his glass, and she knew it.

Dr. Randahl took a sip of his wine. "This wine is good too. Makes me wonder if you taste as good." Kensi's head snapped up, as Dr. Randahl set his glass on the table. Now he was the one avoiding eye contact.

"I concur." She tilted the glass and drank the last sip of her wine. "Looks like I'm in need of another glass." Dr. Randahl was about to get up from the table, but Kensi beat him to it. "No, you sit. Eat. I'll get it." Kensi walked slowly into the kitchen with the same sway of her hips as earlier. She sat her glass on the counter. His comment had thrown her a little off kilter, but she was sticking to her guns. They'd been going back and forth at it since they met. Someone was going to have to give in to put an end to this game, and it wasn't going to be her. She poured a half glass of the wine and then downed it before pouring another. She sat the bottle on the counter and looked around. The kitchen was gourmet, everything was stainless steel, and nothing seemed out of place. She walked over to the island to see what else was for dinner tonight. There was a white glass bowl on the counter piled high with strawberries, grapes, and sliced bananas. Next to it was another glass bowl container with a lid. When Kensi removed the top to see what was in the bowl, the sweet smell of chocolate filled her nostrils. She dipped her finger in the bowl to steal a taste, and it was just as delicious as it smelled.

"Everything okay in there?" Kensi was too busy indulging to realize she had been in the kitchen longer than necessary. Hearing Dr. Randahl's voice gave her an idea. She pulled the lid off the chocolate and tipped the bowl, pouring chocolate down her right leg. Then she smashed the bowl to the floor causing a loud clatter.

Dr. Randahl ran into the kitchen. "What the hell?"

Kensi stood there trying to look innocent with chocolate running down her thigh. "I'm so sorry. I don't know what happened. Do you have a towel or something I can use to get this off?"

Dr. Randahl walked over, picked Kensi up, and sat her on the island. He stood between her legs, not caring that chocolate was now all over his jeans. He grabbed a strawberry from the bowl, ran it down Kensi's thigh, and held it between them. He slowly brought his mouth closer and Kensi followed his lead. Dr. Randahl took a bite out of the strawberry and an even bigger bite out of Kensi. They kissed and it was a long, tongue-twisting, hungry kiss.

"I surrender. You win." Then he picked her up and carried her back into the dining room. He placed her on the dinner table and asked her to lay back.

"Why? What are you doing?"

"What you've been waiting for me to do all night. I'm getting ready to have dessert."

Kensi didn't argue. She lay back on the table, still covered in chocolate that had now spread from her thigh down to her ankle and had ruined her shoe. She had a feeling Dr. Randahl was about to make up for it.

"Close your eyes."

"But I want to see you."

"You'll feel me. Now close."

Without putting up further argument, Kensi closed her eyes.

"Keep them closed or else. Do you understand?"

"Yes." With her eyes still closed, Kensi was trying to use all of her other senses to figure out what was going on. She'd heard his footsteps when he left the room and then re-entered, but she couldn't see a damn thing. Just when she was about to open her eyes, she felt his soft lips trailing kisses-from her jaw to her collarbone, and then she felt his warm tongue as he sucked one of her nipples into her mouth.

"Oh God."

"Feel good?"

"Yesssssssss."

He continued his trail of kisses. Down her stomach, and then slow kisses morphed into slow licks when he got to her thigh. "Chocolate never tasted so good." He continued with the soft kisses and slow licks, lifting her leg off the table. He licked the chocolate from her calf and her ankle, and then he slipped her shoe off and let it drop to the floor. Then he kissed and sucked each of her toes before running his teeth down the spine of her foot and playfully biting her heel, causing Kensi to snatch her leg back in reflex.

" Someone is ticklish I see."

Kensi was still lying there, her respirations were increased, and she was trying her best to keep her eyes closed.

"Turn over on all fours."

"Why?" she asked hesitantly, but when he didn't answer she did as she was bid, kicking off her other shoe in the process. Kensi turned over and got on her hands and knees. Feeling the table shift a tad, she wondered if he was on the table with her, and what was the weight capacity, because Dr. Randahl was no small man. Before she could ask where he was, she felt a sharp sting to her left butt cheek. "Oh!"

"Don't question me again," he said. "Now arch your back."

"What?" *Smack!* "Oh my gosh!"

"I asked you not to question me. Now arch your back."

Kensi dipped her back as far as it would go. She was on her hands and knees with her ass in the air, and she was completely comfortable. The anticipation was killing her, but she was ready to see what was next. The first touch of his tongue to her clit brought goosebumps all over her skin. His palms gripped her ass, holding her in place as he devoured her from behind with his mouth. He removed a hand and slipped a finger into her passage, and it felts so good Kensi couldn't stay still. It felt even more amazing when he slipped in two fingers and bit down hard on her ass cheek.

"Oh my God . . . what are you doing to me?"

Smack!

"Three."

"Three what?"

Smack!

"Ahhhhh!"

"Four. Four questions. You want to ask a fifth one?" Dr. Randahl leaned over to whisper in Kensi's ear. They were skin on skin, flesh to flesh, and he was rock hard. "Are you ready, Kensi?"

"Are you, Kenneth?"

Smack!

"Five." The strikes were delightful, as well as the warmth from his skin pressed against her. He'd gotten undressed when he left the room, and Kensi was regretting not opening her eyes earlier so she could get a look at him. She'd seen him naked in the sauna, but she wasn't able to touch him then. She wanted to see him and touch him more now than ever. She heard the ripping of a package, and a few seconds later she felt his knees nudge her thighs open. He put his hands on her waist and started another trail of kisses up her spine. He bit down on her shoulder and then asked, "Are you ready?"

"Yes!"

"Yes. What?"

"What?"

Smack!

"Six. I asked yes what?"

"Yes, Doctor. Give it to me." Kensi could feel his manhood pressing against her ass. The same manhood she'd salivated over when she watched him masturbate in the sauna. Still leaned over her back, Dr. Randahl rubbed her clit with his hand. "Give it to me damn it! Stop fucking with me."

"Someone's impatient." He didn't slide into home base right then. He had her right where he wanted her and she knew it. He removed his hand and grabbed his manhood with it. He began rubbing it back and forth in her wetness. "You're soaking wet."

"That's because I'm ready."

"You're ready, huh? Ready for what?"

"To fuck! Now give me the peen, or get the fuck off me!"

"Peen?"

"Peen, as in penis, cock, dick, manhood, joystick, fun stick, jackhammer, Johnson, meat popsicle. Damn it, just give it to—"

Before she could finish, Dr. Randahl slammed into her, filling her to the hilt. "Yesssssssssssssss!" He pulled back and slammed into her again . . . and again . . . and again.

"Good?"

"Yes! Don't stop."

He'd moved one hand to her lower back, keeping her at an arch so that he could feel every inch of her and get as deep as possible. He kept one hand free. *Smack! Smack! Smack!*

"I'm about to come."

"Me too," Kensi said.

"I want you to catch it for me. Can you do that?"

"After I come, and I'm almost there." He was doing a slow pumping of his hips, probably an attempt to control himself until she orgasmed, but he was going as deep as he could go. And it felt divine. He grabbed her necklace and pulled it tight, cutting off her oxygen supply to make her orgasm more intense. Kensi's muscles clenched around him, she threw her head back, and exploded. Her juices ran down his leg. When she'd finished spasming around his cock, he let the necklace go so she could catch her breath.

"My turn." Dr. Randahl's movements became more rapid. He had both hands on Kensi's hips as he delivered forceful thrusts. The impact was so intense they began sliding forward on the table. "You ready, because I'm about to explode any minute." Without further delay, he pulled out, jumped down from the table, and snatched off the condom. He walked around in front of Kensi, still fisting his cock.

"Open your eyes," he demanded. She did as she was told, and the view was just as it was that night she watched him in the sauna. Back and forth, viciously. It was so animalistic. Kensi sat back on her legs. She grabbed her breasts, not daring to break eye contact.

"Play with your clit," Dr. Randahl ordered, and Kensi slowly slid her hand down, massaging her clit in circular motions. He licked his lips, still stroking himself back and forth, faster and faster.

"You ready?" he asked, still fisting his cock, as Kensi vigorously rubbed her clit. "Open that pretty mouth." Kensi leaned forward just in time to catch every drop of his hot release. She gripped his throbbing manhood and deep-throated it to the hilt. "Damn, girl!" Then she pulled back and swirled her tongue around the head before releasing him.

Kensi sat back on her heels to get another look at the man standing before her. He looked like he was sculpted to perfection, from the top of his head to the bottom of his feet.

"What are you thinking about?" he asked.

"Nothing."

"You're thinking about something. What is it?"

"I'm thinking that I should've brought an extra set of clothes. I'm going to need to borrow at least an old shirt and gym shorts. You mind if I take a shower first?"

Dr. Randahl held out his hand. He helped her down from the table, and then snatched her body toward him. Staring down at her, he said, "You won't be wearing any clothes, because you're not going anywhere. I've got you for the entire night. You're more than welcome to shower. Just know I'll be showering with you, and then I'm going to fuck you in the shower. Twice if you're not too worn out."

Kensi didn't argue. She'd set out to get fucked, and Dr. Randahl wasn't letting her down.

Chapter Forty One

"Martin. We've been over this. We're not going to have strippers at this event. I understand that men and women love to see each other dance naked. However, we're not just selling sex or just entertainment. What we're selling is a combination of both, but with exclusivity. This is a high-class private event, not a bachelor party, okay?"

"It was only a suggestion. It'd be nice to see what you can do on a pole."

"Oh, so not only did you think there were going to be strippers there, but you were hoping I'd be one of them?"

"Hell yeah. Blonde bombshell on a pole. Who wouldn't want to see that? We could get you one of those cowgirl outfits. One with a hat and a lasso."

"Or I could just wear what I have on now."

"And what's that?"

"Nothing but the watch you gave me."

"Vanity, I am trying to respect the boundaries you've set for me as your employer, but another comment like that and I won't be responsible for my actions."

"Hey, you're the one who started it, but back to the event. I'm just about done with everything major that had to be taken care of. Now I'm just staffing, and I have a vacancy in the hostess department."

"I thought you were going to be the hostess."

"I will be, but we still need someone else. I'll have my hands full welcoming guests, introducing myself, shaking hands, listening to our patron's interests, and trying to gauge their likes and dislikes. It would be nice to have someone else available to do my light work. Just in case there's something that has to be tended to and I'm unavailable to do so."

"And who do you have in mind?"

"I was thinking Felicity. That's if you can spare her for the task. I'm not really familiar with her job duties, but I do believe she'd be a good fit. She's attractive, she carries herself well, and she's abreast of what we're trying to do. Felicity would be perfect."

"Let me guess, you would like me to ask her if she'd be available?"

"Yes. I figure she would be more likely to say yes if the proposal were coming from you."

"Well, she's handling a delicate matter for me at the moment. When she checks in with me later this afternoon I'll ask her and I'll get back to you."

"Thanks. I'd really appreciate it."

"Vanity?"

"Yes, Martin."

"In the event Felicity is unable to assist you, I'd be more than happy to co-host with you for the evening. If you promise to send me a photo of you wearing my watch, and only my watch."

"Nice try. Good-bye, Martin."

Martin laughed. "Hey, can't blame me for trying. I'll speak with Felicity and get back with you. Good-bye, Vanity."

They disconnected the call, but before Vanity could make the next call her phone rang. She looked at the screen and recognized the number immediately. Her mind told her not to answer, but curiosity killed the cat.

"Hello, I was calling to speak with Vanity."

"This is Vanity."

"Vanity, this is your manager, Carol Ganton. How are you?"

"I'm fine," Vanity answered, rolling her eyes. This new manager had replaced her old one, and they had butted heads before Carol had been there a full thirty days.

"Great. I was calling because it was brought to my attention that you were supposed to work Saturday night but you didn't come in."

"No, I'm not scheduled to come back in until next Wednesday."

"Well, they had you on the schedule to work this past Saturday. Were you not aware that you were on the schedule?"

"No. This past Saturday I had an engagement, so I know I didn't put down that day to work. If I was on the schedule it's because someone put me on the schedule without my knowledge and without asking me."

"So, you didn't schedule yourself for this past Saturday?"

What is she a fucking parrot? "No, I did not."

"Well, it left the floor short, and as you know, we have to make sure the unit is covered. Are you available to come in possibly tomorrow morning?"

"No, I'm sorry I have prior engagements."

"Well, what day works best for you?"

"I can come in the next day I'm scheduled, which is next Wednesday."

"Do you have any availability before then?"

Hell fucking no! I'm not driving past that damn hospital a nano-second before my next shift. "I don't."

There was a long pause before her manager spoke again. "How is next Wednesday at two o'clock. Does that work for you?"

"Will you be taking me off the schedule for that evening, because if I work that night I'll need to be sleeping all day?" Vanity knew she was pissing her off, but she didn't give a damn. Her manager was always nitpicking and calling her with bullshit.

"Yes. I'll have to take you off the schedule for that shift. As a matter of fact, you won't be able to pick up any more shifts here at Ellerton until we sort out this matter."

"Okay, that's fine. So, we're meeting next Wednesday at two o'clock."

"Yes, we'll meet down in human resources."

"That's fine."

"Okay, Vanity. We will see you then."

Vanity didn't even reply; she just hung up the phone. This was just added bullshit, something else to worry about, and she didn't have time for that. She'd deal with it Wednesday, and not before then. Vanity sat down at her desk to make her last few phone calls, but she was too pissed off. She decided to fix herself a drink instead.

Diary Entry #14

I love being a nurse, but I can do without all the extra bullshit. The point of being per diem is being able to make your own schedule. I wasn't a fucking no call, no show. So, somebody needs to get their story straight and their shit together. Gianna was right about everything. I

should venture out on my own. I can start my own business, throw my own parties, and utilize the contacts that I already have. It'll take some time, it'll be a lot of work, but it will be worth it in the end. I'm pretty sure Alex would be an investor if I decide to do this. Maybe Martin will be interested, but with him, there's still the issue of mixing business with pleasure. We're already riding the "all business" wave, but that may change after this event. I got to see the laid-back version of him, and that's a side of him that I really like. It made me want him right then and there. However, the situation with Alex kept me from being impulsive. I'll be damned though; every time I think back to dancing, laughing, and having a good time with Martin, Paul's face pops in my head. It's been a couple of days since I called. He hasn't called me back, and I'm not expecting him to. Just like I'm sure he's not expecting me to pop up at the club this week to see him. V.C.

Chapter Forty Two

Nadia rolled over and basked in the feel of the soft black sheets she was tangled in. She'd been at Alex's house for the last couple of days but had chosen to sleep in the guest room. The doctor's orders were for him to take it easy, and if they were going to follow them, they had to sleep separately. Nadia told herself it was for Alex's own good, but she knew she was nearly depleted on her bank of restraint also.

Wrapped in the sheet from the bed, Nadia got up and padded over to the window. She pulled it open and let the ocean breeze smack her in the face. Alex had recently purchased one of the beautiful beachfront homes at Manhattan Beach. It was three stories, six bedrooms, had hard wood floors and direct access to the beach. She'd assumed Vanity either decorated it or hired the usual decorator, because his pad was laid. Usually when men decorated their homes themselves they ended up looking like a cross between a fraternity house and a hostel. However, this place was both elegant and comfortable. Nadia took a few extra moments to look out at the ocean and gather her thoughts and then set about getting the day started.

After following her daily grooming ritual, Nadia followed her nose down the winding staircase. The smells from the kitchen had awakened her appetite, and she couldn't wait to see what was cooking.

"Good morning," Nadia called, watching Alex from the doorway. He moved around in the kitchen like a gourmet chef, and for a sick man he sure was fine as hell. When he turned around, he pinned her with his extraordinary blue eyes. He still had "sleep hair," but he was clean-shaven and shirtless, with a pair of rugged jeans on and he was barefoot. There was something about a barefooted man in the kitchen that was just damned sexy!

"Morning yourself. How did you sleep?"

"Like a rock . . . again. I don't know why I'm so tired. It's like all my energy is gone. You'd think I was the one who had gotten drugged."

"Don't talk like that. I'm glad it was me and not you."

"Did you find anything on the security footage?" Alex's head of security had come over to the house yesterday and brought Alex the footage from the night of the incident. Nadia had stayed awake as long as she could so she could watch along with Alex when he reviewed them. However, last night her tiredness had gotten the best of her, and she'd fallen asleep. Hopefully, he hadn't watched it yet.

"We're still reviewing everything."

Nadia was getting ready to tackle the subject full on when the doorbell rang.

"Are you expecting someone?" Nadia asked.

"Yeah, Julien is stopping by. Could you let him in for me?"

"Sure." Leaving Alex to finish up in the kitchen, Nadia went to open the door. Julien really was an attractive young man. He stood at the door with perfect posture, wearing a black AC/DC shirt showing his defined muscle in his arms, his hair was light brown and mussed but sexy, with a boyish grin that showed his dimples, and astonishing sea-green eyes.

"Morning. I came to see Alex. I don't think we were properly introduced the other night. I'm Julien." He held out his hand. Nadia had opened the door, but not her mouth. She had been enjoying the view and forgotten her manners.

Holding out her hand, she said, "I'm sorry, where are my manners? I'm Nadia. I'm a friend of Alex's and Kensi."

"Nice to meet you. Can I come in?"

"Of course." Nadia stepped back and allowed Julien to come in. He and Alex had a similar walk. It was one of confidence, but it was done with such ease. Nadia made a mental note to text Kensi to get the 411 on him. She pulled herself from her thoughts and went back into the kitchen.

"Nadia, this is my cousin Julien. Julien, this is my girlfriend Nadia."

"First of all, we've already introduced ourselves, so you're late. Secondly, I'm not your girlfriend."

"Whoa, bro. Did you just get shot down?"

"I guess I did," Alex said. Then, he turned to Nadia. "I stand corrected. Julien, Nadia is my future girlfriend. Better?" he asked Nadia.

Nadia rolled her eyes and took a seat at the bar next to Julien. "Changing the subject, this smells delicious."

"Yes, it does," Julien agreed.

"Eggs, bacon, French toast, and fresh fruit. There's plenty. You should join us for breakfast," Alex encouraged, taking a seat at the bar on the opposite side of Nadia.

"I'd love to, but I have a prior engagement. I'm picking Kensi up in two hours and taking her to lunch."

"Oh, a date?" Nadia asked, taking a sip of orange juice.

"Yes, the first. Hey, what kind of flowers does she like? I was going to stop and pick some up on the way. Didn't want to show up to the door on a first date empty handed."

"Well ,aren't you a gentleman? I'm not sure what her particular favorite is, but you can't go wrong with roses. White ones. Pretty, long-stemmed white roses."

"Thanks. I'll pick some up on the way. Alex you ready to show me what we talked about on the phone?"

Nadia looked back and forth between the two men. *Show him what? And what the hell did they talk about on the phone? Maybe this is about the tape.*

"Yes, I'm ready. Nadia, baby, we're going to step into the study. You finish eating, and feel free to help yourself to more if you desire."

"Actually, I'm going to have to eat and run. I need to run home and get some things, and I need to make a stop by Vanity's house. I'll be back tonight though."

Nadia was barely able to finish her sentence before Alex leaned in and kissed her. "You're coming back tonight, right? Because I have a surprise for you."

"Yes, I'll be back tonight."

"Good. I'll see you then." Alex leaned in again and placed a chaste kiss on Nadia's jaw. He got up from the bar and grabbed his glass of OJ and his plate. "You ready Julien?"

Julien was sitting there with a full on smile on his face. "Bro, you got it bad."

"Shut up, and come on," Alex said, heading to the study.

Julien got up from the bar to follow Alex. "Nadia, it was a pleasure seeing you again."

"Likewise," she called behind him. Nadia sat at the bar and finished her breakfast. She had racked her brain trying to figure out what kind of surprise Alex had for her but came up with nothing. She had to admit she was a little bit excited. She cleared the bar and wiped up the area before heading back upstairs to grab her phone, keys, and purse. Tip-toeing by the study door, she stopped briefly to see if she could hear what was going on. Nadia was pretty positive they were discussing the security tape, and she wanted to see what, if anything, she could find out. She stood outside the door for a few minutes, and right when she was walking away the door opened.

"Nadia," Alex said, his tone suggesting he suspected she was eavesdropping.

"Alex. I was just about to come in and tell you I was leaving, but I changed my mind. I didn't want to disturb you."

"No bother at all." He snatched Nadia to him and smiled. He held her to him tightly, but didn't say a word.

"Why are you smiling?" she asked.

"No reason." Then he kissed her again, but this kiss was different. It was softer and intimate. Nadia placed her hands on his bare chest, he took little nips at her mouth, the corners of her mouth, and then he softly bit her bottom lip before releasing her. He stepped back and said, "I love kissing those lips. Go before I lock you in and never let you go."

"You try and take it easy while I'm gone. I don't want to come back and find you passed out again, but from exhaustion this time."

"Yes, ma'am."

Nadia headed up the stairs to get her things. She didn't know what his surprise for her tonight was going to be, but she'd have one for him also.

Chapter Forty Three

Diary Entry #15

I'm still sore from being with Dr. Randahl. His sex game is A-game, I'll give him that. He sexed me until the sun came up. Hell, I didn't even get any damn sleep. I'm still a little tired right now. Even though the sex with Dr. Randahl was great, as soon as I walked out of his house, my mind reverted right back to Julien. The images of his dimples and playboy smile danced around in my head, making me grin like an idiot. And that mouth—his mouth and that accommodator—has already been filed away as one of my favorite memories of us. Hopefully we'll be making plenty more memories like that. K.D.

Kensi was in the bathroom attempting to manager her hair. Being Filipino and black gave her a good grade of hair that looked beautiful, but in reality it was extremely difficult to manage. It was a major contrast in how it really was and how people perceived it. Deciding that her hair was as groomed as it was going to be, she started in on the eyeliner. She had barely finished lining the other eye when the doorbell rang.

"Shit. Who the hell is on time anymore?" Kensi took one last look over in the mirror before heading out of the bathroom and down the stairs to answer the door. When she opened the door, she was taken aback for two reasons. The first was relative to Julien being so handsome, and the second was because of the beautiful flowers he was holding.

"These roses are beautiful," Kensi said, reaching for the bouquet.

"They're not nearly as beautiful as you."

Kensi was wearing her bandeaux-style white summer dress with matching white strappy Sergio Rossi's. Her look was casual but she'd jazzed it up to be sexy. She hadn't finished her makeup yet, and her unruly hair had barely been tamed, but she blushed at the compliment anyway.

"Thank you. Would you like to come in?"

Julien stepped past Kensi into her foyer, giving Kensi the opportunity to get a good look at him. His stride was so confident, as if he owned a piece of the world. His toned arms alone were evidence of the incredible shape he was in, and his killer smile with the dimples probably got his way with a lot of women.

"Nice place."

"Thank you. Nice shirt," she said, taking notice of his AC/DC shirt. "I take it you're a fan."

"I am. It wasn't exactly my era, but great music is timeless."

"Agreed." Kensi walked Julien to the living room area. She hadn't expected him to be on time, so she needed a few extra minutes to finish getting ready. He could wait; a little waiting never hurt anyone.

Leaving a waiting Julien in the living room, Kensi went into the kitchen and put her roses in a vase before heading to her bedroom to finish getting ready. She finished her makeup, choosing to keep it light with lipstick, eyeliner, and mascara only. Then, she spent another ten minutes with her hair before throwing in the towel. After twenty minutes of perfecting her look, Kensi grabbed her cell phone and her purse and headed downstairs to a patiently waiting Julien.

Julien looked up from his phone, flashed Kensi with his boyish grin, and asked, "You ready, beautiful?"

"As ready as I'll ever be."

Chapter Forty Four

Nadia stood outside Vanity's door waiting for her to answer, but she was surprised when she was greeted by another familiar face.

"Hello, Felicity. What are you doing here?"

"Vanity and I are finalizing everything for the party. You look nice today, Nadia."

"Thank you," Nadia said, stepping inside. "I've been staying at Alex's, so I don't have access to all my things, but I made do with what I had."

"Well, you look nice. Very nice," Felicity said, stepping forward and pulling at a strand of Nadia's kinky black hair and watching it spring back into place. "I'd say you were very well put together." Nadia didn't miss the fact that Felicity was flirting with her, but she also wasn't in the mood to flirt back.

"Thank you, Felicity. I try. Where's Vanity?"

"She's right through there," Felicity answered, pointing. "She's the one with her face buried behind the computer and barking all the orders."

"That sounds like Vanity." Nadia headed through the doorway and spotted her friend doing just as Felicity said. She had her face hidden behind her computer screen, and she was on the phone barking orders and demands at someone. Nadia lightly tapped on the doorframe to alert Vanity that she had arrived. Vanity held up her finger for Nadia to give her one minute, and then gestured at the seat across from her for Nadia to have a seat. Taking a seat, Nadia used that time to check her texts. She had one message from Alex.

Alex: *Missing your presence already.*

Nadia smiled to herself and replied: *Don't worry, you'll see me later on.*

Alex: *I'm counting the minutes.*

Grinning, Nadia put her phone back into her purse and when she looked up, both Vanity and Felicity were staring at her. "What the hell are you two gawking at?"

"I asked you a question," Vanity said, still staring at Nadia.

"Well, I was texting. I didn't hear you. What is it?"

"I asked you about Alex. How is he? I've talked to him a few times, and he says he's taking it easy, but I know Alex can be very stubborn at times."

"Yes, how is Alex?" Felicity chimed in.

"He's fine. I had to distance myself and sleep in the other room, but other than that he's been the perfect gentleman and he's been listening to everything I tell him. I got him to stay in the bed the first day, but that was only because I allowed him to have his laptop. I didn't realize he wore so many hats. It's been difficult for him to take it easy, but I've been there to enforce doctor's orders. There's no telling what he's doing now that I've stepped away though, but for the most part, he's doing fine."

"Thank goodness you have the time to look after him, because I'm up to my elbows in planning. Felicity has relieved some of the pressure by helping with some things, but this planning has been strenuous. Not to mention, our boss Carol called to let me know I was a no-call no-show the other night."

"Excuse me?"

"Yeah, you heard me right. Apparently, someone put me on the schedule this past weekend, and I knew nothing about it."

"But that's the point in being per diem. You make your own schedule."

"Exactly. She asked me to come in, and I told her the earliest I could come in is next Wednesday. Not a damn minute before then."

"What happened between you two? She really has it out for you. Kensi and I don't have these kind of problems with her."

"She's just being a bitch. I'll tell you what—I'm not signing a write-up or any damn thing of the sort. If she gives me any bullshit about this other than chalking it up to be a misunderstanding, I'm going to hand her that fucking badge and she can find herself someone else to toy with."

Vanity was all serious and Nadia knew it. She'd hate to see her friend quit, but in all actuality Vanity and the manager were like oil and water. It was a known fact on the unit that those two were not mixing.

"On another note, do you have anyone you'd like to invite to the party?" Felicity asked, switching the topic back over to business.

"Actually, yes. I'd actually like to invite Amber. We exchanged info the other night, and I told her she should come to one of your events, if that's okay with you two."

Felicity and Vanity looked at each and nodded their heads. "It's fine with me," Felicity said.

"I don't have problem with that either," said Vanity. "I'll add her name to the list."

"Great. I'll call her with the details and let her know."

"Here's the information." Vanity slid her notepad toward Nadia. "Let her know she is officially on the guest list, and each invited guest is allowed to bring a plus one."

"Will do." Nadia pulled out her phone. "I'll call her right now and let her know. Is there anything you need me to do? Anything I can help with?"

"No, just make sure Alex is taking good care of himself. That's enough for me. Everything else has been taken care of."

Chapter Forty Five

Julien drove a metallic gray four-door, full-sized Dodge Ram pickup truck. Despite the vehicle being large, he navigated it with ease, something else Kensi took note of. They pulled into the parking garage at Santa Monica Place, and took the short walk to Del Friscos.

"I've been meaning to come here," Kensi said after they were shown to their table and seated.

" I'm glad your first time could be with me."

Kensi grinned but chose not to reply to Julien's remark. She felt his eyes on her, but kept her eyes on her menu. "So, I take it you've been here before."

"Several times. The cheesesteak egg rolls are to die for."

"I think I'm going to have a VIP to drink. I love all things pineapple."

"I'll keep that in mind."

"Good afternoon," the waitress interrupted. "My name is Casey and I'll be your server. What drinks can I get started for you folks?" She spoke as if she was greeting both of them, but Kensi didn't miss the fact that the waitress's eyes had landed on Julien and stayed there.

"I'll have the VIP," Kensi said, but the waitress still didn't look in her direction.

"A VIP for the lady, and I'll have an old-fashioned and an order of the cheesesteak egg rolls."

"VIP, old-fashioned, and cheesesteak egg rolls. Got it. I'll let you two finish looking over our menu while I get those drinks and appetizer going for you."

"Thanks," Kensi said, making an attempt to grab the waitress's attention and failing.

"You're welcome," the waitress replied, with her eyes still glued to Julien.

Kensi looked over at Julien ,who seemed completely oblivious to the waitress and her fascination with him. "So, I'm guessing that happens a lot."

"What?" he asked, not having a clue what Kensi was referring to.

"The waitress didn't take her eyes from you for a second. She was practically drooling over you."

"Oh, I didn't notice." Julien dismissed what Kensi was saying and turned his attention to the ocean. "I love coming here, especially when it's not so crowded. I'd like to take you for a walk down Santa Monica Pier if your shoes will allow."

Kensi had stolen a peek out at the ocean herself, but quickly turned her attention back to Julien. "I'll have you know, I'm a veteran when it comes to these heels. I can walk for miles in these shoes."

" I guess that's that. Santa Monica Pier after lunch it is. We'll see how well those sexy stems you call legs hold up."

"You said you wanted to get to know each other, so I have a question. What is it that you do for a living?"

"A lot of things, actually. I joined the navy right out of high school. I moved up the ranks and had the opportunity to serve my country as a navy seal for a year and a half before being honorably discharged. I then came home and got into business with my cousin. I've been a silent partner in a lot of his endeavors, and they've all been quite lucrative."

"Really. So, club Pandemonium?"

"Yes, club Pandemonium. Another successful project Alex, Martin, and myself all had our hand in."

"What about brothers, sisters, your parents? Tell me about them."

"Quid pro quo, Kensi. Your turn to tell me about you."

"Okay. Shoot."

"I know you're a nurse, but for how long? What made you want to become a nurse?"

"I've been a nurse for a couple of years now. My mom died when I was six, but before that, she was in and out of hospitals a lot. I remember seeing the nurses and thinking how I wanted to do that when I grew up. I wanted to be a nurse and help people, just like the nurses that were helping us. Now, here I am, all grown up and a registered nurse."

"And?"

"And what?"

"Is it everything you thought and hoped it would be?"

"Ah, quid pro quo. Back to my question. Brothers, sisters, your parents?"

"I have one older sister, two younger twin brothers, and my parents are deceased. They died a few years back within six months of each other, father of lung cancer, and then my mother of breast cancer six months after him. It's been me and my . . ." Julien's voice faded off into the background. Kensi had turned her attention to the perfectly poised woman and the pudgy balding man who had just come into view. "Kensi?" Julien asked.

"Yes. I'm sorry. I thought I saw someone I knew."

Julien turned around, then turned back to Kensi. "Must've been a hell of a someone, because you look like you've seen a ghost."

"No, I'm fine."

"You're sure?"

"Yes, I'm sure."

"Okay well like I was saying my—"

"On second thought, I think I need to run to the restroom. I'll be back."

Before Julien could get up properly from his seat, Kensi was out of her chair and headed in the direction of the woman she could have sworn was her stepmother. She opened the bathroom door and there was Sara primping in the mirror. Sara didn't even flinch when they locked eyes in the mirror.

"Kensi, dear, I thought that was you."

"Sara, what are you doing here? And who is that man you're with?"

"You're quite the inquisitive one." Sara ran her hands through her hair, retouched her lipstick, and spot-checked her eyebrows. She didn't have a hair out of place and she knew it. Sara was putting on a show for Kensi.

"I just figured we could save some time by bypassing the fake greetings and chitchat. So, who is he?"

Sara didn't answer; she just continued primping in the mirror. "I just thought it would be nice to have a name to go with the description. Make no mistake about it, I will be telling my father about this."

Sara crossed her arms and faced Kensi. "People in glass houses shouldn't throw stones. You go ahead and tell your father whatever you like, but then

I just might have to tell him what I know. I just might have to open my big mouth and tell your father that his sweet, innocent, little girl likes to venture over to the dark side. About how she likes to go to sex parties and sleep with random men. You know he's been having issues with his heart lately. I'd hate to have to be the one to deliver such heartbreaking news."

Kensi didn't say a word. She smoothed out her dress, then walked over to the mirror to do her own makeup check. "You know the difference between you and me, Sara?" Kensi turned around to face Sara. "My father will forgive me for anything and you for nothing." Kensi didn't say another word. She left Sara in the restroom and headed back out to the table with Julien.

Julien stood and pulled Kensi's chair out for her. "Are you all right?"

Kensi looked up and spotted Sara returning to her table. "You see that woman right there?"

Julien looked over to where Kensi was discreetly pointing. "Yeah, I see her. What about her?"

"That's my stepmother, but the guy she's with is not my dad."

"Oh shit. Really?"

"Yeah, really."

Julien took a swig of his drink and snuck another look at the table where Sara and the gentleman were sitting. "You recognize the guy she's with?"

"No, I don't recognize him. Who is he?"

"He's one of the best damned divorce lawyers in Los Angeles. His name is Withers, from Echols, Weinstein, Withers, and associates. I hope your father has good representation, because she sure does."

Kensi had barely touched her drink, but after hearing that, she downed the entire glass.

Julien's eyebrows were raised in concern. "Are you sure you're all right?"

"Yes, I am."

"Okay." Julien picked up his drink and turned his attention back toward the ocean.

"You know what. I'm not all right. I'm really not feeling well. Do you mind taking me home?"

Julien placed his hand over Kensi's. "No problem at all."

***

The drive home was quiet, with Julien making the occasional joke every now and then to elicit a laugh from Kensi. Most being unsuccessful, but Kensi noted the effort. Julien, ever the gentleman, opened Kensi's door and helped her out of his massive pickup truck and walked her to her front door.

"Well, Ms. Kensi, even though our time together was cut short, I really enjoyed our lunch date and I'm hoping we can do it again soon."

"I'm sorry. I just . . . I just was not expecting to see her. Then she was with another man, and I kept thinking about how this is going to be an awkward conversation to have with my dad."

"You don't have to explain. I can't say that I can relate, because I've never had a stepparent before, but I can imagine how uneasy you must feel being in this position."

Kensi already had on four-inch sandals, but she still had to stand on her tip toes to place a kiss on Julien's cheek. She unlocked her front door, and then turned back around to face Julien. "Would you like to come in?

It's still very early, and I'm going to fix myself a drink when I get inside. Perhaps you could keep me company. You know, never let a friend drink alone type of thing."

Julien flashed Kensi his boyish grin. "Sure."

"Great." Kensi turned around and unlocked the door, but she was not ready for what she saw when she stepped inside. Kensi dropped her keys and purse at the sight before her. Her home had been completely trashed. All of her things were smashed or broken. The walls had the word "whore" written in purple paint over and over again. Her couch cushions and accent pillows had been cut, and the remnants from the inside were strewn across the floor. Kensi walked into her kitchen, with Julien trailing behind. The dishes were all smashed, the kitchen table had been flipped upside down, and the kitchen walls were covered in groceries along with the word "whore." Kensi bent down to pick up a piece of one of the smashed glasses on the floor, but Julien stopped her.

"Don't touch anything. This is all evidence, and it may have fingerprints on it." Kensi just nodded, unable to get any words past the lump that had formed in her throat. She headed out of the kitchen toward her bedroom, and was confused when her room came into view. Everything was intact. A picture of herself that she kept on her nightstand was on her bed with a purple bra and panties laid out next to it. She stepped closer and looked at the bed, noting that there was also a clear slimy substance next to her lingerie. Kensi placed her hand across her mouth and almost jumped out of skin when Julien placed his hand on her shoulder.

"Oh my God! Is that what I think it is?" Kensi turned her face into Julien's shirt and sobbed. "I need to get some tissues from the bathroom." Kensi walked into the bathroom and stopped dead in her tracks at the message written on the mirror. Perfect handwriting in purple lipstick read:

"My fantasy will become a reality, and pleasure will be certain."

Julien came up behind Kensi and looked at the message left on the mirror. "The police are on the way. Do you know who did this?"

"No, but it's probably the same person who's been sending me notes." Kensi grabbed a tissue and walked out of the bathroom back into her bedroom. Careful not to touch anything, she used the tissue to open the bottom drawer of her nightstand. She pulled out the previous letters she'd received and handed them to Julien.

"How long have you been getting these? Has someone been sending them to you here?" Julien asked.

"I've been getting them for the past few weeks. I've been getting them at work, and I got one at the party. That's why I asked you if you sent me any notes other than the one you sent with the dress. I thought you may have sent me these too."

"What? No Kensi. Of course not. And what party?"

"The party where we first met. Right after we met, actually. One of the servers brought me some clothes, because you ripped my dress, and the note was in the clothes they bought. I tried to see who it was, but they were already gone when I re-opened the door." Kensi's voice broke as she was trying to finish her thoughts. Julien came over and wrapped his arms around her to give her some since of security.

"Does Alex know about this?"

"No, I don't think so. I've only told Nadia and Vanity. Vanity got me a list of the servers at the party, but I didn't recognize any of the names, and everyone was wearing a mask."

"I'll look into it."

Kensi craned her neck to look up at Julien whose facial expression had completely changed. The boyish grin with the dimples was gone and had been replace by an unflattering scowl. "What do you mean you'll look into it?" Before Julien could answer, the doorbell rang.

"That's the police. Come on, the sooner we file this report, the sooner we can get your place cleaned up and back the way it was. "

"I don't think it'll ever be the way it was."

***

Kensi and Julien had been tied up for hours talking to the detectives. After the detectives left, she changed clothes and made an attempt to clean up and restore her home, but it was still a wreck. Julien gave her the option of him spending the night, or her staying at his home. Feeling like her home had been desecrated, she chose the latter.

"Did you take pictures of the damage and the other letters that were sent?"

"Yes, I've got it all on my phone."

"Good, send them to me."

"What are you going to do with it, and where are we going?"

"I'm going to use all of my resources and contacts to find out who the hell is doing this. We're headed to Pasadena. I'm going to link up with some friends of mine. They're my brothers from the navy; maybe they can help you find out who this is."

"The police said they'd look into it, Julien."

"I'm sure they will, but I can guarantee you murders, rape cases, and robberies take precedent over stalkers and vandalism. This is not a priority case for them, but it is for me, so let me help you, okay?"

Kensi didn't argue; she didn't have the strength to put up a fight. She leaned on the door and rolled down her window. She let the wind hit her face and whip through her hair, and the comfort of Julien's words relaxed her.

They finally made it to downtown Pasadena and pulled into a parking garage. Julien whipped his Dodge Ram into a parking space next to a massive black Hummer. Julien killed the engine and told Kensi to give him a few minutes. She took out her phone and began checking her texts and missed calls. Dr. Randahl had texted, but Kensi was not in the mood to talk. She put her phone back in her purse and looked out of the window at Julien and his friends talking. The two men standing with Julien were in the same physical condition as he was, but their facial expressions read, "Do not fuck with me." Julien's boyish grin and easy-going personality made him seem so harmless, but looking at the two men he called his "brothers" made her wonder what type of mean streak Julien was hiding.

Kensi waited in the car patiently for Julien and his friends to end their conversation. She was stressed, and she needed some stress relief. After running into her step-monkey at Del Frisco's and coming home to her vandalized home, her fix from Dr. Randahl had worn off. Julien wanted to wait, and she had waited long enough.

Julien opened the door and hopped back into the truck. Kensi looked out the window at the two men Julien called his brothers. They both gave a hand gesture, to Kensi and she returned their kind gesture with a wave. "They're on it. If they can't find who did this, nobody can." Julien put the key into the ignition, but Kensi grabbed his hand and stopped him before he could start the truck.

"What's wrong?" he asked.

"I need you."

"I'm here."

"No, I need you."

Julien sat there and stared at Kensi. She undid her seatbelt, took off her jacket, and threw it into the backseat of the truck. Kensi quickly climbed over the console and straddled his lap. Julien wrapped his arms around her waist, and Kensi ran her fingers through his mussed hair. "I want you right now, right here in your truck."

"We're in a parking garage, Kensi."

"I know exactly where we are. It doesn't change the fact that I want you."

Julien took his time and kissed Kensi slowly and sweetly. "Someone might see us."

Kensi kissed Julien, taking slow small bites at his bottom lip. "I don't care who sees us."

Julien opened the driver door and slid out of the truck, taking Kensi with him. With her legs still wrapped tightly around his waist, he opened the back door of the truck, sat her on the seat, climbed in, and closed the door behind them.

Julien slid his hands under Kensi's shirt and pulled it over her head. He licked his lips, and Kensi felt her temperature go up. Julien started a trail of wet kisses down Kensi's body. Moving from her lips, down her neck, to her collarbone, and then her breasts. He ran his hands over her shoulders and slowly pulled down her bra straps. He sucked one of her nipples into his mouth, eliciting a soft sigh of pleasure from Kensi.

"Feel good?"

"Yes. Don't stop."

"I don't intend to." Julien continued his trail of kisses down Kensi stomach. When he got to her jeans, he gripped the back pockets with his hands. Then he undid the button and pulled down the zipper with his teeth. He leaned back, pulled off Kensi's shoes one at a time, and then removed her jeans. He licked his lips again as he admired the view before him. Kensi lay on the backseat bared to Julien, with her bra pulled halfway down and her matching panties. "Your under garments look expensive. Are they?"

"It's La Perla. Why?"

Julien leaned down and slowly nipped at Kensi's hip.

"For a minute I thought you were going to rip my panties off like you ripped my dress the night we met."

Julien looked up at Kensi, flashed her his dimpled grin, and said, "Send me the bill." Before Kensi could stop him, he grabbed her panties with his teeth and ripped them off. He put one arm behind her back, yanked her up from the backseat, and pulled her onto his lap. "Your hair is a mess of beautiful curls. Don't ever change it."

Kensi ran her fingers through Julien's hair. "Shut up and kiss me."

He did just that. In the back of Julien's four-door pickup in a public parking garage, he and Kensi were a tangle of bodies, kisses, slow licks, and soft bites. The windows were fogged up and they had almost exhausted each other before Julien had a chance to penetrate her. Breaking the final kiss, he pulled back and asked Kensi, "Are you ready?" Kensi didn't say a word; she simply nodded her head. Julien donned a condom, grabbed Kensi's hips, and lifted her onto him, but he didn't slide into home just yet. He let her dangle with his manhood resting at her entrance.

"Don't tease me, Julien." Without further delay, he removed his hands completely, letting Kensi drop down, taking all of him in one swift move and filling her to the hilt. "Oh my God!"

"No, baby, it's just me."

Kensi wrapped both her arms around Julien's neck and rode him up and down slowly. She felt stretched to the max, but the pleasure outweighed the pain. Julien attempted to wrap his arms back around her waist, but Kensi grabbed them and pushed them onto the seat.

"No hands."

"Yes, ma'am," was all Julien said, but she could see from his face that he wanted to be the one in control. He wanted to put his hands on her waist to control the pace, but Kensi was on top and she wanted to be in full control. When she knew he was close to orgasm, she put her hands on Julien's shoulders, tightened her vaginal muscles, and picked up the pace.

"Damn, girl."

A cocky Kensi replied, "I know." Then, she tightened up some more and watched as Julien's forehead wrinkled, as his abdominal muscles tightened, as he gripped the backseat, as his breathing increased, and as . . . he came. Kensi was right with him; she nibbled on his ear to suppress her own moaning, gripped her breasts with her hands, and threw her head back as her orgasm washed through her.

When Kensi caught her breath, she looked into Julien's eyes.

"What are you thinking right now?" he asked, but before she could answer, there were three loud taps on the window followed by the flashing of a light.

"What the hell?" Julien said, turning his attention to the window.

"Security. You folks are going to have to take that elsewhere. I'll give you five minutes to get out of here. If you're not gone by then, I'll have to call the authorities."

Kensi and Julien just looked at each other and started to laugh. Kensi grabbed her shirt and jeans and started to get dressed. Julien climbed over the console and back into the driver's seat, and when Kensi was somewhat put back together, he helped her to climb back into the passenger seat. After primping for a few moments, she noticed Julien staring at her and grinning from ear to ear.

"What the hell are you smiling about?"

Julien put his keys into the ignition and started up the engine. "I can't wait to get you to my house and fuck you over and over again. Remember when you said 'no hands' and I abided by your rules?" Julien's smile was replaced by a look of pure seriousness. "Let's hope you can be as obedient as I was."

A tingle ran up Kensi's spine, as she smiled at the promise in Julien's voice. He couldn't wait to get her home, and she couldn't wait to get there.

Chapter Forty Six

Nadia followed the trail of lovely white rose petals from the front door, up the stairs, and out to the balcony. The balcony was covered in white rose petals, with a vase of long-stemmed white roses, and two lit candles waiting on a table. Alex stood next to the table watching and waiting, with his hands tucked in cream-colored linen pants, and a matching white linen button down. Nadia had stopped by her home and changed into a tight strapless jean dress with a small split up the back and royal blue Manolo Blahniks.

"Did you wear that for me?" Alex asked, slowly taking steps toward Nadia.

"Did you wear that for me?" Nadia asked.

When he was close enough, he snatched her to him and held her in his arms while he stared into her hazel eyes. "Yes, I did," Alex answered without shame, still holding Nadia in a tight grip. "You know a man can get lost in those eyes of yours."

"Well, hopefully he'll be able to find his way back." Nadia stared into his eyes. "Your eyes aren't that bad either, sir. I may get lost in yours and be the one who is unable to find my way back."

"I'd come get you."

"Would you now? And what would we do when you found me?"

Alex spun Nadia around with her back to his front and began a very slow sway. "I'd hold you just like this and make you dance with me just like we're doing now."

Nadia smiled. She was enjoying spending time with him. It had been a while since she enjoyed the company of a man for more than a few hours. "So, I take it this is the surprise you had for me."

"I just figured since you had taken care of me so well over the past few days, I should return the favor. It's a nice night, so I thought you may like to dine out here with the ocean and the stars. I heard what you told Julien about him not being able to go wrong with pretty white roses, so I ordered two dozen as soon as you left. They're not as lovely as you, but they'll do."

"I love them," Nadia said, smiling at the fact that Alex was still swaying with her in his arms even though there wasn't any music playing. "You know there's no music playing, right?"

Alex spun her around to face him. "We don't need any. You and I make our own music."

"Is that right?"

"Yes, it is. How do you like your surprise so far?"

"I'm quite pleased, Alexander."

Alex reluctantly let Nadia out of his grip, walked over to the table, and pulled out her chair. "Please, have a seat." He removed the porcelain plate cover from her dish. "I've prepared blackened salmon, pineapple slaw, and asparagus with a parmesan butter glaze."

"Looks and smells delicious."

"Tastes even better. I promise." Alex took the seat opposite of Nadia. "Did I tell you how beautiful you look tonight?"

Nadia just blushed and picked up her fork, "Quite the charmer, aren't you?"

"I try."

"Well, this is all very nice. I almost forgot that I have a surprise for you."

"Really? For me?"

"Yes. You've been quite patient, a true gentleman, and very hospitable over the past few days, so I figured you deserve a reward."

"And what might that reward be?"

Nadia leaned in and Alex followed her lead. She lowered her voice and said, "I decided panties didn't compliment my outfit, so I didn't wear any."

Alex didn't move while Nadia, feeling all the more cocky, put a bite of salmon into her mouth.

"This is quite delicious, Alex," Nadia said, smirking.

Alex removed his napkin from his lap, dabbed the corners of his mouth, and slid his chair back. He grabbed the champagne from the bucket of ice, two glasses, and then Nadia by her arm.

"But, we haven't finished eating, Alex."

Alex stopped mid-step and turned to Nadia. "I haven't even started."

Nadia smiled as Alex led her from the balcony to his bedroom. Nadia stood waiting in the doorway, taking in the scene before her. Red candles and white rose petals surrounded his California king-sized bed. Alex sat the two glasses on the dresser and popped the cork on the champagne. He poured them both a glass and handed one to Nadia, who was taking very slow steps into the room.

She accepted the glass of champagne. "Alex, all of this is too much."

"That's funny. I didn't think it was enough at all."

Alex took a sip of his champagne and continued to stare at Nadia. Then Nadia downed her entire glass before sitting it on the dresser, kicked off her heels, and stormed toward Alex. She kissed him—hard. Alex pulled back, then looked at Nadia in her eyes before kissing her again. When he grabbed Nadia's ass, she wrapped both legs around his waist and kissed him again. He slowly walked them both over to the bed.

When they tumbled onto the bed, Nadia rolled him over and got on top of Alex. She grabbed his hands from her ass, pushed them above his head, and said, "Don't move." Just when she was about to start her process of seduction, Alex rolled her over and put her under him.

Nadia's forehead wrinkled in confusion. "What are you doing?" Alex took each of Nadia's hands and put them above her head. "Alex, what are you doing?"

"This is supposed to be an evening I put together for you. You were trying to steal my thunder."

"I wasn't trying to steal your thunder. I was just feeling a little frisky, that's all."

"I know we've talked about this. You told me that I should come and find you when I was ready to kneel before a real woman, remember?"

"Yes, I do."

Alex stood up and grabbed Nadia by her knees, pulling her to the edge of the bed. He kneeled down between her legs; he ran his hands up her calves and thighs. Nadia sat up on her elbows to take in the sight before her, and Alexander kneeling before her was a sight to see.

He slowly pushed her jean dress up and said, "I have no problems kneeling before you, but it's not to be your submissive. It's to show you how it could be if you submitted to me." He hooked his fingers into her panties and slowly pulled them down. He raised her leg and sucked one of her toes into his mouth while he massaged the bottom of her foot. Nadia sighed in pleasure as Alex teased her. He worked his way up her leg, with soft bites on her ankle, and slow licks and kisses up her thigh. Just when Nadia thought he was about to give her what she'd been craving, he came to a complete stop.

"Alex, we both agreed that neither of us would make any attempts to make the other person submit. So, what the hell are you doing?"

"Waiting on you to change your mind. This is just one night. It's only me and you here, and I know you want this as bad as I do. Let me give you a night filled with pleasure that you'll never forget."

"One night?"

"One night. That's all I ask."

"Okay," she moaned. Alex's eyes lit up at her response. "One night, that's all."

"Understood."

"Now get back to what you were doing. I was enjoying that."

"With pleasure."

Alex grabbed Nadia's legs and flipped her onto her stomach. He slowly unzipped her dress and pulled it off. Nadia lay naked before him, and it was a satisfying sight to Alex, whose hard-on instantly returned. He unbuttoned his shirt and discarded it along with his linen pants. He leaned over and ran his hands up Nadia's forearms. She could feel his manhood pressing against her bare ass through his boxer briefs, and it was huge. Alex bit her shoulder and sucked and licked his way up to her neck. When he bit down on her earlobe, Nadia was in ecstasy.

"That feels good."

"Baby, I'm only getting started." Alex kissed Nadia from her neck to her shoulder, and then down her spine. When he got to her ass, he didn't stop; he bit down on one of her cheeks and gave a hard smack to the other cheek. Nadia raised up slightly, but Alex quickly pushed her back down on the bed, then flipped her over.

He pushed back her legs and placed kisses to her inner thighs. Nadia was already dripping wet from the anticipation. "Let's see what you taste like." Alex licked her at her core, and Nadia's entire body lifted off the bed again. "Do I have to tie you down?" Nadia fell back onto the bed, and Alex continued his intoxicating torture. He licked at her clit slowly, then he added more pressure and picked up speed. Nadia was close to orgasm when Alex suddenly stopped. "You taste divine."

"Then why the fuck did you stop?"

"Did you forget who's calling the shots? I can turn you back over and remind you," Alex said, raising his eyebrows. When Nadia didn't reply, he got up from the bed and stood at the edge. In one fluid movement, he grabbed Nadia's ankles, pulling her to the edge of the bed. He dropped his briefs, walked over to the nightstand, and grabbed a condom from the top drawer, allowing Nadia a chance to get a look at his manhood. He was very well endowed, and Nadia was ready to take on every inch of him.

Alex positioned his cock at her entrance, but he didn't waste any time; he slid all the way home in one thrust. Nadia closed her eyes from the sudden deep penetration, but Alex was the one doing the heavy breathing. He balled his hands into fists, leaned down with his arms on each side of her, and asked, "Are you okay?"

Refusing to stroke his ego, Nadia looked into Alex's blue eyes and said, "If you're going to fuck me, then fuck me. Don't play around in the pussy, Alex."

Alex stood up and straightened his back, then he slammed into Nadia over and over again. Her hands pulled at the bed sheets, her back bowed off the bed, she screamed his name, but she didn't want him to stop. Instead, she said, "That's all you got?" Alex pulled out and flipped Nadia over onto her stomach. "Maybe I should nickname you spatula, since you keep fucking flipping me!" Without instruction, Nadia arched her back perfectly, raising her ass all the way in the air.

Alex decided to try a different approach. He slowly slid back into Nadia's swollen flesh, and he moved back and forth at a snail's pace. When Nadia realized what he was doing, she started to throw it back. Alex gripped her waist and stopped her. "I'm calling the shots, remember?"

"You're being a son of a bitch, Alex."

"And you are not being a very good submissive, Nadia."

In a snotty tone, Nadia said, "Please forgive me, it's my first time."

Alex smacked Nadia on her ass, again and again. Then he leaned over and said, "I can do this all night."

Nadia turned her head to meet his stare. "Looking forward to it." She knew what he wanted her to do. He wanted her to wave the white flag and give into him, but that wasn't an option. She'd agreed to submit. What she didn't agree to was defeat.

Alex slid into Nadia to the hilt, but he didn't move. He grabbed her hair and pulled her neck back, keeping his other hand on her waist. Then, he pulled back and slammed into her. Nadia couldn't move; all she could do was take it. And that she did. Alex pounded into her, and she was taking every thrust, every inch, every pump and not saying a word. Just when Alex thought he wasn't having an effect on her, she tightened her walls around his cock.

"Are you close to coming, Nadia?"

"Yes, so close."

Alcx stopped and said, "Beg for it."

"What?"

"Say, 'Please, Alex, make me come, and I'll give you what you want.'"

Nadia lay there weighing her options. She could either refuse and miss out on an orgasm, or she could give in, as she already had when she agreed to submit and give Alex what he wanted. Choosing the latter, Nadia said, "Alex, make me come."

She intentionally left off the "please," but Alex didn't push the issue. He dived right back into Nadia, pounding into her. Before she knew it, she came, pulsing around Alex's cock. Alex's breathing sped up, and he gripped her waist tighter. He let Nadia's hair go and slowed down his thrusts as he came.

Alex leaned over Nadia and was trying to catch his breath when she said, "I'm ready for round two. You did say all night, right?"

Alex pulled the condom off and walked to the bathroom. Nadia was probably going to be his biggest challenge yet.

Diary Entry #16

I'm not a submissive. I like to give the orders, because I've never been good at taking them. Alex wants me to submit to him, and I obliged. But he'll be tired as hell trying to tame me. I'm going to make damn sure of that! N.H.

Chapter Forty Seven

Vanity had spent hours getting dressed and ready for Pandemonium, and it had been worth every minute. Dressed in a skintight LBD, with six-inch heels, and her long blonde hair pooling around her shoulders, she was going to turn heads tonight. With her agenda already in mind, she walked right in and snatched a seat at the bar. She surveyed the bar, but she didn't find the familiar face she was looking for. A little disappointed, she ordered a glass of champagne and looked out at the crowd. Pandemonium was jumping tonight. Vanity was glad to see she was able to get a handle on the media attention that surrounded the previous weekend's fiasco. The club was just as packed tonight, as it was then, if not more crowded.

"Champagne for the lady."

Vanity turned around and was happy to see Paul. Feeling instant gratification about her decision to pop into the club tonight, she shot her signature bad-girl grin, but he didn't bite. He simply sat her drink down and turned his attention to the next customer. *Two can play that game*, she thought, as she contemplated her next move. How long was he planning to give her the cold shoulder? She watched as he disappeared behind the black swinging doors of the bar. She decided to call and ask him to meet her upstairs in the manager's office. Vanity took out her phone and made the call, but she didn't get an answer. She'd come to the club with intentions of getting laid, and it being by Paul. Deciding not to waste anymore of her precious time, she drank the rest of her champagne and headed through the black doors behind the counter.

The kitchen area was bustling. Everyone was busy, as they should be, so she grabbed the first person she could get her hands on.

"Excuse me. Did you happen to see a man a couple of inches taller than me, Italian, broad shoulders, thick black hair, killer smile."

"I did!" the young woman exclaimed, a little more excited than Vanity's liking. "He went outside. He goes out there sometimes to smoke."

Smoke? I didn't know he was a smoker. "Thanks," she said, dismissing the woman in front of her. Vanity threw her hair back, squared her shoulders, and headed toward the side door. When she stepped outside, she felt a slight chill, but she'd forgotten about the breeze as soon as she spotted her target across the alley. He was taking puffs from a cigarette just like the young woman predicted. Vanity strutted over to him and pulled the cigarette from his grip. She took a puff from the cigarette and blew the smoke out slowly. Then, she threw it down on the ground and stepped on it with her stilettos.

"I've been looking for you," she said, and then she gripped his collar and laid a kiss on him. He didn't even attempt to fight back, but then again, Vanity, was a very attractive woman. It was men's fantasies to have a blonde bombshell show up and seduce them.

Vanity pulled back, giving him the opportunity to say something.

"Hello to you, too," he said.

Vanity didn't come for small talk. She tightened her grip on his shirt. "Are you ready to give me what I came for?"

"Well, that depends. What exactly did you come for?"

"Always the gentleman." Vanity walked further down the alley, pulling him by his hand now instead of his shirt collar.

They stepped between two buildings and she backed herself against a wall. Pulling him close to her, she told him, "I want you to give it to me. Right here. Right now." Vanity ran her hands through his thick black hair, and put her other arm around his neck. "Your hair has grown since the last time I saw you."

"I . . ." he stammered.

"Don't say anything, just kiss me."

Without further delay, he bent forward and kissed Vanity. The kiss was rough and aggressive, not the usual soft, seductive way Paul usually kissed her, but she liked it all the same. His hands slowly moved up her thighs while pulling up her dress. Vanity came to fuck the bartender, so she figured why bother with any under garments tonight. Feeling his hands on her ass, Vanity locked her arms around his neck as he lifted her off her feet and pressed her against the brick wall. She threaded her hands through his hair and made the softest of sighs while he sucked at her neck and nibbled at her earlobe. The small tear of a package was faint as Vanity awaited the penetration she'd been craving. He lifted Vanity some more and then slowly let her slide onto his erection. With her back pressed against the wall, and him holding all her weight, Vanity simply enjoyed his fluid movements. *In, out, up, down . . .* Vanity was in heaven, and her orgasm wasn't far off.

"Are you real? You feel so damn good. I don't know how long I can hold it off," he said, sounding like a man who was about to lose control.

"Me too. I'm about to . . ." Before she could get the words out, Vanity was coming, and he was right behind her with his climax. Standing in the alley, tangled with each other, he slowly let Vanity slide down his body as he slid out of her. Vanity straightened her dress, while he zipped up his pants. Without saying another word to each other, they both headed back down the alleyway to the back entrance of the club. When they opened the door, the atmosphere was the same. The hustle and bustle hadn't halted because those two had snuck off, and nobody was paying them any attention as they walked through as if nothing had happened. Vanity's seat at the bar had been claimed by a woman clearly not interested in the guy standing in front of her, which was fine because she didn't plan on staying anyway. Feeling her phone vibrating in her purse, she pulled it out and smiled when she saw the name on the screen. It was Paul. "Yes?" she answered.

"Vanity?"

"Yes, it's me. Are you calling for more?"

"I was actually calling you back. I saw your missed call."

"Well, I'm going to get out of here. Is your . . ." Vanity stopped mid-sentence. She'd turned around facing the bar and was staring at the six-foot slab of beautiful flesh who had just dicked her down in the alley, but he wasn't on the phone. "Paul?"

"Yeah, I'm still here."

"Where are you right now?"

"I'm at my apartment. Where are you?"

"So you're not at Pandemonium?"

"No, I'm not." Paul said, causing Vanity to almost drop the phone. "My brother is though. He bartends there on the weekends."

"Your brother?"

"Yeah, I have a twin. Patrick. We're identical actually. Besides our names, you can't really tell us apart. My parents . . . " Paul's voice faded off into the background with the thunderous music. Vanity could hear the blood rushing in her ears, and she all of a sudden felt nauseous. She ended the call with Paul and watched as his brother, whom she'd just slept with, continued tending to the bar. She'd come to the club with the intention of having a make-up fling with Paul and instead she'd fucked his brother. Unable to stomach what Paul had just told her, Vanity hightailed it out of the club and didn't look back. What had she done?

Chapter Forty Eight

Diary Entry #17

The last few days with Julien have been amazing. I always thought I'd feel smothered under the care of a man, but Julien just makes me feel safe, which means a lot considering some psycho I don't know is out to get me. Julien's two friends, whose names I've learned are Jacob and Eli, haven't found any new info yet. Or maybe they do know something and they've told Julien but not me. The detectives don't have any leads either. A lot of help they've been. Not! I'm dreading telling my dad about my step-monster or the break-in. He's got enough on his plate already. K.D.

Kensi pulled up to Ellerton Memorial and killed the engine. She'd really enjoyed the past couple of days with Julien, but it was back to work tonight. With twenty minutes to spare before her shift, Kensi pulled out her iPhone and called her dad. After the third ring, she heard the voice of one of her favorite people on the line.

"Dumas residence."

"Maddie!"

"Kensington, how are you, sweetie?"

"I'm fine," Kensi lied. "Is Dad home?"

"He's not, but I'm sure you can get him on his cell."

"No, that's okay. I don't want to track him down if he's out."

"Are you sure? You don't sound like your usual self."

Kensi could never get anything past Maddie. She always knew when something was wrong. "It's because I'm not my usual self." Kensi sighed. She'd been dreading having this conversation. "Someone broke into my home and vandalized it."

"What? Are you all right? Were you at home? Did they hurt you?"

"No, no, no, Maddie. I'm fine, but whoever did this murdered the dishes, groceries, and my sofa."

"Kensi-bear. I'm so sorry to hear that. Your father will be devastated. Are you going to stay the night here? I can get your room ready for you."

"No, I've been staying with a friend of mine. This happened a couple of days ago. With everything going on, I really didn't want to bother Dad. I know he has a lot on his plate right now."

"That witch of a wife has proven to be an even bigger pain in the butt. Her and her son."

"What's Blake done now?"

"Your father spoke with the DA on Blake's behalf and got him a plea deal. Blake didn't even bother to show up in court."

"You're kidding!"

"I wish I were. Now there's a bench warrant for his arrest. The police have been here looking for him. Your father and I haven't seen him. Sara claims she hasn't seen or heard from him either. Your father doesn't believe her. Neither do I."

"Speaking of Sara, I had the pleasure of seeing her and some fancy divorce lawyer out to lunch the other day."

"Did you now?"

"Yes, I did. She was pretending to be all perfect, and not a hair out of place."

"That sounds like Sara."

"That's the other reason I was calling. When I was home, Dad mentioned he'd contemplated divorce but hadn't filed yet. The lawyer I saw her with is considered one of the best in town."

"Well, I don't mean to let the cat out of the bag, but your father is at his lawyer's office now. They are planning to have Sara served with divorce papers, as well as a notice to vacate the premises. She may have *one* of the best divorce lawyers, but your father hired *the* best divorce lawyer. But you didn't hear any of that from me."

"Hear what?"

"That's my girl. I'll tell him you called when he gets in. He's going to be livid when I tell him about your apartment."

"Yeah, I'm not looking forward to that phone call at all."

"Where are you right now?"

"Sitting outside the hospital in my car. I'm working tonight."

"Well, you have a good night at work, dear, and I hope to see you soon, okay?"

"Okay, Maddie. I love you."

"Love you too, Kensi."

Kensi ended the call, grabbed her tote, and started her hike across the parking lot. She had to gather all of her willpower to keep from turning back around and walking through the sliding doors. Kensi headed to the time clock to punch in, but her pace slowed when she saw Dr. Randahl waiting casually in the hall. Sure that his presence was not coincidental, Kensi walked right up to him and said, "What can I do for you, Dr. Randahl."

"You can meet me in the doctor's lounge on your break," he replied pulling at Kensi's employee badge and watching it draw back into place. "That's if you're not busy."

Kensi got up close and pressed her body against Dr. Randahl's. "Dr. Randahl, as much as I would love to watch you jack off again in the sauna, I'm going to have to pass. That night at your house was nice, really nice, but it was a one-time thing."

"Understood," was all Dr. Randahl said before turning and walking away.

Kensi stood there watching and hoping this wasn't going to make their work relationship awkward.

Chapter Forty Nine

Diary Entry #18

I fucked Paul's twin brother. I've been saying the words silently to myself since that night. I've been trying to keep busy with the event planning, but my thoughts keep taking me back to that night. It's not as if we were exclusively dating or anything, but it's also not as if what I did was a small mistake either. On top of that, I'm headed into a meeting with my manager. I'm definitely not in the mood for any bullshit, and I'm a tad stressed out. If she says this is anything other than a misunderstanding, I don't think I should be held responsible for my actions. V.C.

Vanity was in the human resources waiting area when the desk attendant called her name.

"Vanity. They will see you now. Just go straight down the hall and it's the last door on the left."

"Thanks," Vanity said. She'd pasted on a fake smile to cover up her actual mood. Hopefully, she'd be able to keep up her nice-girl charade throughout the meeting.

Vanity made it to the end of the hall, and when she walked into the office, two pairs of eyes landed on her. The first pair belonged to her manager, Carol, but the second pair of eyes were unfamiliar.

"Hi, I'm Melanie Ingram, human resources director," the unfamiliar woman said as she stood up from her chair and held out her hand.

Accepting the woman's kind gesture, Vanity shook her hand. "I'm Vanity Carter." She wasn't going to say it was nice to meet her, because it wasn't. Vanity had a million other things she'd rather be doing.

"Vanity, have a seat please," Carol said. "I've filled Melanie in on the situation at hand. We spoke on the phone and I was letting you know we had you down for a no-call no-show. You stated you weren't scheduled, but we've pulled the schedule and it does show you as scheduled for the seven p.m. to seven a.m. shift. So, if you would just walk us through what happened."

Straight faced, Vanity looked across the table at Carol and said, "There's nothing to walk you through." Vanity took the skeleton scheduled she'd printed from when she put her schedule in. "This is a copy of what days I scheduled myself. If someone else changed these days, that's not my fault."

Carol took the paper from Vanity and examined it. "This isn't the actual schedule. This is just the schedule before changes are made."

"But I'm per diem. Whatever days I put in are not to be changed," Vanity interrupted.

"Yes, but it's your responsibility to receive a copy of the actual schedule. If you had seen the final schedule, you would have noticed that you were scheduled on the wrong day. It may have been a computer glitch of some sort, but you not knowing resulted in you not showing up, and that left the floor short. The unit must be covered."

Wanting Carol to cut the shit, Vanity turned to the human resources director. "So, what happens now? It seems like I'm being held responsible for something that was out of my hands."

"Well, we wanted to make sure we get your side of what happened. As of today, we're going to have to place you on an official suspension pending investigation," Melanie replied.

"Excuse me?" Vanity asked. "What exactly is being investigated?"

"Well, we need to see if the computer system switched your dates, or if someone possibly switched their days on the skeleton but did it under your name by accident, or if one of the head nurses accidentally changed the dates. We just need to make sure we have fully investigated before we make any decisions," Carol said.

"Okay," Vanity said. "No, you know what? It's not fucking okay." Vanity snatched her badge off and threw it on the table. "Ellerton may be a great hospital, but when they put pains in the ass like you Carol in charge, it destroys the culture. You've had it out for me since you got here." Vanity stood up from the table. "I wouldn't be surprised if you were the one who deliberately switched my days to put me in this predicament."

"I beg your pardon," Carol said, her eyes flashing in anger.

"Beg all you want, bitch, but I'm done. Melanie, I'm sorry we had to meet under such unpleasant circumstances. You have a nice day. And you, Carol, can take a long walk off an extremely short pier."

Vanity opened the door and walked out of the office with her head held high. She'd quit her job, but she had never felt more relieved. The smile that spread across her face was larger than life. When she got to the sliding doors at the entrance of the hospital, she donned her sunglasses and stepped outside, feeling relieved as she exited Ellerton Memorial Hospital without looking back.

Chapter Fifty

Diary Entry #19

I quit my fucking job, and I feel great! I'll take peace over conflict with a bullshit-ass manager any day. I haven't told Nadia and Kensi I quit yet, but we're hanging out today, so I'll fill them in. It's time that I take my savings, put these contacts I've made to good use, and start my own business. On top of everything Paul's called me every day, two and three times a day, but I can't bring myself to answer the phone. It's going to be an awkward conversation, and I'm just not ready. I'd rather remain on my high from quitting my job a little while longer. V.C.

"So, what's new, you guys?" Nadia asked with a glow that could not be ignored.

"Well, I slept with Dr. Randahl and then I told him I was no longer interested. Julien and I were almost arrested for indecent exposure in a parking garage. I caught my step-monkey having lunch with a prestigious divorce lawyer. The psycho who's been leaving all these notes has broken into my house, trashed the place, and then masturbated on my bed. What about you guys, anything new?" Kensi said with a straight face.

Nadia stood there with her mouth agape, trying to process everything Kensi had said. Still not able to conjure up any words, she turned her attention to Vanity's direction.

"Don't look at me. Looks like Kensi is going to be the recipient of the juiciest gossip award today," Vanity said. "Do you know who broke into your home?"

"I have no damn idea. There was writing in the bathroom on my mirror and the wording and handwriting matches the notes I've been getting. It's still a mystery, but Julien and his guys are looking into it."

"Julien and his guys? And what do his 'guys' look like?" Nadia asked.

"Nadia," Vanity said.

"What? Alex and I are not in a relationship, and I'm keeping my options open."

"Really? Not in a relationship? Can't tell by that glow you're wearing."

Nadia looked herself over. "I am not glowing."

"Bullshit," Kensi chimed in. "If the lights in this place go out we could just suspend you from the ceiling. Your face alone could illuminate this place."

"Why do we have to wait until the lights go out? I'd gladly let you suspend me from the ceiling with the lights on."

"Nadia, you are such a freak," Kensi said.

"What are we doing here anyways?" Nadia asked.

"I still have some party favors to pick up, and Secret Desires has always been my adult store of choice. Plus, the owner is always really nice."

"Well, thank you," a voice chimed in from behind them. "Vanity, I thought I saw you come in. I've got a box up front with your name on it."

"Thanks. These are my friends, Kensi and Nadia."

"Nice to meet you," she said. "You ladies feel free to have a look around, and let me know if you need anything."

"Actually, " Kensi interrupted, "would you happen to sell accommodators?"

"Sure do. Right this way."

"The accommodator? Is that something Dr. Randahl introduced you to?" Nadia inquired.

"No, it was actually Julien. I really won't be seeing Dr. Randahl again. He was sort of just an itch I had to scratch."

"Here they are. They come in all different lengths and widths. If you ladies need anything else just let me know."

"Thanks," they said in unison.

Nadia walked over to the wall and grabbed one of the accommodator boxes. "Damn, girl. Julien used this on you?" she asked Kensi

"Yes, and it was amazing," she said, snatching the box from Nadia. "Just the one I was looking for. Thanks, Nadia."

"You're welcome," Nadia said and she snatched one for herself. Kensi and Vanity were staring at her. "What?"

"You're such a freak," Vanity said with a grin.

Nadia put a hand on her hip. "Kensi's the one who turned me on to this accommodator thing, but I get called the freak."

"We know I'm a freak, but Vanity was just pointing it out for you in case you didn't hear me when I said it to you earlier."

"If you two are done, I have news," Vanity interjected.

"Oh, spill. Is it a new guy? Do we know him?"

"No, it's not about a guy," Vanity said. "I went in for a meeting with our manager and the human resources director."

"Hold on," Kensi said, raiding her hand. "When and why did you have a meeting with our manager?"

"Long story short, Carol called me in because she says I was a no-call no-show one night. I went in and sat down with her and the human resources director. Carol mentioned suspending me pending investigation, and I just wasn't having it."

"So, what happened?" Nadia inquired.

"I quit. Actually, I cussed Carol's ass out, and then I quit."

Kensi and Nadia stood there in shock.

Wanting to hear their thoughts, Vanity said, "Well, say something."

"Okay, you quit your job. What's next? I know you have a plan. You always have a plan," Kensi said.

"For the first time in a long time, I don't have a plan. Monetary-wise, I've made a lot of money hosting events. Actually, I've made more money doing that than I did as a nurse. I'm thinking about going into business for myself. I've been brainstorming about some different avenues I can take, but I don't have any concrete thoughts right now."

Kensi said, "But I—"

"I think that's great," Nadia interrupted. "We think it's great, don't we, Kensi?" Nadia looked at Kensi.

"Yes. Great," Kensi said with an unsure smile.

Nadia continued, "Whatever you decide to do we're with you all the way, Vanity."

"Thanks," Vanity said. "And Kensi, you don't have to say it. Yes, I love nursing, and I'll miss it. However, it's time for me to venture out and do something else. You guys have nothing to worry about. If I know one thing about myself, it's that I always land on my feet."

Kensi pulled Vanity into a hug. "I wish you the best in anything you decide to do. Whatever your next step is, Nadia and I will be right there with you." She pulled Nadia into the group hug.

"You guys are my best friends. As long as we stick together, we can make it through anything," Nadia said.

"You guys are going to make me cry," Vanity replied. "Let's get what I came here for—you two purchase what you have, and let's spend the day at Burke Williams."

"I'm in!" Nadia said without hesitation.

"Yes! Between my stalker, crazy-ass step-monster, and all this sex I've been having, I need a spa day."

"You'll have to fill us in on what happened with your step-monster, Nadia said, putting her accommodator on the checkout counter.

"Will this be all for you?" The owner asked Nadia.

"Do you carry the stuffoscope here?"

"Yes, we do."

"Great. Could I get one of those please? Also, I'd like a pair of the electric gloves and a vibrating tongue if you have it," Nadia said.

"I'll go grab them. I'll be right back."

When Nadia turned around, Kensi and Vanity were staring at her. "Freak," was all Kensi said before the three of them burst into laughter.

***

Just before they could walk into the spa Vanity's phone rang.

"Vanity, are you with Nadia?"

"Yes. Why?"

"Step away for a minute. I need to talk to you about something."

"You two go ahead. I need to take this call, and then I'll be right in," Vanity called to Nadia and Kensi who were already walking into the spa.

"What's up Alex?"

"She's insatiable. I always knew a woman would be the death of me, and I think I've finally met her."

"Let me guess. You're talking about Nadia?"

"Yes, I spent hours trying to break her, waiting for her to give in, or at least tire out."

"And?" Vanity asked.

"And nothing. The woman is a machine."

Vanity laughed.

"It's not funny. She's a sex machine. I finally got her to submit to me for one night."

"And I'm guessing that didn't go to well."

"It was a total disaster, at least for me, anyway. She probably feels victorious," Alex responded .

"Alex, I know Nadia. From what I do know, I would say she's really not a submissive. Plus, she's told you that before, and you've now witnessed it firsthand. Maybe you need to accept her for who she is, or . . . let her go."

"That's not an option. Then, she has this sick fantasy that I'm going to submit to her." Alex laughed at his own statement. Vanity on the other hand did not, she remained completely silent.

"I know what you're thinking Van and you can fucking forget it. Alexander McCoy will never submit to a woman."

"You know as well as I do that submission can be done in many ways. As long as trust is one hundred percent given, the rest can be tweaked to fit the couple. I'm just saying maybe you're thinking too much about her tying you up and flogging you. Maybe all she wants is for you to beg her, worship her, give her a little power in the sex situation."

"I did fucking worship her. For hours, might I add. Besides, Nadia knows it's the submissive who holds all the power."

"If you really want her the way you say, then you'll figure out a way to make it work. You know, merge both of your sexual interests."

"I'm taking relationship advice from a woman who refuses to be in one. I must be pussy-whipped," Alex said.

"Hey, you said it, not me."

"Change of subject, Alex. What are you doing about the woman, you spotted on the video, who drugged you at the club?"

"Haven't quite figured that out yet. I don't recognize her, but that doesn't mean she doesn't know me. And she was standing there talking to Nadia, so I'm not sure if she meant to drug me or her. You haven't said anything to Nadia about it yet have you?"

"Not yet. Have you showed Nadia the video?"

"No, I haven't. I was trying to resolve this without involving her."

"Nadia needs to know Alex, just in case she was the target. That way, in the event that she and the woman on the footage come in contact with each other again, Nadia's guard will be up."

"I am clearly off my game. Looks like you've got all the answers, and I'm barely focused."

"Not all the answers," Vanity said, thinking about the situation with Paul.

"Well, I'll let you ladies get back to whatever you were doing."

"Okay, and If you need anything else, or if you just want to talk call me."

"Thanks, Van. How in the hell did I manage to get involved with such a difficult woman."

"You haven't heard? It's usually the ones who are difficult, that turn out to be the most worth it."

"Touché," Alex said.

Vanity shook her head as she put her phone back in her purse and headed into the spa.

Chapter Fifty One

After spending a few hours at the spa with her best girlfriends, Vanity pulled into her driveway behind a car she didn't recognize. She opened her car door to get out and the mystery car's driver side door opened. When Vanity got a look at whom it was, she screamed.

"Oh my goodness! Gianna, when did you get here?" Vanity asked, hugging her friend.

"Just touched down an hour ago and came straight here. How are you? You look great!"

"Thanks. Let's grab your bags and go inside and I can tell you all about it."

"Bags? You know me better than that. I've got my purse and a small carry-on. I shop when I land, nothing's changed."

Vanity just smiled. "Oh, my friend. I've missed you so much," she said as she and Gianna ventured up the walkway and into her home. "Make yourself at home. Of course you're staying here, so I'll show you to your room later. But first, Vanity walked over to her buffet and grabbed a bottle of Moet, "let's have a drink."

"I see you're still harboring bottles of Moet like they're going out of style."

"Of course," Vanity replied, smiling at her friend. "It's been months since I last saw you. You look good, G."

Gianna put her hands on her hips and spun around. "Thanks. I try." Gianna was a few years older than Vanity, but still just as gorgeous. Standing two inches taller than Vanity at five foot eight, Gianna had a sleek jet-black bob, stormy gray eyes, and her perfect toned body was covered in tattoos that were being concealed by her clothes.

"One for you, and one for me," Vanity said, handing Gianna a champagne flute and taking the other.

Gianna took a seat on the couch, kicked off her shoes, pulled her legs up, and tucked them under her. "Hey, blondie. You going to join me or just stand up the whole time?"

Vanity kicked off her heels and slumped down into her oversized chair. She reached behind her and grabbed her throw, re-arranging it several times before getting it exactly how she wanted it.

"Okay, Vanity, what's up?"

"What do you mean?" Vanity asked, taking a sip of her champagne.

Gianna sat there in silence.

Vanity took another sip of her champagne. "I hate that you know me so well."

"I know," Gianna said, taking a sip of her drink.

"I am no longer a nurse," Vanity answered in a cracked voice before completely emptying her champagne glass.

"And how do you feel about your decision?"

"I don't know." Vanity shook her head, but she didn't say another word, and neither did Gianna.

After a few more moments of silence, a tear rolled down Vanity's face.

"Oh, Vanity. Girlie, don't cry," Gianna said, walking over to the chair where Vanity was sitting.

"I'm not a nurse anymore. I worked so hard to put myself through school for nursing, but I'm missing something in my life Gianna. This last year working in the hospital was more stressful than joyful. I used to be so happy going to work, helping people, and knowing that I'm making a difference in someone's life. But honestly, I just don't feel like that anymore. I switched from full-time to per diem, thinking that if I wasn't in the hospital so much I'd begin to miss it. I thought maybe the happiness would slowly come back, but it hasn't. I'm ready to move on and do something new, but I don't want to feel like I'm abandoning my calling in life."

Gianna pulled her friend into a hug. "Vanity, you will always be a nurse. You've earned the degree and you've dedicated time that you can't get back to helping people. Now it's time for you to chase a bigger dream. And if all else fails, we can move to Vegas and open a brothel. We'll have all the girls wear nurse uniforms so you feel right at home."

Vanity stopped crying and burst into laughter. "Prostitutes in nurse uniforms?"

"Yes! They'll be sexy lingerie-type nurse uniforms. We'll even have a section called the ER, but not for emergency, more like erection room."

"Really, G?" Vanity asked, still laughing.

"Shit yeah, girl! You know how much money we'll make? We'll call it the Ho-spital."

Vanity laughed even harder and this time Gianna laughed with her.

"I'm glad you're here," Vanity said, wiping at her tears.

"Of course. I came to handle business and have a little fun. We're some bad bitches, Vanity, and we've both escaped the worst and made something out of nothing. Tears are something we don't have time for, so wipe them away, and let's start thinking about the future. Deal?"

"Deal." Vanity agreed, hopping up from the couch and grabbing her glass. "Refill?"

"You know it," Gianna said, stealing Vanity's chair. "And you can forget about getting your seat in this chair back," Gianna said, leaning back in the chair and getting comfortable.

Chapter Fifty Two

So far everything was perfect and the police station had been immaculately transformed. The floors were polished to perfection with a black oriental rug that began at the entrance and broke off into several directions to take guests to different rooms, with the main pathway leading to the grand room where the majority of the guests had gathered. There were large vases filled with black pansies and snow-white tulips everywhere, and the walls were covered in erotic artwork of men and women embracing their nakedness and sexuality. Black, white, and gray-colored drapes hung from the ceiling, covering the entire location. The lighting was dim, but not dark, just enough light to find your way around. The servers were not masked this go around, but were still well dressed in white button-down shirts, with black slacks, and matching black button-down vests. The party had only begun an hour ago, but the majority of the guests had arrived. The evening was already a partial success, everything was going as planned, and Vanity was hoping it remained that way.

"You've really outdone yourself this time, Vanity," Alex said.

"Thanks," Vanity said. "You're looking good for someone who had a near-death experience." Alex had rolled up the sleeves to his gray button-down shirt that was lighter in color in comparison to his dark gray-hued slacks.

"Not bad yourself, Van."

"Thanks." The plan was to gain more contacts throughout the evening, so Vanity had chosen to keep as much concealed as possible while still remaining sexy. She'd decided on a white backless, round collar, fish-tail dress. Vanity was completely covered, but the dress was skin tight and showed all of her curves. "Where's Nadia?"

Alex grabbed two of the champagne flutes from the waiter passing by and took a couple of sips before answering. "She said she thought it would be best if we arrived separately. Something about her not wanting to feel obligated to remain monogamous tonight since we're not a couple. A bunch of bullshit I don't understand."

"So, she thinks if you arrive separately it will give you both some room to freely explore your sexual interests for the evening?"

"Something like that."

"She obviously has no idea that you don't give a damn about that," Vanity said, taking a sip of her champagne. "Did you talk to her about the video at all?"

Alex finished off his glass, caught the next waiter coming, and exchanged his empty glass with another full flute. "If she thinks she's going to engage in any sexual activities tonight with anyone else she's in for a rude awakening. As far as the video goes, I still haven't shown or told her about the woman on the video. I was planning on bringing it up, but then she brought up coming here tonight separately, and it slipped my mind."

Vanity took another sip of her champagne, but stopped the glass midway to her mouth when she spotted who'd just walked through the door. "Excuse me, boss, but I've got work to do."

"As do I, Van." Alex strolled off, and Vanity started in the direction of the Attorney General's daughter, Bethany Mildred.

"Good evening, Bethany. I'm Vanity Carter. I'm so glad you could make it this evening," Vanity shook Bethany's hand.

"Yes, Vanity, it's so nice to meet you. This place looks spectacular."

"Glad you like it. However, there is so much more to see," Vanity said, grabbing a champagne flute from one of the waiters and handing it to Bethany. "A glass of champagne to start the evening."

"Beauty, brains, and hospitable. Triple threat, I see."

"I try, "Vanity said modestly. "I'll let you take a look around and catch up with you again sometime during the evening to see if everything is to your liking."

"Thanks, Vanity."

"You're very welcome." Vanity was just about to question the whereabouts of her other boss when she felt a hand snake around her waist.

"I believe tonight is the end of our business relationship."

Vanity turned around to see Martin standing there in a tailored navy blue suit. "I wouldn't say that quite yet."

"And why wouldn't you say that yet?" Martin asked, pulling Vanity in closer to him.

"If all goes as planned, I'll have a business proposition for both you and Alex."

"I'm listening right now, but it's kind of hard to focus with you wearing that dress."

"Exactly, which is why we'll have this conversation in a more appropriate setting, like an office perhaps," Vanity said, easing Martin's hands from around her waist.

"I thought you two were keeping your relationship strictly professional," Nadia said as she approached. "Good evening, Martin. Looking just as debonair as the last time I saw you."

"Thank you, and you look just as breathtaking as the first time I saw you."

"But I'm not holding a candle to Vanity, am I?" Nadia asked.

"Yes, she is beautiful," Martin said, giving Vanity a full look-over. "Vanity, we'll talk more later. Nadia, it's been a pleasure seeing you again. Enjoy yourself."

"Thanks, Martin," Nadia said, pulling at the hem of her dress.

"Pull at it all you want, but unless your legs get shorter, that dress is not going to look any longer," Vanity said jokingly.

Nadia was dressed in an off-the-shoulder teal bandage dress that was a couple inches too high to be considered mid-thigh. "I thought this dress was rather appropriate for tonight, thank you very much."

"I was just joking, Nadia. You look fabulous as always. A few minutes earlier and you would have run into Alex."

"That's exactly what I'm trying not to do."

"What's the problem? Just the other day you were glowing all over, and tonight Alex tells me it was your idea for the two of you to come here separately."

"Yes, it was. Look around, Vanity." Nadia and Vanity looked around at the many people engaged in play. "This isn't exactly a dinner party. I didn't want him to feel obligated to be glued to my hip."

"You didn't want him to feel obligated, or is it you that didn't want to feel obligated to him?"

"Good question. If and when I find out the answer I'll let you know."

"Well, of course you know my work is never done, so if you need anything just let me know, or Felicity, she's co-hosting with me tonight."

"Will do." *Maybe Felicity wants to play tonight*, Nadia thought as she walked over to one of the private rooms.

***

Nadia quietly slid into the room with the other onlookers and became even more impressed with what Vanity had done with the location. There was a two-way mirror separating the room she was in from the room everyone was looking at. The room had a St. Andrew's cross, sex bench, and an Esse chaise. However, it wasn't the equipment in the room that grabbed Nadia's attention; it was the woman standing over a very attractive blindfolded man. The submissive was kneeling before her with both of his hands wrapped around her leather boots. As he sucked on her inner thighs, she rewarded him by running her hands through his hair and lightly pulling at the roots. But when his mouth became too greedy for her liking, the dominatrix struck him with her riding crop across his back.

"Is that what you want to do to me? Strike me with a riding crop," Alex whispered in her ear.

"It's not just that," Nadia said. "It's the mental and the physical. The obedience and the worship. It's the way a man looks up at you like you're a sex goddess that I find so intoxicating. It's . . ." Before Nadia could finish, Alex had grabbed her by her arm and led her down the black-carpeted hallway. "Alex, where the hell are you taking me?"

"I'm taking you to our own private room so we can settle this."

"We've already tried, Alex. Our tastes are different. It just won't work."

"Well, we'll stay in here until we make it work," Alex said, pulling the sliding door and slamming it shut.

Alex had led her into a prison cell and closed the door. The room was decorated like a plush bedroom with a small Zeppelin lounger in place of an actual bed. But as plush as the decorations were, it was still a cell nonetheless.

"Are you fucking crazy? Open this door right now!" Nadia demanded.

"Can't. I don't have a key. Besides, it has to be opened from the other side."

"You have lost your fucking mind. Help! Help! Somebody help!" Nadia screamed.

"You going to stand there and yell all night, or are we going to work this out?"

Nadia narrowed her eyes at Alex, who had taken a seat on the lounger and crossed one leg over the other.

"This is going to be a long night."

"Indeed, "Alex replied. "Let's start with why you think it's so terrible to submit to me?"

"See, you're not listening. I didn't say I thought it was terrible at all. That's an assumption made by you. I simply said that it's not my thing. I'd rather have a man kneeling before me than vice versa. Do you get it now?" Nadia asked, completely irritated that Alex was holding her hostage in a prison cell.

Alex got up from the lounger and grabbed one of the riding crops from the wall. He walked over and stood in front of her.

"Alex, I swear if you touch me with that I'm going to kick you in the nuts."

Alex smiled. He obviously loved Nadia's fire. Hiking up his pants, Alex bent down and kneeled. He grabbed her wrist, put the riding crop in her hand, and said, "I'm here to worship you and to be obedient to you both mentally and physically. If this is how you need me, then you have me. You've had me from the first time I met you, and I'm not leaving this room until we get this, whatever this is, right."

Nadia didn't know what to say, so she didn't say anything. She bent down and pulled Alex up to his full height. "You'd submit to me just to keep me around?"

"Yes, I would." Before Alex could say anything else, Nadia had jumped all over him. They fell back onto the lounger, mouths glued to each other, and limbs tangled.

Chapter Fifty Three

"About time. I was beginning to think you weren't coming, " Vanity said, giving Kensi a hug. "Nice to see you again too, Julien."

"Likewise," Julien replied. "Have you seen my cousin?"

"Earlier. If I know Alex, he's probably somewhere looking for Nadia. You find her, and I'm sure Alex won't be far behind."

Julien gave Kensi a peck on the cheek and said, "I'm going to go find Alex. You'll be okay?"

Kensi rolled her eyes. "I'll be fine, Julien, just go." When Julien was out of sight, Kensi turned to Vanity and said, "He's way more paranoid than I am."

"Well, he's attentive; I'll give him that."

"Yeah. Very attentive." Kensi grinned.

"I'm sure a dress like that can make any man pay attention," Vanity said. Kensi had chosen a knee-length, long-sleeved lace dress. The dress was deep purple, with a plunging neckline and completely see-through. Instead of wearing a colored lingerie set underneath, Kensi was wearing skin-toned boy shorts and a matching bra. If you weren't looking closely, you'd think she'd come to the event commando.

"He probably stopped paying attention to me to steal a few looks at you. Where did you get that dress?"

Vanity was about to answer, but the couple walking toward them made her lose her train of thought. "Amber," Vanity said, "and with Dr. Randahl I see."

"Yes. Nadia said it was plus one," Amber said.

Kensi and Dr. Randahl stared at each other. Vanity was watching the staring match between the two and trying to hold a conversation with Amber. "Yes, it is plus one. Well, I hope you and Dr. Randahl have a nice time. Kensi, if you don't mind, I need your help with something."

"No, you don't," Kensi said, refusing to be the one to break eye contact first.

"Yes, I do." Vanity grabbed Kensi by the arm and hauled her away. "What the hell was that about? I thought you told him you didn't want to see him again?"

"I did, and five minutes later he shows up to a party thrown by my friends with 'the help' on his arm."

"Kensi, did you forget that you came here with someone else too? Does the name 'Julien' ring a bell? Get a grip, get a drink, and just enjoy the party."

Felicity walked up and said, "Hi, you two. Vanity, I've been looking for you. There's some guests who would like to meet the woman who coordinated this event."

"Okay, I'll be right there. Kensi, try to have a good time, okay?"

"I will, girl. The two of them just caught me off guard. I'm fine. I promise." Vanity and Felicity headed off, leaving Kensi to her devices.

Deciding to use her time alone to explore the grounds, Kensi headed into the great room. There were multiple sex scenes in play, but one scene in particular had the majority of everyone's attention. Kensi walked over toward the scene and was in immediate shock. Pop star, Lili Cassidy, was straddled on top of one of the waiters. She'd secured his hands above his head, strapped his legs down to the other end of the table, and was riding him in reverse cowgirl for everyone to see. She recognized a few of the other guests as well. Plastic surgeons with celebrity status, musicians, politicians, professional athletes, and a few TV personalities were present. Vanity had really brought out some big names for the evening. After surveying the crowd to see whom she recognized, Kensi moved along. She left the great room, and headed down the hall where the private rooms were. When she got to the cellblock she halted, but her curiosity willed her to keep walking. Kensi stopped to peek into one of the cells and was amazed at what she saw. The cell had been transformed to a small playroom. Kensi stepped inside to get a full look around the transformed cell. She ran her hand across the whips, the bondage chains, the rope, and the pansies and tulips that were in a vase on a small table in the corner of the room. She walked over to the sex swing to get a closer look, but then the door slammed, making her jump.

Kensi turned around and was shocked. "Blake? What are you doing here?"

"You always were the living and breathing definition of curiosity killed the cat." Kensi's stepbrother looked like a disheveled, sleep-deprived maniac. He had on a uniform that resembled the other waiters, but it was also disheveled. His eyes were red rimmed, his hair was a mussed mess, and he looked like he hadn't shaved in forever. "I came to see you, Kensi."

"Came to see me? What the hell are you talking about, and why the hell did you close the door?" Kensi walked toward the door, but before she could reach it, Blake grabbed her arm and pulled her toward him. " Let me go, Blake! What the hell are you doing?"

"Don't fight me, Kensi. I came here for you. For me. For us."

"What the fuck are you talking about? Let me go!"

Holding on to Kensi's arm with a death grip, Blake said, "Kensi, it's me! I'm the one. The one for you. All these years I've been waiting on you to come to me, to choose me, and then it dawned on me. I needed to make you see. Do you see now, Kensi? Do you?"

"See what?" Fear lodged in her throat. "And let go of my arm, you're hurting me."

"Us! Me and you. We should be together. Become one. You've always been the girl of my dreams, the girl of my fantasies. And when fantasies become a reality, pleasure is certain."

Kensi stopped trying to wiggle her way out of Blake's grip. A look of confusion crossed her face, followed by one of comprehension. "You. You've been leaving me all those letters. You're the one who broke into my home." Blake's grip had eased up just enough for Kensi to snatch her arm away. "You sicko. You sick son of a bitch. You broke into my home! You destroyed my things and masturbated on my fucking bed. You sick fuck!"

Kensi picked up the vase and knocked Blake over the head with it. Blake dropped to his knees in pain, rubbing his temple where Kensi had clobbered him.

Kensi stepped around him and started banging on the door, screaming for help, praying someone could hear her. She turned around to make sure her attacker was still down, but Blake had risen back to full height and was headed toward her. Kensi frantically beat on the door, but Blake snatched her and threw her down onto the Zeppelin lounger. Kensi tried to wiggle her way from under him, but he'd put all his weight into holding her body in place, and had both of her arms pinned above her head.

"You're going to give me what I want," Blake said while planting a slimy kiss on Kensi's neck. Kensi closed her eyes, turned her face toward him, and bit his nose. Blake screamed as blood gushed from his nose, and Kensi took the opportunity to knee him in the balls. When she got up, she kicked him in the gut with her stilettos, and then again in the face.

"I'm not giving you anything, you sick fuck! You stay away from me!" Kensi screamed, and then she started banging on the door again, yelling for help.

Chapter Fifty Four

"Do you hear that?" Nadia asked, untangling herself from Alex.

Alex sat up. "What the hell is that?"

"Someone is yelling for help. Alex, we have to get out of here."

Alex pulled a set of keys from his pocket and walked over toward the door.

"You liar! You've had the key to get out of here this entire time, and you held me hostage."

"Yes. I'm willing to do anything when it comes to you, Nadia," Alex said, unlocking the door.

Nadia was first out of the cell and headed in the direction of the banging. When she got closer, she recognized the voice that was yelling for help. "Kensi! Kensi is that you?"

"Nadia! Can you hear me? I'm down here! Help!"

Nadia followed Kensi's voice and stopped in front of the door. She could see Kensi's face through the small window of the door, and she was panicking. "I'm here, Kensi. It's okay." She turned to Alex. "Hurry up and open the door."

Alex stuck the key in the door and a hysterical Kensi charged out of the doors right into Nadia. "It's Blake. He's the one who's been stalking me."

Nadia peeked around Kensi to get a look, and Blake was still out cold lying on the floor. "Alex, lock the door," she demanded.

"What?"

"Lock the door!" Kensi and Nadia both screamed in unison. Without further delay, Alex slammed the cell door shut.

"Do one of you mind telling me what the hell is going on here?"

"That's her stepbrother."

"So, I just locked your stepbrother in a cell? Anybody care to tell me why I just did that?"

"He's her stalker, Alex. The person who's been stalking her. That's him."

"Your brother is your stalker. That's some . . . some twisted shit."

"Kensi!" Julien yelled, running down the hall.

Kensi ,still frantic and shaking, turned toward Julien.

"Are you okay, Kensi?" Julien said. "What happened?"

Kensi wiped her face and walked into Julien's arms. Then she stepped back and smacked him across the face. "Where were you? I could've been killed." Then she hugged him again and said, "I'm so glad you're here."

Alex leaned over and whispered to Nadia, "And we thought we had problems. Your friends are just as confused as you are."

"I'm not confused."

"Yes, you are."

"No, I'm not."

"Yes, you are."

Vanity, Martin, and security all came running down the hall. The scene before them was Julien consoling Kensi, and Alex and Nadia arguing back and forth. Vanity did a wolf whistle to get everyone's attention. "Anybody mind telling me what the hell is going on here?" Everybody began to speak at once. "One at a time, please."

Kensi said, "Blake is locked in that cell." Vanity and the security men walked over to get a look through the small window on the door. "He's the one who's been stalking me." Kensi tried to keep talking, but her voice began to crack.

"I'm going to get her out of here," Julien said.

"We have to call the police." Vanity stopped Julien. "Take her to the security office for now." Vanity turned to the two security men that had accompanied her to the scene, "Get everyone else out of these cells. Tell them it's a safety precaution, a pipe burst, or something. Just move them all out and block off this area." Vanity turned back to Alex and Nadia, but before she could ask anything Martin chimed in.

"And what do you two have to do with all this?" Martin asked, referring to Nadia and Alex.

"Alex brought me down here, against my will might I add, and locked me in a cell."

"I did not bring her to the cells against her will. She wanted to come down here."

"So, you think I like being held against my will?"

"Yes, I think you like a lot of things—you just fight it. We've gone over this ,Nadia."

Vanity and Martin walked off leaving Alex and Nadia standing there to sort out their disagreement.

Julien had his arms wrapped around Kensi and was walking her to the security office when someone snuck up from behind him and grabbed his arm.

"Get your goddamn hands off my little girl!"

Kensi turned around and her mouth fell open at the person in front of her. "Dad! Dad, what are you doing here?"

"I invited him," Sara said, walking up behind Mr. Dumas. "I thought he should see for himself what type of extracurricular activities his little girl is into."

"You fucking bitch!" Kensi smacked Sara across the face, eliciting gasps from all the guests who were watching.

"Kensi!" her dad yelled. "What has gotten into you, young lady?" He grabbed her by her arm and led her toward the front entrance. "Watch your mouth. I didn't raise you to speak that way. And what the hell do you have on? Is that blood? Are you hurt?" he asked as he frantically checked her over to make sure she wasn't hurt. "I'm taking you home. Now! I can't believe you're in here with these people . . . this trash."

Kensi stopped and snatched her arm away. "I'm not going anywhere, Dad, and these people are not trash. They're my friends! And yes it is blood. The blood of that bitch's son!" Kensi said, pointing at Sara, who was standing there holding her face where Kensi had struck her. "Blake's locked in one of the cells in the back. He's the one who vandalized my home, and he's the one who's been stalking me. Go ahead, Sara. Tell my dad about what kind of sick fucker you raised."

"Kensi!" Mr. Dumas yelled, then turned to Sara. "Is this true?"

"She's a lying, little violent whore. Listen to her, the profanity, that dress. She's not the sweet, innocent little girl you've always portrayed her to be now is she? How are you going to spin this story, Kensi?"

"I can start by kicking your ass!" Kensi said.

"Mouth, young lady!" Mr. Dumas yelled. Sara had taken out her cell phone and headed toward the front entrance.

"Don't run away now. You've been begging for this ass whooping for years, bitch!"

Kensi's dad grabbed her by her arm and pulled her away as she continued to yell at Sara. "Kensi, close your mouth and get ahold of yourself. We are leaving, and you can start explaining yourself in the car."

"No, I'm not," Kensi said, pulling her arm away.

"Excuse me?" her father said.

"I'm an adult. I can make my own decisions. I won't be explaining anything to you. Besides, I should wait until the police get here since Blake assaulted me."

Mr. Dumas grabbed Kensi by her arm again. "Fine, but I'm not letting you out of my sight."

Kensi was trying to wiggle her arm out of her father's grip when a man came from out of nowhere and tackled her father to the ground. Everyone around stopped what they were doing to watch the scene before them. "What the hell? Get off him! Get the hell off him!" Kensi tried to pull the man off, but she had used all her strength up on Blake.

Julien grabbed the man from behind and pulled him off Kensi's dad. "That's her father, man. Ease up," Julien said.

With all men now back on their feet, Kensi recognized the man that had just tackled her father to the ground. It was one of Julien's "brothers." "Eli?"

"Yes, ma'am."

"And just what the hell do you think you're doing?" she asked.

"My job, ma'am."

"Your job, huh? Which is?"

"To protect you at all costs."

Kensi narrowed her eyes at Julien, and then back at Eli. "I'm guessing these were Julien's orders?" When Eli didn't answer, Kensi looked at Julien. "Well?"

"Yes, I asked Eli to look after you as a favor to me."

"For how long?" Kensi asked.

"Not long."

"How long is not long, Julien?"

"Since the day your home was vandalized."

Kensi stood there dumbfounded and not pleased at all.

"Kensi, honey, who the hell is this?" Mr. Dumas asked.

"He's a friend of mine," Kensi answered before turning her attention back to Julien. "Julien, I can't believe you. You should've told me. You don't just ask people to keep an eye on me. I can take care of myself!" Kensi turned toward her father. "Dad, that goes for you too."

Kensi walked off toward the security office. She didn't make it ten steps before bumping into Dr. Randahl. "Oh, just fucking great! And what the hell do you want, another blow job? Or do you want to go into one of the interrogation rooms while I watch you jack off from the other side of the glass?"

Dr. Randahl raised his eyebrows, but he didn't reply.

Kensi did a quick assessment. When she didn't see Amber, she said, "Where's the tart you brought with you, Dr. Randahl? Let me guess, she couldn't stay out past curfew?"

"Kensi, if I didn't know better I'd think you were jealous."

"Well, I guess it's a good damn thing you know better!" Kensi said as she stormed past Dr. Randahl toward the security office.

***

Vanity, Felicity, and Martin were all working diligently to contain the fiascos that seemed to be multiplying.

"Martin, we've already contacted the authorities and they're on the way. Felicity and I will handle the police, but we need you to keep the guests entertained. Create a diversion or whatever you have to do. Just try to keep everyone in the area of the grand room or the hall where the interrogation play rooms are," Vanity said.

"And what kind of distraction do you suggest?" Martin asked.

"I think I can help with that," Gianna said. Vanity had never been happier to see Gianna. "I know I'm late to the party, but better late than never, right?" Gianna was wearing a vinyl leather piece of clothing that could've been mistaken for an extremely skimpy bathing suit. The outfit allowed for the majority of her colorful tattoos to show. She'd accessorized with knee-high leather boots, a leather collar around her neck, and was yielding a whip in hand.

Gianna walked over to Martin and wrapped one of her legs around his waist. "Where do you want me, Daddy?"

Vanity and Felicity just stared at Martin waiting on his response.

"Come on. Don't tell me he's shy, Vanity," Gianna said, jumping up onto Martin and wrapping her legs around his waist. Martin looked over at

Vanity who held up both of her hands and shook her head. Letting Gianna slide down his body until her feet met the floor, Martin readjusted his suit and held out his arm for Gianna to grab ahold.

"Oh, classy, eh? If that's how you want to play it," she said, grabbing Martin's arm.

"You two take care of the situation with the police," Martin said, looking at Vanity and Felicity and then back to Gianna. "We'll run some type of interference."

Gianna pulled at Martin's arm. "Come on. I'll tell you what each of my tattoos mean. Even the one's you can't see," she said, leading him toward the grand room.

Felicity headed toward the security office and Vanity was right behind her when someone tugged at her elbow. Vanity had never been ashamed of anything in her life, but she instantly blushed when she saw who it was.

Standing six feet tall in rugged jeans, a crisp white T-shirt, and a black blazer to accentuate his broad shoulders, he said, "I've been calling you, and you haven't returned any of my calls."

"Paul, what are you doing here, and how did you get in?"

"Is everything okay?" Felicity interrupted.

"Yes, it's fine. You can go ahead to the security office. I'm right behind you. Just give me a few minutes," Vanity said before turning her attention back to Paul.

"Is that all you can spare for me tonight, just a few minutes?" Paul asked, running his hands through his hair and flashing Vanity his playboy smile.

"I asked you a question first."

"I have a few friends who are working here as servers tonight. They might have snuck me in through the back."

"I see. And the answer to your question is yes. Tonight really isn't a good night, Paul. There's a lot going on right now. As you probably already know, I coordinated this event, so it's my responsibility to make sure everything is running smoothly, and right now everything is not. I just don't have the time to have the serious discussion that I know you want to have."

"Stop, Vanity. I know what happened with you and my brother. He told me everything, and look at me," Paul said, grabbing Vanity by her chin. "I don't care. I know you thought he was me, and I can tell by how you're refusing to make eye contact with me that you feel terrible about it. Yes, I want to talk, but not about that. I want to talk about you and me."

With a look of sincerity, Vanity said, "I didn't know he wasn't you."

"I know. I know," Paul said, letting her chin go.

"I have to go. There are some things I have to take care of that cannot wait."

"Okay. I'll let you get back to what you were doing, under one condition."

With raised eyebrows and a slight smirk, Vanity asked, "And what's that?"

"That you promise to call me. I'm not saying it has to be tonight. Just promise me you'll call as soon as you get a chance so we can talk."

Vanity hesitated. "You just don't give up, do you?"

Flashing his playboy grin again, he said, "No, I don't."

Vanity flashed him her million-dollar smile. "Fine. I promise."

Paul bent down to kiss Vanity on her cheek, and then he strolled off with his hands in his jean pockets toward the front doors. His back was just as impressive as his front, and Vanity took a minute to admire the sight of Paul until he disappeared from her view.

***

When Vanity got to the office they were using for security and surveillance, the police were already waiting, and one officer was putting Kensi in handcuffs. "What the hell is going on, and why is she in handcuffs? She's the victim here," Vanity exclaimed.

"I've already tried to explain the situation to them," Julien said. "Just let them do their job. We'll get it all sorted it out."

Felicity stepped next to Vanity. "They're arresting her. It's all one big misunderstanding. Let's just let the police do their job for now. I'm sure the charges won't stick."

"We received two calls. One was from a woman by the name of Sara Dumas saying she was assaulted by her stepdaughter, Kensington Dumas. That is you, correct?" the officer asked Kensi, looking up from his notepad.

"Yes, I am Kensington Dumas."

"And that is the last question my daughter will be answering without a lawyer present. Kensi, don't say another word. My lawyer and I will meet you down at the police station," her father said.

"Technically, we're already at the police station, Dad," Kensi said.

"Don't be a smart ass. Just do as I say, and don't say another word until we get there. Do you understand me?"

"Yes, Dad," Kensi answered.

"Are you in charge here?" one of the officers asked Vanity.

"Vanity! You're the one in charge of this place?" Mr. Dumas asked.

"It's a long story, Mr. Dumas, but yes I am," Vanity answered. "We called the police hoping you would come and assist us in detaining the person who attacked and has also been stalking the woman who is in handcuffs." Vanity walked over toward the two security personnel that were sitting in front of the screens monitoring the cell that held Blake. "Security can escort you down to the cell to arrest the real criminal."

"We'll be needing a copy of those surveillance tapes as well," the officer said.

"Officer, this is not my first rodeo. You'll need a warrant to get a copy of these tapes. Aside from all of the commotion, I am throwing a party with a restricted guest list. It's in my best interest to protect their identities. Surely you understand. Also, there are several entrances at this location. I'd greatly appreciate it if you'd avoid using the main entrance. I don't want my guests to be alarmed should they . . ." Before Vanity could finish her sentence, the sound of three gunshots echoed.

Everyone ran over to the cameras to see what all the commotion was. Both the police and the security guards were on their radios relaying information to each other. *So much for not alarming the guests,* Vanity thought, watching the monitors as the guests ran around frantically. Vanity began to panic herself when she couldn't locate Alex, Nadia, Gianna, or Martin on the cameras. The two security and police officers left out of the office, leaving one police officer behind with Kensi.

"I'm going out there too," Vanity said.

Mr. Dumas looked over at Vanity and said, "You're not going anywhere. The police are here. Let them handle it."

"We'll go," Julien said. "Eli and I both."

Kensi objected immediately, "You will not! Let the police handle it. It's their damn job."

"Kensi, watch your mouth," Mr. Dumas said.

"Dad, I'm not just going to let him go out there and play Rambo. He should stay here." Kensi turned to the officer and said, "You can't let him go out there."

"Sir, she's right. I'm going to have to ask you to stay here. It's for your safety," said the officer, hoping to reason with Julien.

"My cousin is out there somewhere, so that's where I'm going," Julien said.

Julien nodded for Eli to follow him out of the office but stopped when he heard Vanity nervously say, "I think I found them."

Everyone turned their attention to the surveillance cameras, and there was Nadia standing stiffly behind Alex while a female aimed a gun at them both.

"That's the woman from the club the night Alex was drugged. She's the one we caught on tape slipping something into his drink," Julien said.

Mr. Dumas stood there with his arms folded across his chest and shook his head. "What have you kids been out here getting yourselves into?"

Chapter Fifty Five

"Why don't you just let her go, and then you and I can talk about this?" Alex said.

The woman scoffed at Alex's remark. "You men are all the same. All of you think everything is all about you. Well, I'm sorry to disappoint, but it's her I want, not you."

"Scarlett, that's your name. I remember you from Neiman Marcus and I saw you at the club opening night," Nadia said, recognizing the woman who was holding her at gunpoint.

"I lied. My real name is Heather. Heather Kaleb to be exact. Does the name Jeffrey Kaleb ring any bells?" she asked.

Nadia was speechless.

"Ah, I see you recognize the name. So tell me something: exactly how long have you been sleeping with my husband?"

"I'm one of Dr. Kaleb's patients, that's all. I didn't . . . I mean . . . I'm . . .," Nadia stammered.

As Nadia struggled to complete her sentence, the woman aimed the gun at the ceiling and fired two more warning shots. "Don't lie to me! You've got five seconds to step from behind him or I shoot the both of you."

"You don't have to do this, "Alex said.

"Five, four . . ." Heather counted.

"He's right, you don't," Nadia said.

"Three . . ."

"Is he really worth it—a scumbag who cheated on you? Is he really worth you spending the rest of your life in jail?" Alex asked.

"Two . . ."

Nadia stepped from behind Alex and said, "Okay, just don't hurt him."

"Police! Drop your weapon!"

Nadia would've felt relieved that the police had arrived, but the look on the woman's face didn't give her any comfort.

Still holding her gun in Nadia's direction, Heather said, "One."

Several shots rang out. Alex grabbed Nadia, pulling her to the ground, shielding her with his body.

Nadia opened her eyes and was staring at the woman who'd just held her at gunpoint. The woman's eyes were lifeless as she lay in a pool of blood on the floor. Not sure of what else to do, Nadia tried to wiggle out from under Alex, who was still shielding her body with his.

"Alex, you've got to move. Alex. Alex?" Nadia went from calmly nudging Alex to crying his name hysterically. "Alex! Alex!" Managing to wiggle out from under him, Nadia rolled Alex over onto his back. His gray shirt was soaked in blood, and he wasn't moving.

"Alex! Alex, can you hear me? Get up, Alex. Please!" Nadia cried hysterically as she screamed for Alex to answer her, but he didn't.

Hi there,

Thank you for choosing and reading The RN Diaries. I *loved* writing this novel, and I hope you enjoyed reading it just as much! I'm currently working on book two. So, get ready to take a look into the pasts of Vanity, Nadia, and Kensington, and see how they became the fiesty women they are today. You can follow me at the links below to receive the latest news:

https://www.facebook.com/DolynKeys

https://instagram.com/dolynkeys

https://twitter.com/dolynkeys

Email: dolynkeys@gmail.com

Can't wait to connect with you! Until then, try something different. . . You might like it!